THE POPSICLE TREE

THE POPSICLE TREE

a Dick Hardesty Mystery by

DORIEN GREY

GLB PUBLISHERS   San Francisco

Published in the United States by
GLB Publishers
P.O. Box 78212, San Francisco, CA 94107 USA

Cover by GLB Publishers
Photography by Gary A. Brown

Library of Congress Control Number:

2004113662

ISBN 1-879194-55-4

First Published Jan. 2005

DEDICATION

*To those
who can still
see life through
a child's eyes*

CHAPTER 1

Didn't somebody once say 'the only thing consistent in life is change'? So how come so many people are totally unprepared for it? They go through life as if they were driving down a freeway using only their rear-view mirror to steer by. They think they're going along fine, and suddenly: Wham! Something they didn't see coming plows into them head-on and changes their lives completely, sending them spinning off in directions they'd never imagined going.

The best way to handle change is simply to deal with it, and try looking at it the way a kid sees new experiences: as a challenge often filled with wonder. Everything's possible to a child, and 'growing up' shouldn't change that. Just keep your mind and your heart open, and who knows? A Popsicle Tree? Why not?

* * *

"You think they'll like them?" Jonathan asked as we left the apartment with a shopping bag full of presents.

"Of course they will," I said. "We have excellent taste."

"In men, anyway," he replied, grinning. "At least I do. I'm not so sure about you."

"Would this be Bid for Reassurance number 1,209?" I asked.

We were on our way to our friends Tim and Phil's apartment, where we were invited for an impromptu 'Welcome Back' gathering the day after our return from two weeks in New York. It was pretty short notice, and Jonathan had to scurry to get the presents wrapped, but we were anxious to see everyone again—'everyone' in this case being Tim and Phil, Bob and Mario, and Jared and Jake, who formed our inner circle of friends.

They'd said five o'clock, since it was a Sunday and everyone had to work the next day—including me, unfortunately—and to my surprise we arrived exactly on time.

Tim, Phil, Jake, and Jared were already there, and you'd think we hadn't seen each other in two years rather than two weeks. Jonathan discreetly put the shopping bag on the floor next to the door before our exchange of bear hugs with everyone. Phil excused himself and went into the kitchen, returning with a Coke for Jonathan and a Manhattan for me. It was good to be home.

We'd just gotten seated when Bob and Mario arrived. Since Bob owned our favorite bar, Ramón's, and Mario managed Venture, another bar, I realized their being there had involved some serious juggling of schedules, and I appreciated it. As soon as Tim got their drinks and we'd exchanged a toast to long-lost friends, Jonathan couldn't wait any longer. He got up and went to the shopping bag.

"We got you all something from New York," he said. Like Santa Claus with a bag full of toys, he handed out the gifts—one each for Tim and Phil and for Bob and Mario, and separate gifts for Jake and Jared, since they did not live together.

They all expressed surprise and thanks as they took the gifts, and Jonathan, like a little kid, oversaw the opening of each gift in turn. For Jake, a contractor by trade, we'd found a 1923 Sears & Roebuck catalog which featured at least a dozen pages of entire homes you could buy in kit form—a three bedroom cottage went for around $1,000. Jonathan had put a little tab in the catalog to mark the pages.

"Jonathan thought you could get some ideas from them," I said, and Jake looked at both of us and grinned.

"This is great, guys. Thank you." And he pulled Jonathan down to him and gave him another hug.

Don't you wish you'd given it to him? one of my mind voices asked. I recognized it immediately as my crotch.

Shame, Dick Hardesty! Shame! my saintly conscience replied.

Yeah, yeah…whatever.

For Jared, who taught Russian Literature at a small college about an hour north of the city, we'd found an old book of Russian folk tales in the original Russian.

Jared was visibly impressed. He turned through the pages, then looked from Jonathan to me and said: "Where did you ever find this?"

"In a little used book store in Greenwich Village," Jonathan said. "That's where we got Jake's catalog, too."

Bob and Mario had been renovating a great old Victorian house, and we'd gotten them a pair of heavy glass candle holders we thought would go well on their mantle or dining room table.

"They're beautiful," Bob exclaimed, admiring the candlewick pattern.

"We got them at Macy's," Jonathan announced happily.

"Well, they're perfect, and we thank you," Mario said.

"You're welcome," Jonathan said, beaming.

Since Tim and Phil collected exotic tropical fish and had initiated Jonathan's interest in them, we had picked out a large coffee-table photo book from the gift store of the New York Aquarium.

"Thank you, Jonathan. Thank you Dick," Tim said. "Of course you realize we will now have to file for bankruptcy after we go out and get all these fish."

His Santa Claus duties finished, Jonathan came back and sat beside me.

"Now," Jared said, "tell us all about your trip."

And we did.

*　*　*

It was a wonderful evening. As usual there was enough food for a small army, and Jake had brought a Bavarian chocolate cake for dessert, as if any of us really needed it after all the other food.

We sat around talking and laughing until just before ten, when Jared said he'd better get started on the drive back to

Carrington. He'd left his car at Jake's, so they left together, followed shortly by Bob and Mario, leaving just Jonathan and me with Tim and Phil. Jonathan wanted to help Tim with the dishes, but Tim refused with thanks, and we left at about 10:30, heading for home and the prospect of work in the morning.

*　*　*

I spent the entire morning at work returning calls left on the answering machine, and setting up appointments with prospective clients, one of whom was a George Cramer, owner of Cramer Motors, a used car lot in The Central, the business hub of the gay community. He didn't go into detail but I arranged to meet him at his lot at 2:30 that afternoon. A couple of checks had come in with the accumulated mail, so I decided to take a late lunch and run them to the bank on my way to The Central.

Jonathan had been saving money to buy his own car for going to and from work, and we'd planned that I would sell him—he insisted—the car we now had and I'd get a new "family" car. I thought as long as I'd be at Cramer's lot, I might look around to see what was available. Being in The Central, a large percentage of the lot's customers were from the community and I knew a couple of people who had bought cars there and been satisfied.

I parked on the street in front of the lot, and the minute I walked onto the lot itself and passed the first row of cars, I was approached by a guy who did the term "tall, dark, and handsome" a great disservice. Since he was wearing a name tag—'Clint'—I gathered he was one of the salesmen, and wondered what in the world he was doing selling used cars when he could be gracing the cover of any men's magazine in the country.

"Hi," he said, cramming more charm into one syllable than it was meant to hold, and giving me a smile that made me wish I'd brought my sunglasses. "I'm Clint. See anything you like?"

Don't go there, I warned my crotch before it could say

anything.

I was aware that the question was one he undoubtedly used on every male gay prospective customer.

"Perhaps…" *Damn,* that was my crotch talking out loud, not me! "…in a few minutes," I hastened to add. "I'm looking for Mr. Cramer right now."

"Sure," he said, still smiling. "He's in the office. Just let me know when I can be of some help, Mr. …?" He held out his hand.

"Hardesty," I said. "Dick Hardesty."

Yeah, like you had to include your first name! one of my mind voices—the one in charge of being a pain in the ass—snorted.

"And I'll do that," I added as I took his hand. There was just the slightest hint of an extra squeeze before he released it. Damn, this guy was good!

Leaving Clint however reluctantly, I made my way to the office. There were two empty desks, and three doors other than the entrance, two of which were closed. Through the third door I could see a very large man seated behind an equally large desk, who looked up as I approached.

"Mr. Cramer?" I asked.

"Come in!" he said jovially, getting up from his chair and extending his hand.

"Dick Hardesty," I said as I took it.

"Have a seat, please," he said as he walked around me to close the door, then returned to his chair.

"Let me say first off that I am not a bigot," he said, apparently by way of getting right to whatever point he was trying to make. "A man's sexual orientation is his own private business and no one else's. I don't judge a man by who he sleeps with."

And who might we be talking about, here? I wondered. *Me, Clint, or…?*

"I've got one straight salesman," he continued, "Dean Arbuckle, and I suspect he is ripping me off, though I can't prove it. I don't want you to think I suspect him just because he's straight." I smiled, both inside and out. *Ah, the world, it* is *a'changin'*, I thought.

"And you have no other straight employees?" I asked.

He shook his head. "Just one of my mechanics and my niece, Judi, my brother's daughter. She's the bookkeeper."

There was a knock at the door.

"Come," Cramer said, and a rather mousy young woman entered. She seemed startled when she saw me.

"Oh, I'm sorry," she said to Cramer. "I didn't know you were busy." She hastily laid a manila folder on Cramer's desk. "Excuse me," she said and, without ever having looked directly at me, she left.

Judi, I assumed. No wedding ring.

Let's see…straight salesman maybe ripping off the boss + single female bookkeeper…. Gee, ya 'spose?

Well, obviously the possible connection went right over Cramer's head; she was his niece, after all. I looked out the window into the lot.

"How many salesmen do you have?" I asked.

"Six," he said. "There's a photo of all of us on the wall right by the door as you go out. Dean's the third from the left, brown tie. They rotate days and hours—we're open 8 a.m. to 10 p.m. every day. Dean is off today, which is why I was anxious to talk to you without his being around."

"And what makes you think Arbuckle's ripping you off?" I asked.

"Because things just don't add up. I mean, the figures do, I've gone over the books very carefully, but starting about two months after Arbuckle was hired, our profits have been noticeably and consistently down in ratio to our sales. Clint has only worked here about a month, and sales have really increased since he's been here, but the profit margin is still down. Jerry has been with me since we opened, and the rest have worked here for quite a while. No problems until Dean came along, so I'm sure it's him. I just want to find out how he's doing it."

"Have you spoken to your niece about it?" I asked.

He shook his head. "No. Before I hired Judi to do the books, I did them all myself and I know exactly how much profit we should make on every sale. It's been steady for years. And as I said, I just went over them all very carefully in case Judi might have missed something or made some sort of mistake, and all the 'i's are dotted and all the 't's crossed. And I didn't want to stress her…she's kind of fragile."

He paused, looking at me, then said: "So will you look into it? See what you can find out?"

"I'll do my best," I said, "though I can't guarantee…."

"I understand that," he said, "but you have a pretty good reputation, from what I understand. What percentage of your cases would you say you solve?"

Good question! No one's ever asked me that before. I thought a minute. "Most of them," I said. I then told him my rates.

"Fair enough," he said. "It's a lot less than I figure I've been losing lately. When can you start?"

"I just got back from vacation," I said, "so my calendar's clear for the moment. I brought a contract with me, and I'll leave it with you to look over and sign. You can mail it to my office."

"No, no," he said. "I don't want to waste any time. I'll sign it now."

I took out the contract and gave it to him. He read it over quickly, then took out a pen and signed. I signed it too, and he immediately ran a copy on the copy machine next to his desk. When everything was official, I got up and extended my hand, which he rose to take.

"I'll start on it tomorrow," I said, then added: "I don't want to be seen around here too often. I'll keep you posted by phone, if that's all right."

"Fine," he said. "I'm here every day. Let me know if you need anything."

"I will," I said.

I left his office and stopped by the framed photo next to the front door, looking carefully at the third guy from the left in the brown tie. Very nice looking as, with the probable exception of George Cramer, were they all. I had a feeling, given the lot's location and clientele, it wasn't just a coincidence.

Clint saw me as I came out of the office and he hurried over. I noticed another salesman standing by a Volkswagen van, talking with two women.

"So what can I show you?" Clint asked, teeth and eyes sparkling.

Don't ask me that! I thought.

"I'm looking for a good, inexpensive car for my lover," I said, rather hoping to see disappointment reflected in his face when I said the word 'lover'. There was none. Figures.

"I've got just what you want," he said. *Damn!* "Right over here...."

* * *

By the time I was able to pull myself away from Clint after looking at almost every car on the lot and promising to bring Jonathan by soon to look at one or two, it was nearly four o'clock—too late to return to the office and too close to the time Jonathan got off work to try to drive out and pick him up. But I remembered he had given me a grocery list before he left for work, and decided to tend to that on my way home.

When I walked into the apartment, arms loaded with grocery bags, Jonathan was already home. He took one of the bags from me as we went into the kitchen.

"You're home early," I said, setting my bags on the counter and exchanging our evening hug.

"Yeah," Jonathan said, turning his attention to putting the groceries away. "Kyle from work gave me a ride home. Oh, and we've got new neighbors!"

"We do?" I asked. "When did that happen?"

"Apparently that couple upstairs moved out while we were gone," he said. "This new one's a single mom—her name's Carlene DeNuncio and I'm pretty sure she's a family member—and she's got the cutest little boy; his name's Kelly and he's four. They live right above us."

"You met them, I gather," I said.

"They were coming in the same time I was," he said over

his shoulder as he opened the refrigerator door. "She's really nice. Kelly…well, if you think I talk a lot sometimes, you should hear him! He was telling me all about his room and that he goes to school—day-care, actually his mom says—and he waved goodbye as they went on up the stairs."

The minute he'd mentioned our new neighbor's probably being gay and that she had a four-year-old son, I knew he'd be thinking of his own four-year-old nephew, Joshua, and wishing again that we could have kids.

"I sure wish we could have a kid," he said, as if on cue. This was a recurring theme for Jonathan, even though he realized the biological and legal difficulties involved. I wasn't sure whether having a four-year-old neighbor would give him a more realistic look at the problems inherent in raising kids, or if it would simply intensify his wanting one. I hoped for the former.

Our first full night at home after our trip (Saturday didn't count, since we were busy unpacking and coming down from the travel and the entire vacation) was really nice, with just the two of us. We had dinner, watched some TV, and went to bed early—partly because Jonathan, while we were reminiscing about the trip, mentioned the *very* attentive—and *very* handsome—flight attendant on our return flight, suggested we might play a new game he called The Horny Passenger and The Accommodating Flight Attendant. Talk about the Friendly Skies…!

* * *

One of the first things I did when I got to the office Tuesday morning—after attending to my coffee/newspaper/crossword puzzle routine—was to look in the phone book for the address of one Dean Arbuckle. Since he'd been off the day before, I hoped he'd be at work. I took a chance and dialed the number. A woman answered.

"Is Mr. Arbuckle in?" I asked, hoping that he wasn't—if he was, I'd just hang up.

In the background I could hear children arguing. There was a moment's pause while the woman covered the mouthpiece and said something to the children, then came back on. "No, he's at work. Can I help you with something?"

"No, thank you. I'll try to reach him there. Good-bye," and I hung up before she could ask anything else.

On a whim, I consulted the phone book again and wrote down the address, then looked for the number and address of Judi Cramer. There was no Judi Cramer listed, though there were two "J. Cramer"s. I wrote them both down. Since I didn't know whether Judi worked every day or not, I didn't try calling either number—if a woman answered I wouldn't know if it was her or J. Cramer's wife without asking, and I didn't want to have it be her and then have to try to explain why I was calling.

Instead, I decided to take a drive out past Dean Arbuckle's house, to see if there might be any immediately visible evidence indicating a lifestyle above what I might assume to be a normal used-car salesman's means—whatever in hell that might be.

He lived, I saw from looking at the city map I keep in my desk, on the north side of town, near the river. It was a nice day for a drive, and I took my time.

The Arbuckles lived on a quiet residential street of neatly-kept homes. The house I was looking for was much like its neighbors: fake shutters flanking the windows, a twin-dormer roof and a red-brick sidewalk to the front door. As I drove slowly past, I looked down the driveway to the neat two-car garage at the rear of the house, with a basketball hoop over the open double retractable door. The one side of the garage was empty: in the other I caught a glimpse of the grill and front end of what looked to be an expensive and obviously new sports car. I drove around the block and came back, approaching the house from the other direction. Sure enough, that's what it was. A convertible, yet!

Well, it appeared that Dean Arbuckle must be an awfully good salesman to be able to afford a wife, a couple of kids, a nice house, and two cars. (I assumed he drove to work, which meant he had the second car with him. I wondered how new *it* was.)

On my way back to the office, I drove through The Central and down the alley behind Cramer Motors. Four cars were parked directly behind the office building; one a late-model Cadillac—Cramer's, probably—a last-year's model Chevy, an older station wagon, and a Volkswagen around three to five years old. I wondered if Cramer knew Arbuckle had a nice new car in his garage? I tended to doubt it.

* * *

That evening, as we sat watching the evening news before dinner, Jonathan, who had beat me home again—his friend Kyle at work apparently had a girlfriend living near us—said: "Would you mind if I asked Carlene down for coffee and cake after dinner? I don't know if she has any friends around here, and I think you'd really like meeting her."

I set my Manhattan on the coffee table and smiled at him. "...And Kelly?" I added. Sometimes I could read him like a book.

He looked a little like a kid caught with his hand in the cookie jar.

"Uh, well, yeah, of course. We could make it right after dinner since I imagine Kelly probably has to be in bed pretty early."

"Sure, if you'd like," I said.

"Great! I'll run up and ask her, okay?" He said this even as he was getting up from the couch and putting his Coke down next to my Manhattan.

"Okay," I said as he reached the door.

He was back within two minutes. "They're just having dinner now," he said, "but she said that would be nice. They'll be down around seven."

Sitting back down, he picked up his Coke.

"Cake?" I said, taking up where we'd left off. "We have cake?"

"Yeah," he replied. "There's a new bakery right near work, and we don't have cake very often, so I thought..."

Uh huh. "Well, I'm glad you did," I said, "especially since kids love cake."

He blushed. "That transparent, huh?" he asked.

I just nodded and smiled.

"So I like kids!" he said, and I reached around his shoulders with my free arm and pulled him toward me. "I know, Babe," I said.

The news ended and I followed him into the kitchen to set the table while he finished getting dinner ready.

At exactly seven o'clock, as I was drying the last plate and putting it in the cupboard, there was a knock at the door and Jonathan hurried to open it.

"Hi, Carlene," he said. "Hi, Kelly! Come on in."

I came into the living room just as Jonathan was gesturing a rather pretty young woman and a curly-haired little boy toward the couch. The boy was carrying a toy dump truck.

"Hi, Carlene," I said, "I'm Dick."

She extended her hand and smiled, which made her even more attractive.

"It's nice to meet you, Dick."

"And you," I said to the boy, "are Kelly." I extended my hand and, after a quick look at his mother, he let the truck fall to the floor and took it and we shook hands.

Carlene sat down, and Kelly, leaving his truck on the floor, scrambled up beside her, leaning against her shoulder and looking all around.

"Is this your house?" he asked.

"Yes it is," Jonathan said.

"Do you have a little boy?"

Jonathan gave me a...shall we say 'significant'...look before turning to Kelly and saying: "No, I'm sorry, we don't."

You're in for it now, Hardesty, I knew.

* * *

Jonathan made a quick trip to the kitchen to check on the coffee, then returned and sat beside Kelly on the couch.

"Okay if I sit here?" he asked the boy.

"Sure!" Kelly said, immediately scooting off the couch to play with his dump truck and leaving Jonathan, Carlene, and me to get acquainted.

Carlene had moved to Carrington, where her sister lived, and where Jared taught at the college, about a year ago with her girlfriend. They'd been together since before Kelly was born. I gathered, from her reluctance to talk too much about it, that they had broken up very recently and she and Kelly had moved here. She'd found a job almost immediately, and had lived in a furnished apartment until she was able to buy a few basic pieces of furniture, then moved into our building. Kelly was enrolled in a day-care/pre-school run by a pair of lesbian sisters for the kids of gay parents. (Another significant look from Jonathan.)

When we adjourned to the kitchen, Kelly immediately spotted and headed for Jonathan's fish tank.

"Look, Mommy! They got fishes!" he proclaimed, standing on tip-toe trying to touch the tank. Jonathan scooped him up easily and held him in one arm as he pointed out each fish by name. Carlene looked at me with a bemused smile, and I excused myself to go to the bedroom to retrieve an empty hard-cover suitcase to put on Kelly's chair so he could reach the table.

* * *

They left shortly before eight, and we finished cleaning up the kitchen, then went into the living room to watch a little TV. Jonathan had been uncharacteristically quiet, and I was pretty sure I knew why.

"That was nice, wasn't it?" Jonathan asked as we sat on the couch.

"Yeah," I said and, before he had a chance to say it, I added: "And Kelly was very well-behaved. Except perhaps for bursting into tears when Carlene wouldn't let him give the fish some of his cake. But Carlene must be exhausted by the end of the day. I suspect four-year-olds can be quite a handful."

He looked at me out of the corner of his eye, but didn't say anything. It wasn't a very happy look.

You're a real wet blanket, Hardesty, a mind voice said disapprovingly, and I felt just mildly guilty for not being as enthusiastic as I'm sure Jonathan wanted me to be.

I was curious to know more about Carlene—whether she'd been married, who and where Kelly's father was, about the breakup with her partner, which I gathered had not been a smooth one...of course none of it was any of my business, but that didn't make me any the less curious.

* * *

I got up well before seven, managed to get out of bed without waking Jonathan, showered and dressed. I then woke him so he could get ready for work.

"How come you're already dressed?" he asked sleepily, propping himself up on one arm.

"I want to get to Cramer Motors before it opens," I said, "so I can see what sort of car a couple of people drive."

"Why's that?" he asked, throwing the sheet and covers aside.

I tried not to look at him: I knew if I did I might not make it out of the apartment.

"I think I just might do a little basic detective work. I'll take the camera with me, too."

"There isn't any film in it," he said. "I took all the film from our trip in to that photo place near work for developing, and I think the camera's empty."

He came over to give me a hug, and....

"Hey, watch it!" he said. "I've got to get to work, and so do you!"

I hate it when he's right.

* * *

I parked close to the alley behind the lot, where I could watch the employees driving into the small parking area directly behind the office. Cramer's (I assumed) Cadillac was already there. A few minutes later, another car pulled in from the other end of the alley—the late model Chevy I'd noticed before. I couldn't tell who was driving until I saw Judi Cramer emerge. She did not go directly into the office's back door, however, but stood there as if waiting for someone. Sure enough, a few seconds later, an older model Dodge station wagon passed me and turned into the alley. I recognized the driver as Dean Arbuckle. Even from my distance I could see Judi's face light up.

Arbuckle got out of his car, walked over to her, glanced around to see that no one was looking (*I* was, of course, but he obviously didn't see me) and gave her a quick peck on the cheek. She went to touch his arm, but he said something to her, and she went into the building. Arbuckle stayed outside and lit a cigarette, leaning his back against the building.

Damn! I wish I'd had anticipated that little scenario—it would have made a great photo if I'd have known it was coming, and if there'd been any film in the camera. Well, maybe it was a little morning ritual. I'd be back.

OK, that told me all I needed to know at the moment. When Arbuckle had finished his cigarette and gone into the office, I started the engine and drove down the alley behind the parked cars. I slowed down when I passed the Chevy and memorized the license number.

Since I had the camera with me, I decided to take another drive out to Arbuckle's house, in hopes of getting a picture of his new sports car. I had to stop, of course, for film, and on a whim picked up a roll of low-light film along with the regular daylight roll.

When I got to the Arbuckle's house, I saw a woman working on a flower bed beside the driveway. The garage door was indeed open, and the sports car was where I'd seen it before. I drove halfway around the block and parked. Not wanting to appear obvious about what I was doing, I put the camera in the glove compartment, locked it, and walked around the block to where the woman was still busily at work pulling blades of grass from between the flowers. She saw me as I approached, and when I got to the driveway I stopped, looking at the car in the garage as if I'd just noticed it.

"A beautiful car!" I said to the woman, who looked up and smiled.

"Isn't it?" she said. "It's my husband's. He'll let me ride in it, but he won't let me drive it."

I sighed. "I've always wanted one just like it," I said, "but it's way, way out of my price range. And it looks brand new, too."

"It is," she said proudly. "Just three weeks old! My husband is in the car business, and he was able to get it through his employer—sort of as a bonus for all the double shifts and overtime he puts in."

I'm sure, I thought.

I stared at the car admiringly, making a mental note of the license number.

"Well," I said, "your husband is a lucky man." I paused just for a moment, then said: "It was nice talking with you," and continued my walk back to my car.

When I got to the office, I called Bil—yeah, only one "l" for some reason— Dunham, my contact at the DMV, and asked him if he could check on the address of the owner of the Chevy, when the sports car was registered, and if it might have been owned previously. I sincerely doubted it, and as far as I knew Cramer dealt only in used cars.

He said he would and would get back to me within the hour.

I puttered around the office until, a little less than forty-five minutes later, Bil called back with the information. Judi's address, it turned out, was less than three blocks from our apartment. And Arbuckle had registered his *new* car, purchased at City Imports, exactly three weeks ago.

Now, it's possible George Cramer had a very good friend

at City Imports who would be happy to give a hefty discount to one of Cramer's employees, but it's also possible that elephants could fly if they ever thought about it.

* * *

When I got home, I was rather surprised to see Carlene and Kelly in the living room with Jonathan. Kelly was on the floor playing with his dump truck, but both Carlene and Jonathan were not smiling.

Jonathan got up to give me a hug—still without a smile—and said: "I think Carlene needs your help."

We went quickly over to her while Kelly made sounds like a dump truck. I saw she had a piece of paper in her hand.

"What's the problem, Carlene?" I asked and she handed me the paper. On it was written three words: *You're dead, bitch!*

CHAPTER 2

"I tell you what," Jonathan said, "why don't Kelly and I take a walk down to the store? I'm almost out of Coke. That way you and Carlene can talk." He looked at Carlene: "That be okay with you, Carlene?"

"Thank you, Jonathan," she said. "That would be nice. I'm so glad you two live here: Kelly needs to have some men in his life."

Don't we all? I thought, before pulling myself back to the seriousness of Carlene's situation.

"Come on, Kelly," Jonathan said extending his hand. "Let's go for a walk."

Kelly scrambled up off the floor, picked up his dump truck and, tucking it under one arm, took Jonathan's hand with his free hand. "Can we get candy?" he asked, staring up at Jonathan.

"We'll see," Jonathan said, leading Kelly to the door. "But if we do, you can't eat it until after supper, okay?" He looked at Carlene for approval, and she nodded.

When they'd left, I took the chair across from Carlene. "So, what's this all about?" I asked, returning the paper to her.

She shook her head. "I'm sorry to bother you with this, Dick," she said. "I never would have, but we'd just walked in the door and I found it sticking out of my mail box. It just upset me so that I started crying, and just then Jonathan came in and…well, here I am."

"Did the envelope have a postmark?" I asked.

"No. There wasn't any envelope. It was just folded in half and slid partly between the slot on the mailbox door."

"Do you know who wrote it?" I asked, and she nodded.

"It has to be Jan," she said.

"Jan is…your ex?" I asked, and she nodded again. "Has she ever done anything like this before?"

Sitting back on the couch, she said: "Not like this, no, but... she was my very first lesbian experience. My parents were both dead, and Jan was very protective of me—too protective at times—and after Kelly was born, protective became possessive: of both me and Kelly. We always referred to Kelly as 'our' baby, but it got to the point where Jan was taking control of our lives. It was as if she wanted to raise him on her terms, and my opinion really didn't matter.

"We began to argue more and more frequently, and the arguments became more intense. And then, during our last argument, she slapped me, and that was it. I just couldn't take any more. The next day I just wrote her a long letter explaining how I felt, and left.

"Of course I felt terribly guilty about it in a way, for abandoning her. Her father was involved in gambling and loansharking, and was killed when Jan was three. Then when her mother met another man, she just dumped Jan onto an aunt. The aunt raised her as her own, but Jan's never forgiven her real mother, and I can't blame her. What a terrible thing to do to a child. And now I've abandoned her, too, and taken Kelly with me!

"But now she's found me, and I really don't know what to do! She wants Kelly back, and I know she really loves him, and I'm sorry, but I just can't...."

"Is there anything we can do to help?" I asked, for the umpteenth time stepping boldly into something which was none of my business.

She looked at me, as if startled, and quickly said: "Oh, no. No thank you. I'll be fine, really. I just..."

"Look," I said over the protest of my common sense, "do you think it would help if I were to talk to her?"

She looked at me again, her eyes mirroring her anxiety. "I really don't know," she said. "I know *I* can't, but I can't afford to hire a private investigator."

"Don't worry about it," I said. "It won't cost you anything for me to at least talk to her. If you give me her phone number,

I'll see what I can do."

I got up to get a pad and pencil by the phone and brought it to her.

"Are you sure you don't mind?" she asked, and I just shook my head. "She gets home about six," said, "but obviously she was here in town today."

"Well, I'll try to call her a little later," I said. "In the meantime, if you should have any problems tonight, just stomp on the floor and we'll be right up."

She managed a small smile. "Thanks, Dick. I really appreciate it."

At that point the door opened and Jonathan and Kelly came in, Jonathan carrying the dump truck and a carton of Coke, Kelly carrying a small paper bag. Kelly ran over to his mother and gave her the bag. "Jonathan got us candy!" he proclaimed as Carlene opened the bag. "But we have to eat supper first. Let's go now!"

Carlene smiled her thanks and got up from the couch. Jonathan handed Kelly the dump truck.

"Did you thank Jonathan for the candy?" Carlene asked.

Kelly looked up at Jonathan. "Thank you for the candy," he said.

"You're welcome," Jonathan replied, smiling broadly. He walked them to the door and opened it.

Carlene turned, looking from Jonathan to me. "And thank you both for your kindness," she said. Kelly darted out the door and headed for the stairs.

"Kelly! Don't run!" she called as she quickly followed him.

* * *

After we'd had our own dinner, Jonathan said: "Do you suppose we could go for a ride?"

That caught me a little by surprise, but I said: "I suppose. Any place in particular?"

"Yeah, I accidentally threw away my school registration

schedule. Could we drive out there so I can get a copy?"

"Will anyone be there?" I asked.

"Sure, they have some night classes going on all year around."

"Okay," I said. "But first I'd better try to call Carlene's ex."

"I'll go run feed the fish while you're on the phone," he said

When he'd disappeared into the kitchen, I tried calling the number in Carrington that Carlene had given me. There were two rings, then: "I'm sorry, the number you have called is no longer in service." Assuming I'd misdialed, I hung up and tried again. Same message.

"Jonathan," I called toward the kitchen, where I could hear him talking softly to the fish as he fed them ("Hey, they don't get out much," he said once): "do you have Carlene's phone number?"

"I wrote it on the inside cover of the phone book," he said.

I found it and dialed, telling Carlene about the disconnect message and verifying that I had, indeed called the right number.

"That's really odd," Carlene said then paused. "I…I certainly hope she hasn't decided to move and follow me here! But with the note and all…."

"Do you have her work number?" I asked. "I can call there tomorrow to see if she's still working there. It can't hurt. Oh, and I'll need her last name."

A very hesitant: "Are you sure you don't mind? I can't imagine her quitting her job; she's been there since we moved to Carrington. I'm probably just overreacting to all of this." She paused. "Just a minute, I'll get the number for you…. And her last name is Houston: Jan Houston."

When she returned with the number, I wrote it down, then said: "Jonathan and I have to run out for awhile tonight, but we shouldn't be too long. I'd suggest that unless you're expecting someone, you don't answer the door if someone should knock."

"I always check the peep-hole first," she said.

"Good idea," I said. "If you need anything, just call and leave a message on the machine."

* * *

It was a beautiful windows-down night for a drive: warm, with a nice light breeze. After we'd picked up the registration schedule from the college, I remembered that the address Bil Dunham had given me for Judi Cramer wasn't far from our apartment, and asked Jonathan if he'd mind if we made a run over there. There was no particular reason to go, other than it was a nice night for a drive, and I knew I'd probably want to drive by at some point, just to get a feel for where and how Judi lived.

I'd rather expected she lived in an apartment—the area she lived in was mostly smaller apartment buildings sprinkled with older single-family homes. I was rather surprised to find Judi's address was a neat little bungalow on the corner of a block of apartment buildings. The lights were on, and as we turned the corner, I saw a driveway and garage behind the house on the side street. But what surprised me even more was that there were two cars in the drive: Judi's Chevy and, behind it…an older model Dodge station wagon.

Surprise, surprise! I thought. *This must be one of the double shifts Arbuckle's wife said he was always working.*

I drove down the block and pulled into a parking space along the curb.

"What's up?" Jonathan asked as I took the keys out of the ignition to open the glove compartment.

"I need to get a picture," I said, removing the camera and the roll of low-light film I'd been smart enough to buy earlier. I'd only taken a couple of shots on the daylight roll, but figured it was worth the sacrifice, so just clicked the shutter and wound forward until they were all exposed, then took out the roll and replaced it with the low-light.

"Be right back," I told Jonathan.

Getting out of the car, I walked back toward Judi Cramer's house. A streetlight at the corner cast enough light on the driveway to make it pretty sure the pictures would come out. I hoped no one would see me, and especially that Arbuckle wouldn't pick this particular moment to leave.

When we'd driven up, I'd noticed lights on in the front and rear of the house, but now noted that the rear lights (a bedroom, maybe?) had been turned out.

I took several shots from various angles, then hurried back to the car.

"Get what you needed?" Jonathan asked.

"Yep," I said. "I think this will be a fairly short case."

On the way back to our apartment, we stopped at an open drug store for more film, and Jonathan replaced the low-light roll with another daylight roll as we drove. I wanted to be at the lot when Arbuckle and Judi arrived the next morning, to see if history might repeat itself.

* * *

No messages on the machine when we returned to the apartment, so I assumed Carlene hadn't been contacted by her ex.

It wasn't quite time to go to bed, but Jonathan disappeared into the bedroom, emerging a few minutes later with our Polaroid.

"How about a little game of The Oversexed Photographer and the Nude Model?" he asked. "Me photographer, you model."

I got up from the couch. "Well, if you *insist*," I said with a totally fake world-weary sigh, at the same time slowly unbuttoning my shirt. "But I'm afraid we'll have to change the name of the game to The Oversexed Photographer and the Equally Oversexed Nude Model."

"I can work with that," Jonathan said with a grin, snapping the first picture as I slipped my open shirt off my shoulders.

* * *

I was waiting at the lot, camera ready, when Judi Cramer drove into the alley behind the office and parked. While I really didn't use the camera all that much for my work, I was glad that when I'd bought it, I'd spent the extra money for a built-in zoom lens.

Judi sat in her car until Arbuckle's station wagon pulled in a minute or so later. Apparently they had their arrival schedules down pat. They both got out of their cars as I lifted and focused the camera. She came quickly over to him and their faces were about six inches apart when another car turned into the driveway and they quickly moved away from one another. Luckily, I'd already started snapping pictures and figured an almost-kiss was close enough, combined with the evidence of Arbuckle's car in Judi's driveway.

Judi hurried into the office as Clint pulled into a parking spot. Arbuckle was just lighting a cigarette, and they exchanged a few words before Clint entered the office. I couldn't resist taking a shot or two of Clint just on general principles.

Maybe you should have Bil Dunham get Clint's address for you, my crotch suggested innocently.

I told it to shut up.

* * *

I dropped the three rolls of film off at a one-hour photo place near work, and went to the office. I decided to try to call Jan Houston first thing, though I really wasn't sure what I'd say to her if she was there. Oh, well, I dialed.

"Parker Precision Products," the female voice said.

"May I speak to Jan Houston?" I asked.

There was a pause, then: "Miss Houston is on vacation this week," she said. "She'll be back on Monday. Would you care to leave a message?"

"Ah, no thanks," I said. "I'll reach her later." And I hung up.

Vacation, eh? I wondered. *Then why is her home phone disconnected?*

Well, short of driving up to Carrington to try to locate her, there really wasn't much more I could do at that point. I'd just have to caution Carlene to be very careful, and try to keep an eye on her when she was at home.

Around 10:30 I took a walk to the one-hour photo place to see if the film was ready. It was, though the clerk informed me I'd better check my camera because most of the three rolls were blank.

I'll say it again: a good camera's well worth the money, especially in my line of work. Every photo I took turned out, including the almost-kiss, which didn't leave much doubt as to what was taking place. I set the ones with Clint aside, debating what I should do with them. I didn't think Jonathan would be overly happy to have me taking pictures of another guy. I sighed and tore them up.

Woos! my crotch said disgustedly.

When I returned to the office I called Cramer Motors and asked to speak to Mr. Cramer. When he came on, I told him I had some news for him and asked if we could meet for a few minutes somewhere other than at the lot. He suggested Coffee &, a diner in The Central, about three blocks from the lot. We agreed to meet at noon.

The clock over the counter showed 11:50 as I walked in the door of Coffee &. I didn't mind being early because, being in The Central, there were always several select pieces of eye candy around. I wondered if Clint, from Cramer's lot, ate there.

Down, boy! Down!

I took a booth against the wall and ordered a cup of coffee from a cute little waiter who was so androgynous it took me a minute to figure out his gender.

About ten after twelve—why am I always early and everyone else always late?—I saw George Cramer come through the door, looking first at the clock, then around the room for me. Seeing me, he came over.

"Sorry I'm late," he said, sliding into the seat across from me. "Dean needed me to close a sale."

"No problem," I said, as the cute waiter came over with a full coffee pot and another cup.

"Hi, Mikey," Cramer said with a grin.

"Hi, Georgie," Mikey replied, leading me to believe Cramer may be a regular here.

"Did you want menus?" Mikey asked.

"I'll just have the regular," Cramer said: "Small salad with lemon, Fat-Free French dressing on the side."

"I'm proud of you!" Mikey said, grinning. "We'll be swapping tank-tops in no time!"

He then turned to me with a suggestively-raised eyebrow. "And do you know what you want?"

Are those double-entendres really there, or do I just insist on seeing them?

"I'll have a cheeseburger and fries," I said, choosing not to return his serve, if it was one.

"So Arbuckle's a good salesman?" I asked when Mikey had gone off with our order.

"I don't hire bad salesmen," Cramer said with a smile.

"What do you know about him?" I asked. "About his personal life, I mean."

Cramer thought a moment. "Not too much. No reason to. I checked his references before I hired him, same as I always do. He's moved around quite a bit, but that's not uncommon in this business. Got a wife, two kids. And I get a feeling he's got something going on the side."

"Yeah?" I asked. "What makes you think that?"

"Well, a couple of times his wife has called the office on days he wasn't working wanting to talk to him."

"And you told her he wasn't working?"

"No, I don't like getting anybody into trouble. I'd just tell her he wasn't available right then. She called last night, as a matter of fact."

"So you don't have him working double shifts or overtime, then?"

He shook his head. "I might if somebody was out sick, but we've got two salesmen on the lot at all times. I wish we *were* busy enough to need them to work double shifts!"

Mikey brought Cramer's salad and a small pitcher of dressi.

"I'll be right back with your cheeseburger," he said with a really cute smile.

Hardesty!

"Do you mind if I start?" Cramer asked. "I don't like to be gone too long from the lot."

"Please," I said.

He squeezed a lemon slice over his lettuce, then looked at me. "So tell me what you've found out," he said.

I did. About Arbuckle's new car and his wife's explanation of how he got it, about seeing his work car in Judi's driveway, and I had just opened the envelope of pictures when Mikey came with my cheeseburger. When he'd gone, I slid the envelope across the table to Cramer, and he opened it a bit hesitantly. His face went from pink to grey to red as he looked at them, one after the other, then again. Then he sat the photos down and slapped himself on the forehead with the palm of his hand.

"Now," I said before he could speak, "there may very well be a simple explanation for all this. Arbuckle may have come into money from another source—gambling, maybe, and he didn't want his wife to know. And maybe he and your niece are really in love, or...." I shrugged, "maybe he conned Judi into somehow doctoring the books to give him money... 'for a divorce' probably. I don't know, but I really feel you or I should have a talk with both of them to see what's really going on."

"Thanks, but I'll do it myself," he said. "I'll talk to Judi first, and if it's true that she has been shaving money from the company for *whatever* reason...well...." He sat silent for another minute, shaking his head. "Why didn't I *see* it?" he asked, more of himself than of me. "Judi's a sweet kid, way too innocent for her own good. She's always been painfully shy. She's never had a boyfriend, that I know of. And I've noticed...*now* I notice...that lately she seems to have become more outgoing...happier. Why the *hell* didn't I *see* it?"

Two plus two equals four, Cramer! I thought.

"Would you like me to talk to Arbuckle?" I asked.

Again he shook his head. "No. I want to talk to Judi first. If it's true, I'll fire his ass in a heartbeat and call my lawyer to get every red cent back!"

He looked at me and extended his hand, as he started to scoot out from his seat.

"Thank you, Dick! If there's anything more I might need you to do, I'll call. And any time you're in the market for a really good deal on a used car, you come to me, okay?"

"Okay," I said as I released his hand and he stood up.

"Just send me your bill."

"I will," I said, and he walked away much more briskly than he'd entered, leaving me to eat my cheeseburger and fries alone.

*   *   *

Back at the office, I had a call from a straight lawyer I occasionally did work for. His paralegal was in the hospital with a broken leg following an auto accident. He wanted to know if I could do some research for him at the Hall of Records and the library.

Hey, money's money, and I'm not above doing just about anything legal to get it.

I told him I'd be happy to and agreed to drop by his office after work to pick up some materials I'd need. Since his office was on the other side of town from home, I called Jonathan to tell him I'd be a bit late.

I arrived home a little after six to find an excited Jonathan waiting at the door, my evening Manhattan in hand. "I was watching for you," he explained as we exchanged our customary hug.

"Something going on?" I asked as he led me to the sofa, where his Coke was waiting on the coffee table.

"I've got some fantastic news!" he said as he sat beside me. Then he paused, and said: "Actually there may be two pieces of fantastic news, depending on what you think."

"Okay," I said. "You've got me. Now, what's the news?"

He was sitting on the edge of the couch, turned halfway toward me. "I just got off the phone with my brother Samuel, and you remember that contest I told you about when we were in New York and I talked to Sheryl that John Deere was having for its salesmen where the winner got a trip to Hawaii?"

I think I followed most of it, so I nodded.

"Well Samuel *won!* They're going to Hawaii!"

One nice thing about Jonathan is you seldom have to try to figure out how he feels about something. His delight for his brother was written all over his face.

"That's great!" I said, and meant it.

"And they're going to drive out so they can take cash for the airline tickets between Wisconsin and Los Angeles—his boss said they could do that so they'd have more spending money for Hawaii—and they're going to drive out and back. They've never had a real vacation, and I don't think Sheryl's ever been out of Wisconsin much, so this way they can see the country. The Hawaii trip's for a week, and Samuel's taking his other week's vacation and a couple of extra days for the drive!

"And since they have to come this way to get to L.A. they're going to stop here and stay with us for a night. That'll save them some motel money, too! I'm so anxious to see them, even if they can't stay long."

"Are they going to take Joshua with them?"

The speeding freight train of Jonathan's part of the conversation suddenly stopped in mid-stroke. He deliberately took a sip of his Coke before answering, and he didn't look directly at me when he said: "Uh, well, no. I mean, the trip is just for the two of them, and...."

Oh-oh, one of my mind voices said softly. "Will one of your sisters take care of him while they're gone?" I asked aloud.

Another pause. "Uh, Rachel and her family live in Florida, and Ruth already has more kids than she can possibly handle, and Sarah and Sheryl really don't get along all that well, and my dad can't do it, being on the road as much as he is, so..."

"So?" I prompted, knowing full well what the "so" meant,

but not willing to let him off the hook so easily.

His face reflected his anxiety over a perceived rejection, but he took a deep breath and forged ahead: "So I was wondering if it would be okay if we could take care of him while they're gone."

I set my drink down on the coffee table and took his hand, looking into his face until his eyes finally came up to meet mine.

"We both work, Babe."

"I know," he said, "but I was thinking we could put him in the same day-care Kelly goes to. It would only be for ten days.... Samuel and Sheryl will pick him up on their way back...and I haven't seen Joshua for a long, long time, and I know you'll love him, too, and you won't have to do anything. I mean, I'll watch him when we're home, and..." His mounting anxiety was clear in his voice, and I couldn't torment the poor guy any further.

I squeezed his hand and kept my eyes on his. "So you told them we'd do it?" I asked, keeping my voice very calm.

He looked momentarily startled, and shook his head. "No!" he said. "I mean, I told them I'd have to talk to you first, and if you don't want to do it I'll understand, but if we don't do it I don't know what they'll do. Maybe they'll have to cancel their trip, or maybe they can buy another ticket and take him with them, but they haven't had a vacation just the two of them since...well, I don't think they've ever had a real vacation, and..."

"Okay, Babe," I said, with far more conviction than I felt. "Okay, we'll do it *if* we can get Joshua into day-care for those 10 days."

Jonathan threw his arms around me and gave me a lung-emptying hug.

"Thank you, Dick! I'm *so* glad I found you!"

He released the hug and got up from the couch to go to the phone to call Wisconsin.

So it's only ten days, I told myself. *You'll survive.*

* * *

While Jonathan was checking on dinner, I called Carlene and told her what I'd found out about her ex, Jan's, being on vacation until Monday. I asked if she had received any further notes or harassment, and she said no. I was still curious as to why the phone had been disconnected, but didn't bring it up.

Jonathan came in from the kitchen. "Is that Carlene?" he asked.

I nodded.

"Can I talk to her?"

"Sure," I said, and made the transfer.

"Can you go turn off the potatoes for me?" he asked as he took the phone.

"Sure," I said again and went to the kitchen to do it. When I returned, Jonathan was writing something down on the inside cover of the phone book.

"Thanks so much, Carlene," he said. "I'll call them right now. Tell Kelly I said 'hi'. I'll talk with you later. 'Bye."

Hanging up the phone he turned to me. "Can I call them right now, or should we wait until after supper?" he asked.

By "them," I was quite sure he meant the sisters who ran the day-care center.

"Maybe you should wait until after we've eaten," I suggested. "Probably it's their dinner time, too."

"Yeah," he said, a bit reluctantly, "we should eat first."

* * *

"So exactly when are Samuel and Sheryl and Joshua coming?" I asked.

"Didn't I tell you?" he asked, looking surprised. "I'm sorry! I was just so happy to know they were coming, I..."

"That's okay, hon," I said. "So when?"

"Well, Samuel actually asked for an extra day in addition to his extra week. They'll leave Cranston a week from this

Friday, be here sometime Sunday, then leave Monday. And if we can get Joshua in day-care by then, they can come with us…or me, or whatever…when he goes in the first day. I'm sure he'll be more comfortable his first day if they take him in. I just hope Happy Day will take him."

By the time we were about done with dinner I could tell, by frequent glances toward the living room, that Jonathan was chomping at the bit to make his phone call, so I told him to go ahead, and I'd clear the table. He hurriedly finished what was left on his plate and got up from the table, coming around behind me and putting his hands on my shoulders. He bent over and nibbled the top of my left ear. "I love you," he whispered, then went quickly to the living room, and the phone.

While I was more than a little conflicted over the idea of living with a four-year-old for ten days, I knew how important it was for Jonathan. And I was happy to see that he was taking control of the situation by making all the arrangements himself. And I suppose I was also thinking, selfishly, that riding herd on a rambunctious—is there any other kind?—four-year-old boy for ten days might dampen his enthusiasm for our having a kid of our own.

Don't get me wrong: I really love kids, but I just didn't know how I'd feel about being around them 24 hours a day. Ten days I could manage: eighteen years…?

I'd cleared the table and started washing the dishes when Jonathan came back into the kitchen.

"They think they can take him!" he said excitedly. "They don't usually do it, but when I told the one I talked to that Carlene recommended them, and that it will only be for ten days, she said they probably could. They want to see us tomorrow at one o'clock!"

"Us?" I asked.

"Well, she said me, 'cause I was the one who called her, but I'd like you to come. I can take a long lunch, and…"

"I'd like to, Babe, but this job I took on just before I came home is going to stick me in the library and at the Hall of

Records most of the day. But I can take the bus, and you can use the car."

He looked disappointed, but said only: "You're sure?"

"I'm sure," I said.

* * *

Riding the bus to work wasn't bad, but I missed the flexibility a car provided. On the way into town, I thought again about George Cramer, and wondered how his talk with Judi had gone. I'd held off sending him a bill, just in case he might need me again, but not having heard from him, I assumed the situation had been resolved, and made a mental note to send it the next day. And I also thought of George's offer to perhaps give us a break on a car. I'd decided it probably would be better all around if Jonathan didn't buy my car. It's not that he'd blame me if I sold mine to him and something went wrong, but...I could trade mine in on something a little later. And seeing Clint again would be nice, too, my crotch reminded me innocently.

* * *

I was able to stop by the office for about half an hour, just to check mail and phone messages and drop off the materials I'd gotten from the Hall of Records and the Library. I'd put it all together the next day and get it to the attorney. I got home only about ten minutes later than normal. Carlene and Jonathan were having a cup of coffee when I came in, seated on the couch in front of the coffee table, which was almost completely covered by photographs. Kelly was seated on the floor busily playing with several toy cars. He paused in mid-"rrrrrrrrr" to look up at me.

"Hi," he said, and picked up his "rrrrrrrrr" where he'd left off.

"Hi, Kelly. Hi Carlene," I said, moving to the couch to sit beside Jonathan.

"We got *in!*" Jonathan proclaimed, obviously delighted.

"Well, good," I said, still not exactly one hundred percent sure if I was or not and realizing I had no idea how much day-care might cost—though I knew Jonathan would insist on paying for it, even if it meant dipping into his 'car fund.'

"And our New York photos came back!" he said. "They all turned out fantastic! I asked Carlene down to look at them to tell you about Happy Day so you won't think I'm making it up. It's great, Dick. Joshua will love it, and he'll be there with Kelly, and the sisters who run it are really nice."

He leaned over quickly to give me a peck on the cheek. " Here," he said, gathering up all the cards; "I'll put them together so you can look at them a little later." The stack was about four inches high.

"It looks like you had a wonderful time," Carlene said. "Jonathan was telling me all about it."

Gee, what a surprise! I thought. *And he's usually so shy about talking.*

"And he's right about Happy Day, Dick," Carlene said with a smile. "It's really a nice place and they are wonderful with the children."

"How many kids do they have there?" I asked.

"Only eight!" Jonathan said, rising quickly from the couch and moving past me to go to the kitchen. "Be right back."

"I wonder how they can run a business with only eight kids," I said. "They must charge a fortune." Though I realized even as I said it that I doubted that Carlene had a fortune.

"Not really," Carlene said. "They come from a wealthy family, so they don't really need the money. It's really more a labor of love for them. They only accept children with working gay parents."

Jonathan returned with my Manhattan and handed it to me.

"Can I have a cookie?" Kelly asked.

"Not right now, honey," Carlene said. "We'll be having dinner in just a little bit."

"That's okay," Kelly responded. "I can still eat a cookie."

"You can have a cookie for dessert," she said, smiling at him, then turned her attention to Jonathan and me. "I think we'd better go," she said. "Thanks for showing me the pictures, Jonathan. You're a good photographer."

She got up, then bent over to pick up Kelly's cars, one of which he refused to part with, and they went toward the door. Suddenly she stopped and turned around.

"I wasn't going to mention this," she said, "and I probably shouldn't bother you with my paranoia, but...."

"What is it?" I asked.

"Well, today when I came to pick Kelly up at Happy Day, there was a car parked across the street, and the man in it was taking pictures out the car window. He was still there when I brought Kelly out, and I think he was still taking pictures, but when he saw me looking at him, he drove off."

"That's odd," I said, "but given the nature of kids' family situations, I wouldn't be surprised if a non-gay parent checked up on things every now and again."

"I suppose that's true, but...I'm pretty sure I've seen him before."

"Oh? Where?" I asked.

"Here," she said.

CHAPTER 3

"Here?" I echoed.

"In front of the building," she clarified. "A day or two ago. I'm sure it was the same man, but I may be wrong. He was just standing on the sidewalk looking at the building. He didn't have a camera and I just remember thinking: 'I wonder what he's looking at.' I didn't pay any more attention to him and I think he just walked away, but when I saw the man in the car I could swear it was the same man."

Maybe she *was* being paranoid. Maybe she wasn't. And it was the 'maybe she wasn't' that bothered me.

"Why don't you give me a call after you get Kelly to sleep?" I suggested. "I'd like to talk to you a little more about all this."

Kelly was holding her outstretched hand and leaning at about a fifty-five degree angle away from her—I wasn't sure if he was trying to pull her to the door, or was just being a four-year-old boy curious as to how far he could lean without falling over.

"I will," Carlene said and took a few steps toward the door, which apparently caught Kelly by surprise and made him scramble to regain his balance.

When they'd gone, Jonathan returned to his seat next to me.

"How long before dinner?" I asked.

"How long will it take you to cook it?" he asked, then quickly hunched his shoulders and raised his hands in front of his face as if warding off an expected assault and added: "Just kidding! Just kidding! It's already in the oven."

"You're a real card, Quinlan," I said.

He smiled broadly. "I'm glad you think so," he said.

"So have we got time to look at the photos first?" I asked.

"Sure!" he said happily, reaching for the stack.

* * *

At eight thirty, Carlene called, speaking softly. I thought about asking her to come back down, but knew she wouldn't want to leave Kelly alone, and I didn't want to suggest my going up there for fear of waking Kelly. Well, the phone would have to do.

"About this man you saw," I said. "What did he look like?"

"Well," she said, "I didn't really have all that good a look at him either time. It was really hard to tell positively if the man in the car was the same man or not."

Well, that was helpful, I thought.

"But," she continued, "they were both dark skinned—Italian, Greek, or maybe Mexican or Spanish, and they both had jet-black hair and a thick moustache: you know, the kind that makes a sort of horseshoe around the mouth? I'm quite sure it was the same man."

It sure seemed so from her description, however muzzy it may have been. "And you don't remember ever having seen him before he showed up in front of the apartment?"

"No, I'm sure."

"Well, it sounds pretty much like a private investigator to me," I said. "Would Jan be likely to hire a private investigator?"

I knew that was pretty *un*-likely, since if it was her ex who'd left the note, she obviously knew where Carlene lived before the guy with the moustache appeared on the scene.

"No," she said. "Jan spends money as fast as she gets it. I can't see her hiring an investigator. And what reason would she have?"

Point, I thought.

"Anyone else you can think of who might hire one? Your ex husband, for example?"

"Oh, no," she said, "I was never married, and Roy would be the last person in the world to care where I was or what I was doing."

"Well, there's Kelly," I pointed out.

"Roy doesn't know about Kelly, and wouldn't care less if he did."

"How did you meet Jan?" I asked.

"At work," she said.

"This was before or after you met Roy?" I asked.

"I was three months pregnant when I met Jan," she said.

"So they didn't know one another, I assume."

She paused. "Yes, they did, oddly enough. I never did figure out how or why, but I do know that if there was one person in the world Jan loathes, it's Roy. I figured a lot of it was because of Roy's getting me pregnant, but apparently it went back a long way before we met.

"Roy was a stock-car racer," she said, "and I was a starry-eyed teenager who didn't really know what I wanted and, well…to get back to your question, Roy would be the last person in the world to care where I was or what I was doing."

"Well, there's Kelly," I pointed out.

"Roy doesn't know about Kelly, and wouldn't care even if he did," she said. "When I told him I was pregnant, he wanted me to have an abortion…he said he hated kids and wasn't about to have his life ruined by having one. So he gave me the phone number of some guy he heard of who performed abortions, gave me a hundred dollar bill, and said he'd call me in a week or so. I said I'd do it, but I couldn't. When he called the next week I told him I'd done it, but that I never wanted to see him again. And I didn't."

"Sounds like a real nice guy," I said.

"You have no idea. I really wish I knew what he'd done to Jan to make her hate him so, but knowing Roy, I'm sure she had her reasons. Roy's dad was a really shady character who made a ton of money with a string of auto body repair shops, most of which were fronts for bookie joints. Roy bragged that his father had served a couple of years in prison for it. And his mother's a shrew who has every nickle Roy's dad left when he died—Roy didn't get a cent except for what she doled out to him when she felt like it. That's probably why Roy shows her nothing but contempt. I think he started dating me because he knew his mother wouldn't approve, and she most certainly did not.

"Jan really looked after me through my pregnancy, but I think she was afraid that Roy or his mother might find out about it, and when she suggested that we request a job transfer to the Cincinnati office, we did. I didn't tell anyone I knew except my sister, who had just moved to Carrington. She couldn't stand Roy, either, but I wouldn't listen to her."

"Has your sister talked to Jan, do you know?"

"Jan called her a couple of times wanting to know where I was," she said, "but Beth wouldn't tell her. Beth and Jan never got along, either. Both of them were always trying to protect me in their own ways, but their ways were poles apart."

"I appreciate your being so open," I said. "and about the only thing I can think of for now is that if you see the guy with the moustache again, and if he's in a car, try to get the license number. I can track it down from there."

"Thank you, Dick. No wonder Jonathan loves you."

"That's very nice of you to say," I said, "and you're more than welcome. I'll talk to you tomorrow, or if you need to reach me at the office, feel free. I'm in the book under 'Hardesty Investigations.' Have a good night's sleep."

"I will," she said. "And thanks again."

* * *

The next week was a total blur. There were really only two major highlights amidst dealing with a couple of minor cases and Jonathan spending just about every non-working hour getting the apartment ready for his relatives: I received a comfortingly large check from the case I'd worked on while "on vacation" in New York—long story—and, only a small part because of it, Jonathan and I found ourselves at Cramer Motors.

I'd figured that with Joshua needing transportation to and from day-care—even though Carlene would probably be willing to take him in and pick him up with Kelly, it would be an imposition—and Jonathan having been building up his 'car fund' so diligently, it was time we looked into getting him a car of his own. Not surprisingly, Jonathan agreed one hundred percent.

So on Wednesday I picked him up from work and we drove into The Central and Cramer Motors. We parked on the street and as we walked onto the lot, my crotch immediately called my attention to the fact that Clint was on duty, talking with two other guys I assumed to be customers. Ignoring it, we started walking around, looking at various prospects. By mutual agreement, we skipped the high-end cars and concentrated on the more reasonable and practical.

Jonathan had just climbed into a little Volkswagen when Clint appeared.

"Good afternoon, guys," he said, his charm and sex appeal engines running full bore. To my crotch's delight, he recognized me. "Hello, Dick!" he said warmly, extending his hand. "I'm glad you came back!" He bent forward slightly to look into the car at Jonathan who, when he looked up from running his hands over the dashboard and steering wheel, was obviously as impressed as I had been the first time I saw him.

"And you're Dick's other half, I assume," he said. Jonathan reached across himself to shake Clint's hand, returning his smile. When they released the handshake—which they seem to have held for a little longer than I was comfortable with—Jonathan slid out of the car and closed the door.

Sure, Hardesty, one of my mind voices said, *you could drag out a handshake with Clint for an hour and a half, but you get irked when Jonathan holds it half a second longer than you think he should? Can we say 'double standard,' boys and girls?*

It was right, of course.

After asking several questions to get an idea of what Jonathan wanted, subtly buttering him up like a fresh ear of boiled corn, Clint guided us to several other cars. I stayed largely out of it: this was Jonathan's decision after all, not mine.

When we reached the other end of the lot, Jonathan pointed to a neat little gunmetal grey Toyota Corolla sitting in front of the service garage. "What about that one?" he asked, starting toward it.

"That just came in this morning," Clint said. "I don't think Mr. Cramer's even priced it yet. They just finished servicing it."

"Can you go check?" Jonathan asked.

"Well, sure," Clint said. I think he was just a little disappointed that his regular sales charms had not done their job on their own.

"And will you tell him I'm here?" I asked. "I'd talked about a car with him."

"Sure," Clint said. "I'll be right back."

Jonathan and I continued over to the Toyota. "Samuel had one exactly like this!" he said. "Same year, same model, same color. I loved it!"

"Do you really want a four-door?" I asked. "We already have one."

Jonathan started circling the car slowly, bending down to look under the wheel-wells, kicking the tire, checking for dings and dents on the body.

"I like four-doors," he said, continuing his inspection. As I followed him around, I noted that it did seem to be in excellent shape. When he'd circled back to the driver's door, he opened it and got in.

"It's a stick shift, just like Samuel's," he said, then glanced at the odometer. "And it's only got 36,000 miles on it! That's really great for a five-year-old car!"

At that point, Clint came up and said: "Mr. Cramer would like to see you in his office."

"Me?" I asked. "Or both of us."

"Both of you," he said.

And that is how we became a two-car family.

* * *

To continue with the blurred week, there was insurance to get for the car, license plates to apply for, and a lot of hassle trying to figure out where we were going to park it. Parking on the street was possible, but not easy, and of course Jonathan, solicitous for his new car's welfare, wanted to have a garage for it. He went so far as to going from door to door in our building asking if anyone might not be using their assigned garage. By the luck of the Irish—Quinlan being a fine old Irish name—an older couple on the ground floor had just sold their car and did not intend to get another.

So one by one the problems were resolved and the week passed and it was Friday night. Phil and Tim joined us for dinner at our favorite restaurant, Napoleon, and we had our usual great evening. We had taken Jonathan's car, of course, so he could show it to Phil and Tim, who were duly impressed. After dinner he insisted that he drive us all out to Ramón's for a nightcap. It was a transparent ploy so he could show it to Bob Allen. But we pretended we didn't notice.

We didn't get home until late, and found a message on the machine from Carlene, asking me to call her. It didn't sound urgent, and it was really too late to try to call then, so I decided to call her first thing in the morning.

*   *   *

I called Carlene while Jonathan was fixing breakfast. She had seen the man in the car again, outside her office, and she'd managed to get a license plate number, which I took down—I'd check it out with Bil Dunham on Monday. While she was still upset, the man had not approached her, so she was more concerned about why he was following her and who was behind it.

Before I hung up, Jonathan asked to talk to her about the dietary habits of four-year-old boys in preparation for our trip to the grocery store.

The rest of the day was a fairly typical Saturday: Laundry,

dry cleaning, a couple of miscellaneous errands, then another nervous-energy (Jonathan's, not mine) cleaning of the apartment. Pizza for dinner so as not to mess up the kitchen— Jonathan wanted to stay close to home in case Samuel might call, which he did, around nine, saying they were fairly close to the city and should arrive before noon on Sunday.

The last item on our Saturday agenda was a lengthy period of horizontal recreation at my insistence—okay, I didn't exactly have to use brute force to convince him—before what I unhappily suspected might be a rather lengthy dry spell with Joshua just down the hall.

Apparently Jonathan had had the same thought, for as we were getting ready for bed, he took a coin out of his pocket.

"Flip you for a game," he said.

"Well that sounds like fun," I replied.

He laughed. "No," he said. "We might not have much chance to play games for awhile, so we'll flip a coin and whoever wins gets to choose a game."

Games had become an integral part of our sex life, since Jonathan had an extremely vivid imagination and never seem to run out of ideas—and it got to the point where I was contributing several of my own.

"Tails," I said as he flipped.

He took his hand away from the coin and gave me a wide and somewhat downright lecherous grin. "It's heads!" he said, then stepped over to me and pushed me down on the bed, hard.

"What...?" I started to say, but he cut me off.

"Did I tell you you could talk?" he demanded.

"Uh, no," I admitted, already slipping into the role he had, as winner of the toss, assigned to me.

"Uh, no *what?*" he demanded sliding his pants and shorts off in one motion, his eyes never leaving mine.

"Uh, no...*sir!*" I said as he yanked my shoes off and reached for my belt. Usually, when we played this particular game, it was I who was giving the commands. But as they say, variety....

* * *

As we lay in bed after our most rewarding physical therapy session, I turned to Jonathan and said: "This may be a truly stupid question at this stage of the game, Babe, but do Samuel and Sheryl know you're gay?"

He laughed and rubbed his chin up and down on my shoulder (he needed a shave). "Well considering that Samuel and I slept together for years before he got married, I'd assume so."

I knew that "slept together" was a euphemism for having sex, and gave a fleeting thought to Samuel's true sexual orientation. But then I thought back to when I was a teenager and had sex with half (the male half) of my high school class. I was the only one who turned out to be actually gay, but to a horny teenager, sex is sex. I'd imagine it was that way for Samuel. Not that it mattered. Still, I couldn't help but ask: "Just how do you feel about that, now? Has it been a problem between you at all, since he got married? Any temptations?"

Jonathan laughed. "Of course not! I mean, I can understand why some people might not understand, but... well, it just *was*. It was just sex. I love Samuel because he's my brother, but I don't *love* him. We never talked about it, because we never had to. Samuel loves Sheryl and he'd never be tempted by another woman...let alone a man."

Maybe more than a little Jonathan logic in there, but I bought it.

"Okay," I said. "Just curious."

* * *

Jonathan was up by six on Sunday morning. I pretended to still be asleep and did manage to get another half hour or so in before the smell of coffee got me up. Jonathan was standing at the window, coffee cup in hand, looking down at the street.

"I don't think they'll be here just yet," I said, startling him. He came quickly over to me, a sheepish grin on his face, for a morning hug.

"I know," he said. "I guess I'm just a little excited about actually seeing them."

Could'a fooled me, I thought.

We went into the kitchen for coffee for me and a refill for him. I noticed the Sunday paper on the table.

"I went down to get it," he said. The fact that it was on the kitchen table rather than in the living room gave me the subtle hint that our regular routine of having it scattered all over the living room as we read and exchanged sections was a 'no-no' for today.

"Why don't you read the paper while I run in and make the bed and shower?"

"I can make the bed," I said. "You go ahead and shower."

Making the bed was another definitely non-routine project, reserved for when company was coming.

* * *

By ten thirty we'd both showered, dressed—after about six changes of shirt, Jonathan chose the blue-and-white striped crew neck he'd bought in New York—had a quick breakfast, done the dishes, and I'd read most of the paper. Jonathan paced and fussed with the plants in the front window so he could keep an eye on the street. At quarter to eleven, he exclaimed: "They're *here!*" and was out the front door like a shot.

Meeting the in-laws for the first time is always a little anxiety-producing, and I admit I was a little less comfortable than I'd hoped to be. He'd left the door open, and I could hear footsteps coming up the stairs. I carefully put the last section of the paper back in its proper place, folded it, and laid it on the coffee table. I got up from the couch just as the Quinlan clan entered the room.

Sheryl Quinlan was very pretty with long, straight brown

hair that fell over her shoulders. She was carrying a large stuffed rabbit, the birthday present Jonathan had sent Joshua from New York. Samuel was...well, let's just say good looks ran in the family. Just about the same height as Jonathan but slightly heavier. It wasn't hard to tell that he and Jonathan were brothers, though Samuel had a certain ruggedness about him Jonathan lacked.

And holding tightly to Sheryl's free hand was Joshua: a three-foot tall replica of his father right down to the green eyes and long lashes.

Jonathan introduced us, and I shook hands all around, including Joshua, who looked at me solemnly and said: "Who are you?"

"This is Uncle Dick," Jonathan said.

"Okay," Joshua replied.

Samuel had brought in two suitcases and Jonathan had another, and a large open cardboard box from which several toys stuck out.

"Come on, I'll show you your room and the rest of the place," Jonathan said, his happiness reflected in his voice.

The four of them went off to the guest bedroom and I stayed in the living room, since I'd already had the tour.

There followed half an hour or so of general awkward confusion, and we all settled at the kitchen table for coffee...and milk and a cookie for Joshua, who sat in his father's lap, intently watching the fish tank. Jonathan had, as he had done with Kelly, carefully introduced Joshua to all of the fish, at which point Joshua tried to reach into the tank to pet them. He got as far in as his wrist before Jonathan took a step backward, effectively pulling him out of the water. Without missing a beat, Jonathan reached for a paper towel and wiped Joshua's hand.

"I really appreciate your letting Joshua stay with you," Samuel said, looking from Jonathan to me. "I don't know what we would have done otherwise."

"He's really been looking forward to this," Sheryl said, smiling at Joshua. "We've been telling him that now that he's a big boy, he can spend some time alone with his Uncle Jonathan." She turned her smile on me and added: "And Uncle Dick."

So much for 'does she know?' I thought.

"And we told him he'd be going to school and have lots of other boys and girls to play with."

"Which reminds me," Jonathan said. "Later on I'll ask Carlene and Kelly to come down so you and Joshua can meet them."

"Oh, about the day-care," Samuel said. "Do they want us to pay up front or when we come to get him on our way back?"

"I'm not sure," Jonathan said, lying since I knew he had to put down a sizeable deposit. "Don't worry about it now."

Joshua, who had done quite well for himself in the milk department and had offered part of his cookie to Sheryl and Samuel several times, started squirming on Samuel's lap.

"I want down now," he said, and Samuel put his hands under Joshua's armpits and slid him to the floor, where he immediately ran over to the fish tank and tried to climb onto the counter to get to it.

Oh, this is going to be fun, I thought.

"Joshua!" Samuel said sternly, and without a word, Joshua cut off his mountain climbing expedition and raced off into the living room, where Jonathan had left the box of toys.

* * *

It was a very nice day. As I was sure would happen, the more I was around Samuel and Sheryl, the more I liked them, and Joshua, who reminded me very strongly of Jonathan in many ways, was winning me over bit by bit.

We went out for a late brunch to a popular straight restaurant, and Joshua was surprisingly well behaved for the most part. When a game of 'drop the napkin on the floor' was called in the third inning by his father, Joshua became distracted by a baby a table or two away, then by one of the waitresses passing by with a tray of something that caught his eye. And each time Samuel would speak to him quietly but firmly, and he'd go back to either eating or quietly playing with his food.

After brunch we took a drive around the city—though Jonathan had proudly shown off his new car and was obviously delighted by Samuel's approval, it was a little cramped for four adults and a four year old boy, so we took my…make that 'our other'… car. Joshua insisted on sitting in the front seat and sat happily in Jonathan's lap. Jonathan was happy as a clam, pointing out various landmarks, where he went to school, where he worked, and where I worked.

I'm sure Samuel and Sheryl were very tired of riding by the time we got back home.

Jonathan called upstairs to ask Carlene and Kelly to come down, which they did. Kelly brought his dump truck, and he and Joshua were instant best friends despite a few noisy but short-lived squabbles over whose toy was whose, refereed by the moms.

Jonathan asked Carlene if she and Kelly would like to join us for dinner, but she sensed that Jonathan needed time with Samuel and Sheryl, and declined gracefully, saying she had some errands to run. They left after about an hour with assurances to both boys that they would be seeing each other the next day at 'school'.

Naturally, trying to catch up on well over a year of news of family, friends, hometown changes, who'd died, who'd gotten married, etc. took up most of the day's conversations. I certainly didn't mind, and didn't feel left out. Jonathan soaked it all up eagerly. And, of course, Sheryl and Samuel wanted to know all about Jonathan's life since he left home. He discreetly left out his first couple of months here when he'd had to resort to hustling to survive, but they seemed very proud of him for going to school and having a job he loved.

And in the discretion department, neither Sheryl nor Samuel asked how we met.

Joshua, who had removed every toy from the cardboard

box and scattered them about the room, started coming over to his mom and dad, wanting attention. He'd sit with them for a moment, then get down and go do something, then back again, wanting them to play with him.

Jonathan took the cue and got down on the floor with him. "What'll we play?" he asked. Joshua immediately picked up a toy car and began moving it around, and Jonathan followed suit. Soon they were chasing one another's cars around the floor, laughing, crashing the cars into each other, and making various appropriate-to-the-action noises.

After a few minutes, Jonathan said: "I know what, Joshua…why don't you come help me start dinner?"

"Okay!" Joshua replied, scrambling to his feet.

"Let's put your toys away first," Jonathan suggested, and Joshua looked plaintively at his mother, who nodded silently, then started picking up the various toys.

When they were done, Jonathan held out his hand to Joshua and said: "Okay, let's go start dinner."

Sheryl got up from the couch. "I don't think you know what you're getting yourself into," she said. "I'd better come help, too."

"Would you like a drink, Samuel?" I asked when they'd left the room. I instinctively knew not to call him 'Sam', just as I knew Joshua was 'Joshua' and not 'Josh.' Biblical names seemed to be a Quinlan trademark.

"If you're going to have one, sure," he said.

I looked at my watch. "Yep, it's Manhattan time," I said. "What would you like?"

"Do you have a beer?" he asked.

"Sure," I said, getting up. "You want a glass?"

He shook his head, and I went into the kitchen.

* * *

I was glad to have the chance to be alone with Samuel. My crotch would have been rather happy, too, I must admit. There was a lot I didn't know about Jonathan, and Samuel was in a unique position to tell me.

Jonathan had, apparently, always been Jonathan: unbounded enthusiasm for whatever strikes his fancy, naive, trusting, openly sentimental.

"You know," Samuel said, taking a sip of his beer, "so often I'll look at Joshua and think: 'My God, he's exactly like Jonathan was at his age.'"

Samuel was four years older than Jonathan, but their three sisters were considerably older, so they never were overly close to the brothers. As the youngest of the family's five children, Jonathan was the apple of his mother's eye, and he worshiped her. When she became ill, Jonathan did everything he could to help her, holding his emotions in check whenever he was with her, and when she died, he was shattered. He ran away from the funeral and wouldn't come out of his room for a week except to go to the bathroom; Samuel or Sheryl would bring him food, but Jonathan wouldn't let even Samuel come near him. It wasn't too long thereafter that Jonathan announced he was leaving, and he did.

"I was really worried about him," Samuel said, "but he'd call every now and then just to let us know he was all right. And then he met you, and…well, I'm glad he did. He needs someone in his life."

"Thanks, Samuel. That was nice of you to say."

He shrugged. "Truth's truth," he said.

* * *

I'd volunteered to run to the store to pick up a few things Jonathan decided he needed for dinner, and I ran into Carlene and Kelly coming into the building just as I was. Kelly was carrying a large children's book. "Look what I got!" he exclaimed happily, holding the book out to me. Since he obviously wanted me to take it, I did, switching the grocery bag from one arm to another. Its whimsical, bright cover practically jumped out at you: a monkey and a penguin standing paw-in-flipper in the jungle, looking up at a beautiful tree laden with popsicle fruit. The name of the book was *The Popsicle Tree*, and I was surprised that I immediately recognized the artist's style. Sure enough, there under the author's name was 'Illustrations by Catherine Tunderew'—the ex wife of an ex client.

Small world, eh, Hardesty? I thought.

I handed the book back to Kelly with a smile. "That looks like a great book!" I said. "Maybe you'll let Joshua read it sometime."

"Read it to me now!" Kelly urged. Luckily his mother stepped in.

"Dick's busy right now, honey. We'll read it when we get upstairs," she said, then looked at me with a smile. "It's been a long day," she said.

"I can see why," I said, opening the front door for her.

* * *

Dinner was pleasant, and Jonathan had gone out of his way to make it special. It was clear that Joshua was getting tired, since he found it hard to sit still, constantly turning around to look at the fish and played with his food more than ate it. He had insisted that Bunny, his stuffed rabbit, have a chair next to him, and kept trying to give it some of his carrots. And after dinner, as soon as his father told him he could leave the table, he hopped down and raced back into the living room. A few minutes later he came back into the kitchen carrying a children's book. He came over to me...for some unknown reason...and handed me the book as Kelly had done earlier.

"Read me this," he said.

Sheryl looked at him until she caught his eye. "Did you say 'please'?" she asked.

He turned back to me. "Please."

"Well, I'll tell you what," Sheryl said to Joshua. "Why don't we go get you ready for bed, and then maybe Uncle Dick will come in and read to you." She turned to me. "Would you do that, Dick?"

"Sure," I said. I'd noticed all day that both Sheryl and Samuel had gone out of their way to encourage Joshua to feel comfortable around us. I knew Sheryl was strongly torn about this whole vacation thing: on the one hand she was excited about having probably the first chance since Joshua was born to be alone with Samuel for more than a day or two; on the other hand, she was extremely hesitant to be apart from Joshua for ten whole days.

Since we only had two double beds in the apartment, Joshua would be sleeping with Samuel and Sheryl. That way, he'd get accustomed to what would be 'his' room and bed while his folks were gone, and give him a special last night with Mom and Dad.

Jonathan, Samuel, and I were in the living room when Sheryl came out of the bedroom with Joshua, dressed in Dr. Denton pajamas (with the drop-seat feature and built-in slippers) carrying Bunny in one arm and his book in the other.

"Ready for your story?" I asked, and Joshua nodded.

"Can I come, too?" Jonathan asked the boy.

"Okay," Joshua said.

We both got up and escorted him into the bedroom for story time.

* * *

Everyone was up early the next morning to give us all time to shower, get dressed, and have breakfast. Sheryl was nervous, though she tried not to show it, and Joshua was too busy playing with his cereal to notice. Sheryl, Samuel, and Jonathan would take Joshua to day-care, meet the women who ran it, and make sure Joshua was settled in. Then they would come back to the apartment, get their things, and continue their trip to California and Hawaii, while Jonathan went off to work—he'd told his boss he'd be about an hour late.

The four of them left before I did, after a minor tantrum

by Joshua—quickly squashed by Samuel—over the boy's insistence that Bunny go to school with him.

I shook hands with Samuel and got a hug from Sheryl, both of whom thanked me again for letting Joshua stay with us, and then they were gone.

And the adventure begins! I thought.

* * *

At the office I did my morning coffee-newspaper-crossword puzzle routine waiting for the DMV offices to open, then called Bil to ask him to check on the license number Carlene had given me.

He called back within the hour with the information: the car belonged to one Frank Santorini, 10335 Kurt Street. I recognized the name. I thanked Bil, and as soon as we hung up I reached for the yellow pages, looked under "Investigators, Private," and found the listing I was looking for: Santorini Detective Agency. I dialed the number.

"Santorini Detective Agency," a very female voice announced. Well, he obviously was doing better than I was: he had a secretary.

"Is Mr. Santorini in?" I asked.

"He's on the phone. Would you care to wait?"

"For a minute," I said.

There was a click, and the tinny strains of 'Do You Know the Way to San Jose?' came over the wires.

Muzak! One of my mind voices whispered in a dutifully awed tone. *The guy has a secretary* and *Muzak!*

It was a *long* song, and I was about to hang up, having long since determined that not only did I not know the way to San Jose, but had no desire to find out, when there was another click and: "Frank Santorini."

"Mr. Santorini," I began, "my name is Dick Hardesty. I'm a private investigator. I have a client who claims you have been following her. I was wondering what you might tell me about it."

There was only the slightest of pauses, and then: "What is your client's name?"

"Carlene DeNuncio," I said.

Another pause, then: "Sorry, never heard of her. And even if I did, as you know I wouldn't be obliged to tell you."

So much for professional courtesy, I thought. "I see," I said, mildly pissed. "Well, I just hoped you might be able to help me."

He chuckled. "Well, Mr. Hardesty," he said, "that's why we get paid the big bucks. Good luck," and he hung up.

* * *

I was just getting ready to go home a little early when the phone rang.

"Hardesty Investigations," I announced as always.

"Dick. It's Jonathan."

Well, of course it is! I thought, until the tone of his voice sunk in. He was speaking very calmly, but something was definitely wrong.

"What's wrong?" I asked.

"I came to pick up Joshua, and the Department of Children's Services was here. They took Kelly!"

"Took Kelly?" I echoed. "Why?"

"I don't know," he said, his voice still calm, though I knew it was difficult for him.

"Where's Carlene?" I asked.

"I don't know!" he said. "Can you call someone and find out what's going on?"

"Of course I'll try," I said, trying to mask my own concern. "Do you know where Carlene works?"

"Richardson Engineering," he said. "She told me once."

"Well, you take Joshua home, and I'll meet you there. I'll see what I can find out before I come home, so if I'm a little late..."

"I understand," he said. "I'll see you at home."

I immediately looked up Richardson Engineering and dialed the number, hoping someone was still there.

"Richardson Engineering," a woman's voice answered.

"Yes," I said, "I was wondering if Carlene DeNuncio might still be there?"

There was a long pause, and then a very strained: "May I ask who's calling?"

I did not like the way she sounded. "A friend," I said, "and I really would like to speak with her if she's there."

Another long pause. "Let me transfer you to Mr. Richardson," she said quickly.

Maybe Richardson Engineering didn't allow their employees to accept phone calls, and I was about to be chewed out. That's what I'd have liked it to have been, but my gut told me otherwise.

"Emmet Richardson."

"I'm sorry to bother you, Mr. Richardson, but I'm trying to reach one of your employees, Carlene DeNuncio. I'm a friend. My name is Dick Hardesty."

Silence, then a clearing of the throat, and: "I'm terribly sorry to tell you this, Mr. Hardesty," he said, causing my heart to drop into my stomach, "but Ms. DeNuncio was struck by a car on her lunch hour. I'm afraid she's dead."

CHAPTER 4

Oh, JeezusJeezusJeezus!

I left the office immediately and headed for home. I didn't know how I was going to tell Jonathan. I knew how sensitive he was, and how easily his emotions get the best of him. But with Joshua there...I just hoped he could hold it together.

And even as I was thinking this, I knew I was going to be calling Mark Richman at police headquarters to find out everything I could about Carlene's death. It may have been an accident, but something told me it wasn't.

Jonathan and Joshua were in the living room, playing with some of Joshua's toys. Jonathan got up quickly and came over to give me a hug.

"What did you find out?" he asked, keeping his voice low.

"Let's go into the bedroom a minute," I said, and he looked at me with a mixture of questioning and apprehension, but didn't say anything, following me as I left the living room. Joshua was busy talking to G.I. Joe and didn't notice. I closed the bedroom door quietly.

"What?" Jonathan demanded when we got into the bedroom, and I told him. I could just as well have punched him full force in the chest. His eyes went wide and he sat back down on the bed, hard, his eyes filling with tears.

"But what about Kelly?" he asked, his voice breaking. He clamped his lips together tightly so he wouldn't make any noise. I moved quickly over to him and pulled him to his feet and hugged him while he made soft *mmmph-mmmph-mmmph* sounds, his face buried against my neck.

"Uncle Jonathan!" Joshua yelled from the living room. "Come play!"

I sat him back down on the bed and said: "I'll go play with Joshua for awhile while you get it together, okay?"

He nodded and I left the room, closing the door behind me.

"Hi, there, Joshua!" I said, going over to him.

"Where's Uncle Jonathan?" he asked, looking around.

"He's busy for a minute," I said, sitting on the floor beside him. "What are we playing?"

He reached over and handed me a cowboy doll—okay, okay, an 'action figure'.

"Soldiers," he said.

* * *

As he had done with his mother when she was dying, Jonathan did a good job of hiding his feelings for Joshua's sake and I managed to keep my own concerns in check. Dinner itself was something of an extended skirmish. We had to use the suitcase-as-booster-seat so Joshua could reach the table and he took full advantage of his folks not being there to see just what he could get away with.

Jonathan lifted him into the chair and turned to the stove for something. Joshua immediately got down and followed him.

"You've got to sit down so we can have dinner," Jonathan said.

"Why?" Joshua asked.

"Because you can't eat standing up."

"Yes I can," Joshua said matter-of-factly.

"No, you can't," Jonathan replied calmly, picking him up and putting him back in his chair, then turning back to the stove.

As soon as Jonathan's back was turned, Joshua started to swing his legs to the side of he chair, preparing to get down again.

"Joshua," I said, using the same calm but firm tone Samuel used to get his attention.

He looked at me quickly, but stopped in mid-motion.

Dinner itself was macaroni and cheese and hot dogs, which Jonathan had learned from Sheryl was Joshua's favorite meal. As soon as the plate was set in front of him, he grabbed the hot dog and began eating it from his hand.

"Here, Joshua," Jonathan said, reaching for the hot dog, "let me cut that up for you so you can use your fork."

"No!" Joshua said, moving his hand—and the hot dog—out of Jonathan's reach.

This really was not a good time for a battle of wills, under the circumstances, but Jonathan handled it like a pro.

"Big boys always use a fork," Jonathan said. "I thought you were a big boy."

"I am!" Joshua said a bit petulantly.

"Then...?" Jonathan asked, and with obviously great reluctance, Joshua put the hot dog back on his plate, where Jonathan cut it into several pieces for him, and handed him the fork.

After dinner, during which Joshua asked at least sixteen times where his mommy and daddy were and when they were coming back, Jonathan asked him to help do the dishes. He gave both Joshua and me a dishtowel. I got the breakables, and Joshua got the silverware, one piece at a time.

Samuel and Sheryl called from the motel they'd stopped at for the night. They told Jonathan they'd be in L.A. late the next day, and would catch their flight for Hawaii early Wednesday morning. Jonathan then put Joshua on, who, I must say, was rather casual about the whole thing. He talked to both his parents, answering their questions with a brief "yes" or "no", and wanting to know when they were coming back. Then Joshua said "Okay" and handed the phone back to Jonathan while he went back to his toys. Jonathan assured them that everything was going along just fine, but did not mention Carlene's death.

At eight-fifteen, Jonathan said: "Okay, Joshua, why don't we put your toys away now and get ready for bed, and then Uncle Dick and I will read you a story!"

"I want to play!" Joshua proclaimed, though he was obviously slowing down after his busy day.

"All right," Jonathan said, "but if you play now there won't be time for a story later."

"I want a story too," Joshua said.

"Sorry," Jonathan replied. "One or the other: play or story. Which'll it be?"

Pouting, Joshua began throwing his toys into the toy box, causing Jonathan to go over to him.

"Let's *put* them in so they don't break," he said, leaning down to help.

When they'd finished, Jonathan held out his hand and led Joshua into the bathroom to brush his teeth.

* * *

By mutual unspoken agreement, Jonathan and I didn't talk much about Carlene or Kelly, other than Jonathan's concerns about Kelly's having to be in foster care until Carlene's sister could be notified. "He could stay with us until then," he said, though he knew even as he said it that would probably not be possible. I assured him I would check with the police in the morning and find out what was going on.

* * *

Jonathan got up forty-five minutes early to shower and get dressed in time to get Joshua up and ready to go. While Jonathan was getting dressed, I got up and put on my robe, volunteering to get breakfast ready while he saw to Joshua. Normally, in the morning, I'd just run around the house in my shorts, but in honor of company—albeit four-year-old company—I went with the robe.

Only eight more days, I told myself.

Luckily, Happy Day was only a few blocks out of Jonathan's normal route to work, so we all (including Bunny and G.I. Joe to keep Joshua occupied on the ride) left at the same time.

When I got to the office, I checked the paper to see if there was anything in there about Carlene's death, and there was. Page 2, lower left section:

Hit-and-Run Kills Woman

A 32-year old woman was struck and killed by a hit and run driver Monday in front of her office at 3433 Glenlee Boulevard. Witnesses described a late model white Ford van. The vehicle, which had been reported stolen Sunday night, was found abandoned three blocks from the scene. The victim, Carlene DeNuncio, was a single mother of a young son. Anyone having information on the vehicle or its driver is asked to notify the police.

I put the paper aside without finishing it and picked up the phone.

"Officer Gresham," the familiar voice said.

"Marty, hi! It's Dick Hardesty."

"Dick! Good to hear from you...I think. How was your vacation?"

"A long story," I said. "We'll have to get together for lunch one of these days."

"That'd be great," he said. "So *am* I glad to hear from you or not? What's up?"

I told him about Carlene, about the note, and about her being followed by a private investigator.

"A private investigator?" Marty asked. "Which one, do you know?"

I was a bit puzzled, but said: "Yeah, a Frank Santorini. Why do you ask?"

A short pause, then: "Because a Frank Santorini was found shot dead in his office at Santorini Detective Agency this morning."

Gee, what a coincidence, one of my mind voices observed casually.

'Coincidence' my ass! the rest of my mind chorused.

* * *

'...Lunch one of these days' turned into lunch that same day, when Marty called me back and suggested we meet at twelve-fifteen at Sandler's, a restaurant/diner close to the City Building Annex, where the police headquarters were located. Lieutenant Richman and I had met at Sandler's for breakfast or lunch several times when I was on some case that needed a little extra help from the police.

I was, of course, early, and on a whim stopped in at a bookstore a couple of stores down from Sandler's to see about getting another children's book for Joshua—he'd brought three or four along, but he, as his mother had said, knew them all by heart. I remembered the book Kelly had shown me, and asked the clerk if they might have a book called *The Popsicle Tree*.

"Of course," she said, leading me to a huge section of nothing but children's books. She told me *The Popsicle Tree* was on the current best seller list of children's books. I had no idea there *was* a best seller list for children's books, but I took her word for it.

I bought the book and walked into Sandler's at two minutes 'til noon. I told the waiter I was expecting someone and ordered coffee. As I waited, I took the book out of the bag and began thumbing through it, admiring the illustrations. I didn't want to get too involved in the complexities of the plot which, I gathered, concerned a penguin who comes to Africa to find a popsicle tree to take back to Antarctica for his friends. He is assisted on his quest by a monkey. Well, as I say, the subplots and intrigue were more than I had time to deal with at the moment, but, remembering how much I loved storybooks as a kid, I was sure Joshua would love it.

"Are you going to read that to Jonathan, or is Jonathan going to read it to you?" a voice said, and I looked up quickly as Marty slid into the bench seat opposite me.

I grinned as we shook hands. "We're both going to read it," I said, "...to Joshua," and gave a quick, Reader's Digest version of what was going on.

We small-talked for a few minutes between the time the waiter brought his coffee and the menus until he returned to take our order. Marty was looking good, as always; handsome as ever, but married life had put a few pounds on him. His wife was expecting, and he was excited about that, and he was preparing to take the exam for homicide detective. We talked for a minute or so about the case I'd worked on in New York, for which I'd had to call on him for a police report.

When the waiter came with our order, we got down to the purpose for our meeting: Carlene's hit-and-run death and the murder of the private investigator who had, coincidentally or not—and I had the distinct feeling it was *not*—been following her.

"What do you know about Frank Santorini?" Marty asked before taking a healthy bite out of his B.L.T..

"Not much," I admitted, "and what little I've heard about him hasn't been too flattering."

Marty grinned, wiping the corner of his mouth with his napkin. "That's putting it mildly," he said. "Santorini was pretty much a bottom feeder. Cheating spouses, messy divorces, anything that involved digging up dirt were his specialty. I gather this would cover your client, Ms. DeNuncio?"

I shook my head. "I really don't know," I said, telling him what Carlene had said about her relationship and breakup with Jan Houston and the note Carlene subsequently found in her mailbox. "Jan was possessively attached to Kelly," I said, "and I can understand her being upset when Carlene moved out, but what she might have been trying to do I have no idea. She has no legal rights to Kelly."

"How about the ex-husband?" he asked.

"There isn't any. The guy who got her pregnant thinks she had an abortion. He didn't want anything at all to do with a kid, and he doesn't sound like the kind of guy who would change his mind after four years even if he knew about Kelly. Carlene hadn't seen or talked to him since she told him she'd had the abortion."

"Hmm," Marty said, finishing his coffee. "Well, if you have any information on the girlfriend, we can check her out, but given the kind of people Santorini had as clients, I'd pretty much imagine his killer would be somebody he got dirt on rather than a client who hired him to find it."

He had a good point. If Jan Houston, Carlene's ex-lover, had hired Santorini, what reason would she have had to kill him? Maybe Santorini's death was a coincidence after all.

I gave Marty Jan Houston's name, phone number—in case it had been reconnected—and the name and number of her employer. I also mentioned Carlene's sister, Beth—though I had no idea of her last name—in case she might know something.

The waiter returned to remove our plates and ask if we wanted dessert, but we declined and asked for the check, which I intended to pay, but Marty grabbed for it when it arrived.

"You've got another mouth to feed at home," as he put it.

But I wouldn't let him ("And you've got one on the way," I countered), so we ended up going Dutch.

We shook hands outside the restaurant, and I said: "Let me know how all this turns out, will you?"

"Sure will," he replied with a grin. "And you let me know if you come up with anything more."

"OK," I said. "We'll have to do this lunch thing again sometime soon. And give my best to Lieutenant Richman."

With that, we headed on our separate ways.

* * *

I returned to the office to find the light on the answering machine flashing, but there was no message. About ten minutes later, the phone rang.

"Hardesty Investigations," I said, wishing I had a nickle for every time I'd said it.

"Mr. Hardesty," a woman's voice said, "this is Estelle Bronson from Happy Day day-care."

Oh-oh! "Is anything wrong with Joshua?" I asked, rather

surprised by how on edge I instantly was.

"No, no," she said. "The children are having rest time, and Joshua is just fine. I didn't mean to upset you. I would like to talk with you, if I could, about…another matter entirely."

"Carlene DeNuncio?" I asked, though I really didn't need the question mark.

"Yes," she said.

"Of course," I said. "How can I help you?"

"It's a rather personal matter," she said, which immediately piqued my interest, "and I was hoping we could meet privately to discuss it."

"Certainly," I said. "Would you like to come to my office, or…."

"Could you possibly come out to Happy Day…this afternoon, perhaps?"

My curiosity was building rapidly. "Yes, I can do that," I said. "And I can pick up Joshua at the same time, if that's convenient. I'll call Jonathan and let him know."

"Wonderful!" she said. "About four-fifteen, then?"

"Four-fifteen will be fine. I'll see you then."

I called Evergreens, hoping Jonathan was working the yard rather than out on a job somewhere. Luck was with me again and he was able to come to the phone. I told him I had to go out to Happy Day to talk with Estelle Bronson about Carlene, and that I could pick Joshua up while I was there.

"That's okay," Jonathan said. "I can meet you there. It's not much out of the way, and I've got Bunny and G.I. Joe in the back seat—I told Joshua that was his playroom on the way to and from school so he won't insist on getting into the front seat where he can get into trouble. But he can ride home with you, if you want—we can just transfer the toys."

"Well, we can work that out later," I said. "I'll see you at Happy Day, then."

* * *

Estelle Bronson met me at the front door. She turned out to be tall, rather thin, with a nice face and friendly but somehow a sad smile. Probably older than she looked—mid-thirties, her long brown hair was pulled back, held in place by what appeared to be a large rubber band.

"Come in, please," she said, and I did. She let me pass, then closed and latched the folding children's gate across the door. We were in a formal foyer, with a polished wood staircase to the left, the base of which was blocked by another children's gate.

Directly to my right was what obviously had been the living room of the house, now set up as a combination playroom-classroom with children's desks and a large TV at one end of the room, and toys of all descriptions cluttering the other. The walls were lined with low padded benches and bookcases, above which were several drawings in crayon and water colors. To the left, partly-open sliding doors showed a row of padded plastic floor mats with pillows and neatly folded blankets—probably the original dining room.

"Let's go into the kitchen," she suggested, leading the way down a short hall to the back of the house. I could hear kids laughing and shouting, apparently from the back yard, which I could see through a screen door at the end of the hall. A Dutch door to the left showed the kitchen, and to the right a room set with three children's-sized picnic tables and a couple of highchairs.

I looked through the back door to a large porch and the fenced yard beyond where several kids were playing. There was a sandbox, a swing set, a teeter-totter, and small slide, all of which seemed to be in use. I spotted Joshua racing around the yard chasing another little boy, all under the watchful eye of a woman slightly older than Estelle Bronson, who stood by the swings, and a much younger girl/woman in her late teens, sitting on the grass with a toddler in her lap.

Estelle leaned through the open top of the Dutch doors to unlock it, and we entered the kitchen, which was notable largely because of having two large refrigerators.

"Would you like some coffee?" she asked, motioning me to a seat at the round kitchen table by the window.

"Not for me, thanks," I said, and she merely nodded and sat down across the table from me.

"Carlene told me about you," she said, getting right to the point, "and how kind you were to offer to help her."

"I'm very sorry I couldn't have done more," I said, wondering exactly what Estelle Bronson's interest/involvement in all this might be.

I think she sensed my question, because she said: "I'd never met Carlene until about a month ago, when she contacted us about taking care of Kelly. I've never had this happen before, but there was an instant rapport between us."

"And you and she became involved?" I asked, and she gave me that same smile, only sadder.

She shook her head, slowly. "The differences between gay men and lesbians has always fascinated me," she said. "Gay men…probably because they *are* men…tend to move much more quickly with their relationships than lesbians do. So no, Carlene and I were not 'involved' in the sense you might mean it. We were getting to know one another, and growing closer. I hoped—and believe she hoped as well—that something might develop, but it was much too early to tell, especially in light of her recent breakup."

"I'm very sorry you never had a chance to find out where it might lead," I said sincerely. "Carlene, from what little I really knew of her, seemed to be a really sweet person."

A small sigh and the smile. "So I was discovering," she said wistfully.

"So is there anything I can do for you?" I asked.

She looked at me carefully for several seconds, then said: "I'd like to hire you to find out exactly what happened to Carlene, and why."

"Apparently it was an accident," I said. "The police are looking for the driver."

"I don't believe it was an accident," she said.

So I wasn't the only one to think so. "Why do you think it wasn't?" I asked.

She had been sitting with her hands folded on the table, the thumb of her top hand stroking the wrist under it. "Carlene was frightened," she said. "She wouldn't say of what or of whom, and I at first assumed she was just reacting to her general anxiety over her breakup. But then I sensed it was something else. I didn't want to pry, but I could feel it."

The back door opened and she quickly said to me: "I'll call you tomorrow," as the woman I'd seen by the swings appeared at the Dutch door.

"Oh," the woman said pleasantly, "there you are, Estelle. I didn't know anyone was here."

"Bonnie," Estelle said, "this is Dick Hardesty, Jonathan Quinlan's partner. He came to pick Joshua up, and we were just getting acquainted."

Bonnie nodded and smiled and I debated on whether I should get up and cross the room to shake her hand. I decided against it and merely nodded and smiled in return.

"I'm quite impressed by your facility," I said. "And Joshua looks like he's having a good time."

"I'm sure he is," Bonnie said. "He's a charming little boy and we're glad to have him." She then turned her eyes to Estelle and said: "The other parents will be here soon," she said. "I think we should start getting the children ready."

"Of course," Estelle said, getting up quickly. I followed and the three of us went out onto the back porch. The third woman got up from the grass, still holding the baby, and extended her hand to another toddler, who rather obviously wasn't too steady on her feet yet.

The three of them herded the children toward the porch. As Joshua was coming up the steps he spotted me.

"*Hi,* Uncle Dick!" he said brightly. "Is my mommy here?"

"No," I said, walking beside him into the house, "but Uncle Jonathan will be here in just a few minutes."

"Why isn't mommy here?" he asked.

"Because she and your dad are still in Hawaii," I said. "Remember?"

He didn't respond but ran ahead of me into the playroom with the same little boy he'd been chasing in the yard.

I stood in the doorway to the playroom as the first mother arrived to pick up her kid, followed almost immediately by another mother and then a very hot looking single dad, who'd come for the baby. It was sort of organized chaos, and the sisters and their assistant took it all in stride.

"Come on, Joshua," I said. "Let's go wait for Uncle Jonathan outside."

"Okay," he said, coming over to me with a toy tank.

"Is it okay for you to take toys home with you?" I asked.

"Sure!" he said, but Estelle came over to him and said: "Let's put this away until tomorrow, Joshua, okay?"

He didn't look at me as he handed it to her without a word.

"Thank you, Joshua," she said, smiling, then looked at me and repeated her last words to me in the kitchen. "I'll call you tomorrow."

I took Joshua's hand and led him out of the house just as Jonathan drove up.

* * *

When we got home—Joshua rode with Jonathan rather than switch toys from car to car—I fixed my Manhattan and opened a Coke for Jonathan, pouring a small amount into one of the little jelly jars we normally used for juice in the morning. I brought the drinks into the living room, where Jonathan and Joshua were sitting side-by-side going through a magazine, playing 'What's that?' with the ads and pictures. I set my Manhattan on the coffee table and handed Jonathan and Joshua their drinks, then sat down on the other side of Joshua to relax.

Well, 'relax' isn't exactly the word. The first thing I realized was you don't hand a small boy a glass of something unless he has some place to put it, and the coffee table was too far for him to reach. So he'd take a sip and Jonathan would take the glass from him and hold it while Joshua turned the pages of the magazine, which he moved to his lap so all three of us could play.

"What's that?" Joshua asked me, pointing to a car.

"That's an elephant," I said, which he apparently thought was the funniest thing he ever heard and sent him off into peals of laughter. Well, it's nice to have an appreciative audience.

I'd volunteered to help Jonathan fix dinner, but he said one of us should keep an eye on Joshua who had tired of the 'What's that?' game and climbed down from the couch to sit on the floor in order to carry on an animated conversation with Bunny and G.I. Joe.

At dinner, Joshua told us a long, somewhat rambling story—wide eyed and serious as an owl—about how a monster had come into the playroom and started eating up the other boys and girls and how he had chased it out into the back yard and made it go to bed under the sandbox.

"Wow," Jonathan said admiringly. "You're a brave little boy!"

"I'm a brave *big* boy!" Joshua corrected.

After dinner, Joshua wanted Jonathan to go upstairs and ask if Kelly could come down and play. Jonathan explained that Kelly wasn't home, which led to a series of questions as to where he had gone and when he'd be back, which Jonathan managed to deftly sidestep with the grace of a matador.

A few minutes after eight I brought out the book I'd bought him and showed it to him—I knew if I actually handed it to him, he'd drag out looking at the pictures as long as possible to delay the inevitable bedtime. I didn't give him a chance to ask for it before saying: "Now, as soon as you get ready for bed, Uncle Jonathan and I will come in to read it to you."

To my considerable surprise, he got up and started running for the bathroom. He was about halfway there when Jonathan stopped him in his tracks. "Toys," Jonathan said, getting up from the couch.

Joshua turned around and looked at him, but didn't make a move. There followed a brief stare-down contest until Jonathan said: "Come on, I'll help you." It was apparently what Joshua had been waiting to hear, for he came across the room and started picking up various toys and transferring them to the cardboard box.

He's getting us trained already, I thought as Jonathan bent over to pick up G.I. Joe and Bunny.

* * *

As we were sitting in the living room talking after Joshua had gone to sleep—he'd started nodding off about two thirds through the reading, but wouldn't let us leave until we'd finished—the phone rang, and Jonathan nearly tripped over himself getting to it before it might wake Joshua. It was Tim and Phil, inviting us over for dinner Friday evening. They were looking forward to meeting Joshua, and we accepted their offer with thanks and the caution that they might want to consider moving any really fragile items within easy reach of a four-year-old to higher ground.

At three-thirty in the morning, we were awakened by Joshua calling: *"Mommy! Mommy!"* from his room. Jonathan was out of bed like a shot, grabbing his robe from its hanger behind the door, and dashing down the hall. I debated on whether to get up, too, but decided Jonathan could probably handle whatever the problem might be, and drifted back to sleep. I woke up half an hour later after rolling over and trying to put my arm around Jonathan only to find he wasn't there. I got up and started for the door to check on him, when he came in.

"Nightmare," Jonathan explained as we crawled back into bed. "I stayed with him until I was sure he was fully asleep."

As a result, we were all running late in the morning, and I held off my shower, helping Joshua get dressed while Jonathan showered. After a quick breakfast, they left and I proceeded to get myself ready.

* * *

As I was leaving the apartment, I saw a woman I did not recognize in front of the mail boxes the foyer, fumbling with a several keys. The box she was trying to open was Carlene's.

"Excuse me," I said, never one to mind my own business when something got my attention; "Can I help you?"

She'd been concentrating so heavily on finding the right key that I must have startled her.

"Oh!" she said, then added quickly: "No, thank you. I'm just trying to pick up my sister's mail."

"Ah," I said. "You must be…Beth, isn't it? I'm Dick Hardesty. We live directly below Carlene's apartment. I can't tell you how sorry we are for your loss."

She tried for a smile, but didn't quite make it. "Thank you, Mr.….Thank you, Dick. Carlene told me about you and… Jonathan and…Joshua and how kind you were to her and Kelly."

"How *is* Kelly?" I asked. "Is he with you?"

"He's at our home in Carrington, yes. I have two daughters, twelve and fifteen, and the fifteen-year-old stayed home today to look after Kelly while I came into town to start to straighten out some of Carlene's affairs."

"When and where is the funeral?" I asked.

"It will be Thursday at two o'clock, at Evans' Mortuary in Carrington."

I made a note of the name of the mortuary so that we could send flowers. "Jonathan has been very concerned about Kelly," I said. "How is he doing?"

She almost made it with the smile this time. "He's a four-year-old boy," she said. "He's old enough to know his mother is gone, but doesn't quite understand fully, of course. It's difficult for him, but he'll be fine in time."

"Well, if there's anything at all Jonathan and I can do to help, please give us a call." I took out one of my business cards, wrote our home phone number on the back, and gave it to her.

"I will," she said. "And thank you."

We said our good-byes, and I headed for work.

* * *

I was a good half hour late getting to work, and there was a message on my machine from Estelle Bronson, saying that I need not return her call and she would call back later. In retrospect I found it interesting that, when Estelle and I had been talking at Happy Day and her sister Bonnie came in, Estelle didn't mention to her what we were talking about. I wondered what Bonnie might have known—and thought, if she knew at all—about Estelle's budding relationship with Carlene.

I went through the usual office morning routine, took and made a couple of phone calls and at eleven thirty Estelle Bronson called back.

"I'm sorry I missed your call earlier," I said.

"That's quite all right," she replied. "I know you're busy, as am I most of the time. I was wondering if it would be possible for us to meet this evening…say seven thirty?"

A little unusual, but I realized she was tied up all day with the children. "Yes," I said, "we can do that. Shall I come over there?"

"Oh, no!…I mean, I have to come into town to pick up some things. Bonnie goes to art class Wednesday evenings, and I drop her off and pick her up, so…there is a coffee shop on Beech—Coffee &, are you familiar with it?"

I was. It was where I'd met George Cramer for lunch, and it was in the heart of The Central.

"Yes," I said. "I can meet you there."

"Wonderful," she said. "I'll see you there, then. Good bye."

And she hung up before I had a chance to say anything else. For some reason, the whole situation struck me as being a bit more than just passing strange.

When I left the office for home, I was sure to take a contract with me.

* * *

Jonathan normally had class on Wednesday night but the instructor had been called out of town and the class cancelled until the next week. That was fortunate on several levels, not the least of which was trying to figure out what to do with Joshua while Jonathan was gone; and I wouldn't have been able to meet Estelle without having Joshua along, which would not have been a very good idea with Estelle being his "teacher" at day-care.

Parking, which was becoming a real problem in The Central, was a particular bitch for some reason, but I managed to find a spot in front of The Central police substation and walked to Coffee &, arriving only two minutes before seven-thirty. I'd felt guilty about leaving Jonathan with the dishes, but when I'd told him I had to go out, we used the Melmac dishes for dinner so that Joshua could help him dry them without danger of breakage. As it was, I was afraid I was going to be late, thanks in part to a protracted battle of wills over whether or not having two kernels of corn somehow find their way into Joshua's mashed potatoes had contaminated his entire meal. A tendency toward melodrama seemed to be another common Quinlan trait.

Estelle was waiting for me in one of the booths and I hurried to join her. She'd apparently been there long enough to have ordered coffee and finished about half a cup. We exchanged greetings and I ordered coffee.

"Thank you for meeting me here," she said. "I know I'm disrupting your evening, but I have so little time alone, and I really don't want to bring Bonnie into this."

I once again wondered about the Bonnie factor, but hoped she might give me a clue as to why she didn't want her sister involved.

The waiter brought my coffee and refilled Estelle's cup, asked if we wanted anything else. We said "No, thanks," and he left, putting the check on the table. She reached for it, but I insisted that I take it, and she acquiesced with thanks.

She appeared a little nervous, and when she didn't say anything for a minute or so, I stepped in. "You said you wanted me to look into Carlene's death," I said, "but when we talked at Happy Day, you only said you thought she was frightened of someone or something. Do you have any specific reason to think her death was more than what it appears to the police?"

She looked into her coffee cup and shook her head. "Nothing specific, no," she admitted, "other than what little she said about her former partner and their breakup. She said she wished she had not moved here, but wouldn't say why. It's just a *feeling*...but a very strong one. I'm *sure* it wasn't an accident."

Estelle Bronson had known Carlene DeNuncio only about six weeks. I had no idea how much time they actually had to be together one-on-one, but I would imagine from what Estelle had said that it couldn't have been much. Estelle had given me, when we talked at Happy Day, the distinct impression that she thought/hoped that she'd found in Carlene her 'Miss Right', if lesbians use that expression. I would guess that Estelle's and Carlene's relationship was at the early-and-intense stage. Carlene may very well have been, for Estelle, a fantasy left unfulfilled by Carlene's death. As for Carlene's telling Estelle she wished she'd never moved here, I assumed it was because it was still too close to Carrington and her ex.

"Well," I said, "I do know that the police are investigating and they're really quite good at their job. I'll be happy to do anything I can, but at the moment, with nothing really solid to go on, I honestly don't know. And I certainly don't want to take your money if I don't think there might indeed be something or someone behind the 'accident.'"

"Please," she said quickly, "don't worry about the money! Bonnie and I each inherited a sizeable amount from our parents, and we are each in total control of our own share. So money is not an issue." She dropped her eyes to the table again, then said softly: "It's just that I have never had such a strong attraction...and I mean on all levels, not merely physical...to anyone before Carlene, and I could sense she felt the same way.

It's just…it's just so hard to explain."

She looked up at me and sighed deeply. "And now she is gone, and I won't be satisfied until I know for certain exactly why she was…why she died."

I could empathize with her completely. I was quiet a minute, and then said: "Let's do this: I will look into it and see what I can find, but if I find myself convinced that Carlene's death was just a tragic accident, that will be it, and I'll step away. Agreed?"

She nodded quickly, and I gave her my contract. "Look this over carefully," I said, "and if you still want to go ahead, sign and return it."

"All right," she said. "But I must ask you a favor. Please don't let Bonnie know about this. She is my sister and I love her dearly, but she is sometimes…well, too protective of me. I'm her little sister, and ever since our mother died, she's been particularly so."

Aha, I thought. "Did she know about you and Carlene?" I asked.

"I…I don't think so. I wanted to be really sure we were headed somewhere before I told Bonnie. We only met privately when Bonnie wasn't around."

"And you don't think Bonnie would have approved?"

She shook her head. "I'm afraid not," she said. "As I told you, she is extremely protective of me—no one has ever been 'good enough' for me in her eyes."

"So you've never had a relationship?" I asked, and she blushed.

"No," she said. "I did come close one time, several years ago, a very nice woman named Ann, but…"

"Bonnie disapproved?" I asked.

"No," she said, "Ann died."

CHAPTER 5

Excuse me? I thought, before putting my mental ducks back in a row and saying: "I'm truly sorry to hear that. How did it happen?"

Apparently totally oblivious to the unusual coincidence of having two girlfriends die on her, she said: "Ann had suffered a rather bad back injury just before we met, and the medication she was taking just didn't seem to help. So her doctor put her on a new, much stronger medication," she said. "Ann was rather forgetful and apparently she accidentally took a double dose before taking her evening bath. She drowned in her bathtub. An empty glass of wine was on the side of the tub, and the combination of the medication and the wine caused her to fall asleep, and she drowned."

Uh...? I thought. Well, I guess stranger things have happened, but I couldn't think of many at the moment.

She took the contract and put it in her purse. "I'll try to give this to Jonathan when he comes to pick up Joshua, if that's all right," she said.

"Of course," I replied.

She glanced at her watch. "Oh, my, I'd really better go. I've still got a few things to do before I pick Bonnie up at her art class."

We finished our coffee and left.

* * *

By the time I got home, Joshua was asleep, and Jonathan was on the couch in the living room watching TV. I went over to join him.

"How did it go with Joshua?" I asked.

"Fine," he said, putting his hand on my leg. "He dried two dishes and almost half of the silverware before he got bored and wandered off.

"Oh," he added, "Samuel and Sheryl called from Hawaii! They're having a wonderful time and Sheryl sounded so happy. They both thanked us again for letting them have some time alone together." He grinned. "I wouldn't be surprised if Joshua might be having a baby brother or sister in about nine months!"

"I assume Joshua was happy to hear from them," I said.

"Oh, yeah!" he replied. "I sat him on my lap and put the phone between our ears so we could all talk together. I told them what a good boy he was and that he helped us with the dishes. They asked him about 'school' and that set him off for a good two minute non-stop on what he did today and the toys they had, and his new friends. I'm not sure Samuel and Sheryl had much of an idea of what he was talking about, but they told him how proud they are of him and that they couldn't wait to see him. Really nice. And they said to say hi to you."

"That was nice of them," I said. "Were you able to get him to bed after all that excitement?"

He nodded. "It wasn't as hard as I'd thought it would be. We played for a while, and I got him ready for bed without too much fuss. Then we read *The Popsicle Tree* again. He really likes that book, and especially the pictures. So do I."

One of the infinite reasons I love Jonathan is because he instinctively knows when and when not to ask questions. I had told him I was meeting Estelle Bronson in regards to Carlene's death, but he did not ask me how the meeting went or for details of what she wanted. I think he sensed that, since he had to see the Bronson sisters every day, discretion was the better part of valor, and it was probably best for all concerned that he not know too much of what was going on.

* * *

As I had fully expected, never knowing when a four-year-old boy might suddenly appear beside your bed puts a definite damper on certain aspects of a relationship. When we got into bed and I turned to kiss Jonathan goodnight, the kiss rapidly escalated from a quick peck to something a lot more intense. I automatically rolled on top of him, and he suddenly broke the kiss and rolled me off.

"We shouldn't," he said, physical evidence very much to the contrary. "What if Joshua should come in?"

"So straight couples with kids never have sex?" I asked.

"I don't know how they do it," he said.

I immediately got out of bed, quietly closed the door and moved a chair in front of it, taking a robe from behind the door and tossing it on the foot of the bed. "We'll improvise," I said, climbing back into bed and pulling him to me.

"Just watch it," he whispered sternly. "None of those bull-moose-in-heat noises."

"I won't if you won't," I said, reaching for the nightstand drawer.

And we didn't.

* * *

First thing after arriving at the office in the morning—after making coffee and reading the newspaper, of course—I called Marty Gresham at police headquarters. He wasn't in, so I left a message for him to call me.

I really wasn't quite sure just what I might be able to do for Estelle Bronson. If Carlene's ex, Jan Houston, was involved, the police would probably be able to handle it without my interference. If she wasn't—and I'd have to wait until I knew more about what the police had found out about the 'accident' to have an idea one way or the other—then I'd really have to start digging. The only other person I knew who might even remotely be considered a likely suspect would be Kelly's father, …Roy…? Damn, I don't think Carlene ever mentioned his last name!

Well, I could always check with Carlene's sister, Beth.

And what is Beth's *last name?* a mind voice asked sweetly.

Shit!

There goes your 'p.i. of the Year Award'... again, the voice said.

Luckily, the phone cut short this little exercise in mental flagellation.

"Hardesty Investigations," I said, picking up the phone.

A woman's voice said: "Dick...Mr. Hardesty?...this is Beth Erickson calling...Carlene's sister?"

Now that was something of an unexpected if serendipitous call. "Yes, Beth," I said, "what can I do for you?" I jotted her last name down as we talked.

She sounded upset when she said: "I'm sorry to bother you at work, but I was wondering if you could refer me to a good attorney in the city? Our family attorney here in Carrington is...well, I think he would be a little out of his league with this."

Cryptic, I thought.

"May I ask what type of lawyer you're looking for—in what area of expertise, I mean?" I asked.

"I got a call this morning from Roy D'Angelo, Kelly's biological father, saying he wanted to come pick Kelly up now that Carlene is dead. 'Pick him up,' like he was a suit at the dry cleaners! Of course I told him 'no', and he announced that he intends to file for custody! On the day of Carlene's funeral! I can't let him do that! Carlene would fight him every inch of the way, and so will my husband and I!"

"How did he even know Carlene was dead?" I asked.

She sighed. "Somehow, his mother must have told him."

"His mother?" I asked. "How would she know? Don't both of them live in Kentucky?"

"Yes, but right after Carlene moved from Carrington, she told me that she swore she saw Mrs. D'Angelo on the street, and that she was certain Mrs. D'Angelo had seen *her*, though of course they didn't speak."

I was confused. "So what would Mrs. D'Angelo be doing here? It's a long way from Kentucky."

"Carlene said she remembered Roy mentioning once that his mother has a sister here whom she visited regularly."

So the mother had seen Carlene on the street, subsequently read about her death and the fact that Carlene was "a single mother", put two and two together, and contacted her son.

But why would either one of them care? And again, why Roy D'Angelo's rush to "get back" a son he'd never technically had?

I gave her Glen O'Banyon's name and office number and said I didn't know if he handled custody cases or not, but if he didn't he could probably refer her to someone who did. I also asked for her phone number, just in case I needed it.

She thanked me and we said our goodbyes.

I immediately dialed Glen O'Banyon's number and asked the receptionist if he was in. He was in court, so I asked to speak to Donna, his private secretary, and gave her a brief background of the situation. She said she would pass the information on as soon as she could.

* * *

Again I couldn't help but return to the fact that Carlene had been dead less than four days and suddenly Roy D'Angelo crawls out of the woodwork to seek custody of a son Carlene didn't think he knew he had? If Frank Santorini's death may have been coincidental to Carlene's, I'd bet my bottom dollar that this was no coincidence at all.

The phone rang again.

"Hardesty Investigations," I answered.

"Hi, Dick, it's Jonathan…"

Well of course *it's Jonathan*, I thought. *Does he think I don't recognize his voice after all this time?*

"Hi, Babe," I said. "What's up?"

"I hate to ask," he said, "but could I have your credit card number? I want to order flowers for Carlene's funeral. My boss knows a florist in Carrington and he says they do really nice work, so I'm going to call them, but I'll have to have a credit card to do it."

"Sure," I said, reaching for my wallet. I read him the number and he repeated it after he'd written it down.

"I'm going to have them put all three of our names on the card because I know Joshua liked her too."

"That's a very nice idea," I said, and it was. I wondered if I would have thought of it.

"Well, thanks for the number. I'll call them right now. See you tonight."

When I hung up from Jonathan, my mind went back yet again to the very suspicious timing of Roy D'Angelo's demand for custody of his son. I was very curious as to how he knew not only that Kelly was with Beth but where she lived. In any event, the timing could not have been worse, and it clearly underscored the fact that the guy was a world-class jerk.

I truly, deeply hate funerals, but I was suddenly tempted to take a ride up to Carrington. I could wait outside the mortuary to watch who came in, then maybe drive out to the cemetery to see who showed up there. I wondered if Jan Houston would be there—not that I'd know her if I saw her—and I especially wondered whether Estelle Bronson would show up. I was pretty sure she would, probably on the pretext of representing Happy Day. The one person I was certain *wouldn't* be there was Roy D'Angelo.

Looking at my watch, I saw it was just past ten thirty. The funeral was at two. I *could* make it.

You'll have to go home and change first if you're going, my mind-voice in charge of social etiquette—very seldom heard from, I might add—said.

But I'm not going to actually go to the funeral itself, I countered.

Ah, I see, it replied. *So you're going to drive two hours round-trip to see who shows up at the funeral of a woman you knew personally—albeit briefly—and liked and risk being seen by her sister, whom you've met, and Estelle Bronson, whom you also know, and you don't have the guts to go in to the funeral to pay your respects? You're a strange bird, Hardesty.*

* * *

Okay, okay, so I left the office at eleven-thirty and went home and got into a suit and I went to the funeral.

At about eleven, Marty Gresham had returned my call, saying the Carrington police had been unable to talk to Jan Houston since her phone was still out of order, she was still on vacation from work, and no one was home when they stopped by her apartment. They'd looked in through the windows to verify that everything seemed in order, indicating she apparently hadn't moved out. Maybe I'd have a chance to talk to her if she was at the funeral.

I called Jonathan before I left the office and left a message telling him where I was going and that I might possibly be late getting home. I knew he'd have wanted to go too, but this was a spur-of-the-moment thing, and I was sure he'd understand.

* * *

As I said, I hate funerals. The intimations of mortality are far too blatant. I did not, however, approach the casket. I find viewing the dead—painted and primped manikins from which the human being they once were had long since departed—one of the more ghastly and repugnant of our social customs.

Just as I'd pulled into the parking lot beside the mortuary, I saw a car pull up at the entrance and watched as Beth emerged with her two daughters but, I was greatly relieved to see, no Kelly. The car moved off around the building, and a few moments later a man I assumed to be Beth's husband came from the direction the car had gone, and entered the mortuary. I waited outside, watching the arrivals enter, dreading going in myself. I knew no one, of course, but noted there were a disproportionate number of women among them, covering the full range of the lesbian spectrum from totally-unrecognizable as being gay to a few stereotypical "butch" types.

Just as I was reluctantly getting out of the car, I saw Estelle

Bronson coming up the walk, alone, wearing an attractive but simple dark grey dress with a matching shoulder bag, her hair pulled sharply back. She seemed both startled and relieved to see me, and we entered the mortuary together.

We went up to Beth and her family, who were standing far too close to the coffin to suit me, to express our condolences. I introduced Estelle, whose face was calm, but whose eyes were clearly misted. Kelly, we learned, was staying with a friend until after the funeral and burial. Beth thanked us for the flowers, and pointed out two very pretty arrangements: one from Jonathan, Joshua, and me and one from Happy Day. I wasn't close enough to read the cards, so had no idea which was whose, but it didn't matter.

We then excused ourselves and moved to seats in the back of the room.

The atmosphere was a Sargasso sea of funereal calm, with only a tiny ripple now and then, as if a pebble had been dropped onto the surface. An unreal calm, heavy and almost overwhelming. I'd never been to a funeral that wasn't.

I hadn't wanted to ask Beth directly if Jan Houston might be there, but I carefully looked at each of the mourners to see if I could spot someone I thought might be her. I couldn't.

* * *

Most of those from the mortuary joined the procession to the cemetery, and I questioned yet again why I had come. I'd learned absolutely nothing.

The grave site was near the foot of two tall, cylindrical evergreens standing closely side by side—I remember seeing a picture of that kind of tree in one of Jonathan's landscaping books and always liked the name: Arborvitae Pyramidalis. They reminded me of very large, green popsicles, and I couldn't help but think of Kelly and Joshua, and a much happier *Popsicle Tree*.

As the crowd gathered around and under the canopy over the open grave, I stepped back to where I could keep an eye on just about everyone. Odd, but for someone who so hates funerals, I find a great sense of peace in cemeteries, and in reading the tombstones and epitaphs, and trying to visualize who the people were who lie beneath them.

While thusly distracted, I glanced past the crowd by the canopy to a tall tree about a quarter of a block on the other side, and noticed a figure standing alone, partly hidden by the tree. A woman.

I instinctively headed toward her, and when she saw me approaching, she started walking away. I walked faster, and slowly closed in on her. She wasn't looking back at me, but walking purposefully toward a lone, battered old car on one of the side roads that meandered through the cemetery.

"Jan Houston!" I called when I got close enough, and the woman stopped short and turned.

"What?" she demanded.

"I need to talk to you," I said as I came closer.

"Who the hell are *you*?" she asked.

I took a good look at her as I got closer. Medium height, just this side of stocky, with short greying hair and large hoop earrings, wearing slacks and a denim long-sleeved shirt.

When I got close enough I could see her eyes were red, but her expression was defiant and angry.

"My name is Dick Hardesty," I said, "and Carlene lived in my building. I didn't see you at the funeral."

"*Funeral?*" she spat. "I wouldn't be caught dead at that bitch's funeral!"

"Then what are you doing here?" I asked calmly.

"I didn't come here for her!" she said, her voice still tight with anger. "I came to see Kelly. He needs me now."

"He's with some friends of Beth's family today," I said.

"And he should be with *me*!" she said vehemently. "*I'm* the one who was there when he was born! *I'm* the one who protected him and looked after him from the first. And then *she*..." she gave a contemptuous heads-up nod toward the canopy..."takes him away from me without a word. I come home from work one night and he's gone! He's *mine*, too, and she took him just because she's..."

His mother? I thought.

She abruptly stopped talking and glared at me. "And what the hell business is this of yours, anyway?" she...well...demanded.

"I'm a private investigator," I said, "and Carlene was very upset when she got that note in her mailbox. It *was* your note, wasn't it?"

She looked away for just a moment, then brought her eyes back to mine. "Yes, I wrote her a note. She thought she was going to just take Kelly out of my life and I'd never find him again, but I did, and I just wanted her to know that she wasn't going to get away with it."

"But *'You're dead, bitch'*? Threats don't come much clearer than that!"

She shook her head. "That's not what I meant!" she said. "I meant she was dead to *me*."

Nice try, I thought, then said: "Well, it sounds as though you were angry enough to kill her."

She glared at me. "Yes, I was!" she admitted. "But I didn't. I could never hurt Kelly like that, much as I hated her for what she did to me."

"The police are trying to contact you," I said.

She shrugged. "So?"

"So where were you the day Carlene was killed? I know you were on vacation from work this week, and your phone has been disconnected."

She glared at me, not speaking for a full ten seconds. "It's none of your damned business where I was or when I'm on vacation or whether I pay my phone bills on time," she said defiantly.

"The police will want to know," I said.

"Fine. Let *them* ask. *You* just keep out of my face!"

And with that, she turned around and strode off.

Well, that *was fun,* I thought. I stood there a moment,

watching her, then walked back in the direction of the canopy just as the gathering was beginning to disperse.

I said my goodbyes to Beth and her family, and Beth thanked me for the referral to Glen O'Banyon. I started for my car, having looked around for Estelle Bronson without seeing her, so thought she'd already left. But as I was walking away, I heard my name being called and turned to see Estelle hurrying up to me, opening her shoulder bag. She'd obviously been crying.

She handed me an envelope. "Here is the signed contract, and a check for your retainer," she said, also withdrawing a tissue which she dabbed under her nose. "I was going to give it to Jonathan this afternoon if I got back in time, but since you're here...."

I took it with thanks.

"Was that Jan you were talking to?" she asked. "I saw you go over to her."

"Yes," I said.

"Did she tell you anything?"

"Not really," I said, adding: "Not that I expected her to under the circumstances. She seems quite upset, which isn't surprising. I may try to talk with her again, later."

She nodded, then closed her bag. "Oh," she said, "and I must ask you again to please not mention anything about our...arrangement... to Bonnie. She simply would not understand."

"I won't," I promised.

I walked her to her car, then returned to my own and headed for home.

* * *

When I got home, only about half an hour later than normal, Jonathan was in the kitchen with Joshua, feeding the fish. Jonathan was holding Joshua in one arm with the can of fish food in his free hand. Joshua would hold out his hand and Jonathan would sprinkle a small amount into it and let Joshua drop it into the tank. Joshua, of course, was enthralled to watch the fish scrambling to the surface to eat the flakes, and mimicked the fish's open-mouthed gulps. I hoped he wouldn't be tempted to eat the flakes himself, but obviously Jonathan had that under control.

Still carrying Joshua, Jonathan set down the can of fish food and came over to give me a hug.

"Me, too!" Joshua said, leaning forward to put an arm around my neck and give me a squeeze.

"Thank you both," I said as Jonathan lowered Joshua to the floor.

We didn't say anything about the funeral until after we'd gotten Joshua to bed and read him a story. When he was asleep, we went into the living room.

Jonathan, of course was full of questions about the service, if I knew anyone there, and particularly about Kelly. He seemed relieved when I told him Kelly wasn't there.

"I'm glad," he said. "I couldn't imagine bringing a four-year-old to his mother's funeral! I know some people do, but…I'm really glad Carlene's sister didn't."

I told him about Estelle's being there, which he'd guessed when she hadn't been at Happy Day when he picked up Joshua, and about meeting Jan Houston. He asked about the flowers we'd sent and I told him they were perfect—which they all were, even though I didn't tell him I did not know which specific arrangement was from us. He seemed pleased.

* * *

Friday morning I made a stop at the bank's night-deposit box on the way to work to deposit Estelle Bronson's check. When I got to the office I thought about calling Marty Gresham to let him know I'd run into Jan Houston at the funeral, but then thought better of it. The Carrington police would find her eventually.

I wasn't quite sure what I thought about running into

Carlene's ex. She was clearly a lot more than unhappy and, belligerent as she'd come across, I really could see her point of view. She'd helped to care for Kelly since the day he was born, and to suddenly be cut off from him entirely...well, it would be rough. But it was hard to see much beyond the anger and get a better idea of just who this woman was. Trying to talk with her again would be a little tricky, since she'd made it perfectly clear that she and I weren't about to become good friends.

I thought I might try getting in her good graces—although I really wasn't sure if I might want to be there or not—by talking first to Beth to see if she would be amenable to letting Jan see Kelly from time to time, and if she agreed, approach Jan as an intermediary. But if Jan was involved in Carlene's death, that probably wouldn't be the sharpest of ideas.

The phone startled me out of the whirlpool of my thoughts.

"Hardesty Investigations," I said, after practically knocking the receiver off the cradle while reaching for it.

"Mr. Hardesty," the voice I vaguely recognized but could not place said, "this is Bonnie Bronson. Could I speak with you about a very sensitive matter?"

Bonnie *Bronson? This should be interesting,* I thought. "Of course," I said.

"I understand my sister has hired you to look into the death of Kelly DeNuncio's mother."

And just how did you come by that information? my mind asked.

"Estelle and I had a talk last night after she returned from Ms. DeNuncio's funeral," she continued, answering the question.

"And?" I asked.

A slight pause, then: "And I was wondering if you would be kind enough to just tear up Estelle's check—we insist on reimbursing you for the time you have already invested, of course—and consider the contract voided?"

Not so fast, lady!

"Please don't think I'm being rude," I said, "But may I ask

why Estelle doesn't ask me herself?"

There was a long, deep sigh. "No, I don't think you're being rude at all," she said, "and this has nothing to do with your qualifications as a private investigator. But I'm afraid you...well, you don't know my sister well enough to fully understand her. Estelle is a sweet, wonderful, and compassionate woman, but her compassion too often gets the best of her. Ms. DeNuncio's death was a tragic accident, but I'm sure that's all it was: an accident. I truly hate to see you waste your time"...*and Estelle's money,* my mind added..."looking for something that isn't there."

It was my turn for a pause before saying: "I can certainly appreciate your position, but I must point out that the contract is between your sister and me, and she is the only one who can terminate it. When I agreed to look into Carlene's death, it was with the understanding that if the time came that I was reasonably sure it was an accident, I would withdraw. I don't like to waste either my time or my clients' money on a case I believe is groundless."

"As this one is," she said.

"Quite possibly," I said, "but it is obviously very important to your sister to be sure. That's what I intend to find out," I replied.

She sighed. "Very well," she said, sounding totally unconvinced. "But I will not let it drag out forever—no offense intended."

"None taken," I said. "But think of it this way: we entrust Joshua to your care; I'd appreciate your entrusting Estelle's concerns to me."

There was only the briefest of pauses before she said abruptly: "Well, I really must go. Goodbye."

I couldn't help but wonder just how tight a leash Bonnie Bronson had on her sister, and why? The fact that Estelle kept her budding relationships from her sister gave me the definite impression that Bonnie wasn't too keen on the idea of Estelle's having someone else in her life. I wondered just how far she might go to prevent it. And perhaps it was just my suspicious nature, but the fact that the two relationships Estelle had mentioned had ended with the death of the prospective partner struck me as being more than a little...well, unusual.

I decided to call Marty anyway, just to see if anything more had been found out about the stolen van and its driver. Just as I was reaching for the phone, it rang.

Busy day.

"Dick. Marty." *E.S.P. lives*, I thought. "I just thought I'd let you know the Carrington police talked to Jan Houston last night. She admits to writing that note, but denies it was meant to be a threat. And she claims she was at a friend's cabin at Lake Verde, alone, the day Ms. DeNuncio died. Says she went up there Sunday and came back Wednesday, when she heard about the accident. She doesn't have any witnesses, though."

"Are they going to follow up on that at all?" I asked.

"Well, they called the cabin's owner, who verified that she'd given the key to Ms. Houston Sunday afternoon, and it had been returned Wednesday night. The owner says she hardly ever goes up there herself, and Ms. Houston always mows the lawn and cleans up when she's there."

"So did she?" I asked.

"Did she what?" he countered.

"Did she mow the lawn?"

A rather long pause, then: "Jeez, I don't know. Carrington's got a pretty small police force, so I doubt if they have much time to send officers out of the county just to see if a lawn was mowed."

"Well," I said, "if the lawn *was* mowed, Jan Houston has a stronger alibi. If it wasn't...."

Another pause. "You're right." he said. "But don't forget, she wasn't driving the van that killed Ms. DeNuncio."

"Granted it was a guy who ditched it," I said, "but it's possible she could have stolen it and been driving it. Did witnesses at the scene say it was a man driving?"

"Six witnesses, four stories. One *said* it was a man, one

thought it was a man, and one thought it *could* have been a woman…or not. One claimed there were two people in the van. The other two saw Ms. DeNuncio being hit but were too shocked to notice the driver."

"So could someone on our force go up to Lake Verde and check?"

"Jeez, Dick, I really don't know. It's kind of a long stretch, and unless we had something stronger to go on…."

"I understand," I said, and I did. "But do you think you could get me the address of the cabin? I can take a run up there myself."

"Yeah, that I think I can do. We did run a check on her for any criminal record. She's apparently clean, at least in Carrington and here. Where did you say they moved here from?"

"Cincinnati, I think," I said, "I saw her at the cemetery after the funeral, way off by herself, just watching."

I gave him Beth's phone number and last name, and asked him if anything had been found out about the guy who ditched the van.

"We got a description from some kids who were playing on the sidewalk when he ditched it: short, stocky, middle-aged white guy with a slight limp. Wearing overalls and a work shirt. The description doesn't fit any of our 'regulars'. Lots of fingerprints in the van—way too many, as a matter of fact. It's a rental stolen off a lot—one of those cheapy places where they don't bother to do much more than run a vacuum through it and wash the windows between rentals. And most of the prints were overlapping, on areas like the steering wheel and door handles. It's going to take forever to sort them out…and all this assuming the guy has his prints on file and that he wasn't wearing gloves."

"If he hot-wired it to get it started, was there anything on the lower steering column or the hood?" I asked.

"He didn't have to hot-wire it," Marty said. "It's the kind of place they leave the key under the sun visor."

"Hmm," I said. "So the van was stolen Sunday night. What would a guy wearing work clothes be doing driving it around in broad daylight on a Monday right after lunch if he wasn't working?"

"Good question," he said. "We're going to try to find that out. That's what we do, you know."

I laughed and we talked for a minute or so more, then hung up, with the usual promises to keep each other informed.

**

About two thirty that afternoon, Marty called back to give me the address of the cabin on Lake Verde—too late to drive up there and make it back in time to go to Tim and Phil's for dinner. I thought we might drive up there on Saturday and take a look—maybe even let Joshua go swimming. That was something Jonathan and I had never done yet. Maybe have a picnic.

Won't that be sweet? one of my mind voices said sarcastically. *A family outing! Just like the straight folks.*

I told it to knock it off.

I planned to leave work a little early so I could stop by my favorite bakery, about two blocks from work. I'd told Tim we'd bring dessert, and had ordered one of the bakery's specialties: a Devil's Food whipped cream cake that Tim, Phil, and I loved. (To say that Jonathan loved it too would be slightly redundant, since there was very little other than fresh lox that he didn't love.)

Just as I was getting ready to leave, the phone rang, and I was surprised to hear Glen O'Banyon's voice on the other end.

"Glen, hi!" I said. "To what do I owe the honor?"

"Are you by any chance investigating the death of a Carlene DeNuncio?"he asked, getting right to the point.

"As a matter of fact, I am," I said, curious as to why he might be asking.

"Just what do you know of this child custody case involving

Kelly DeNuncio?" Another rather odd question, I thought.

"Not too much, really," I said. "Carlene DeNuncio, Kelly's mother, was killed in a hit-and-run and all of a sudden his biological father, who Carlene thought didn't even know about Kelly, called Carlene's sister, Beth Erickson, who had taken Kelly in, to announce that he wants Kelly. Very odd timing, if you ask me, especially considering he apparently wasn't even aware he had a son—and even if he was, he'd never shown any interest at all in him. Are you going to be able to help the Erickson's?"

"I'm not sure," he said. "Child custody cases aren't my specialty, and with my schedule as full as it already is...."

"I'm sure they'll understand if you can't take it," I said. "I told Beth to call you just in case, and that if you couldn't take it you might refer her to someone who could."

"Yes," he said, "she did call and I set up an appointment for her with one of my associates here in the office, largely because you recommended me to her. She's coming in shortly, I believe."

"That's really nice of you, Glen," I said, and it certainly was considering that he is one of the busiest and best lawyers in the city.

"But here's where it get's interesting...." He said, then paused.

"How so?" I asked with my usual inability to just keep quiet until he was ready to continue.

"I know quite a few attorneys in Louisville, and I asked Mrs. Erickson the name of the attorney who'd filed the papers. It turns out to be Kelsey Bowman, probably the best criminal defense lawyer in Kentucky. What in hell *he*'s doing handling a child custody case is beyond me, but I'd say Roy D'Angelo must have pretty deep pockets."

Deep pockets? From what very little I knew about Roy D'Angelo, I somehow doubted that he had the kind of money a high-class attorney would demand.

But maybe his mother would.

CHAPTER 6

If Carlene's death was not an accident, Roy D'Angelo's timing in filing for custody put him right up there with Jan Houston in the probable-suspects list. The guy by all accounts was a jerk, but was he just being monumentally insensitive in the timing, or could he possibly be so incredibly stupid as to murder Carlene and then turn right around and file for custody? If indeed he first learned of Kelly's existence from his mother's reading the newspaper report of Carlene's death, it had to be the former.

And how did Roy's mother fit into all this? From what Carlene had said, I gathered mother and son were not terribly close, and that she'd strongly disapproved of Roy's even seeing Carlene. Why would she immediately jump to the conclusion—correct though it was—that Carlene's son was Roy's? And why would she ante up the money for a high-powered lawyer?

Well, the thing about the lawyer was, I suppose, understandable. Roy D'Angelo didn't exactly strike me as being great parent material, and any court would probably see it right off the bat. But never underestimate the power of a good lawyer!

I definitely should talk with Roy D'Angelo, and maybe his mother as well. But how could I reach either one of them if I wanted to?

I pondered these questions to my usual excess while leaving the office, picking up the cake at the bakery, and driving home.

* * *

I got home about ten minutes before Jonathan and Joshua—just enough time to wash up and change my shirt before I heard Joshua's voice at the door saying: "Let me! I can do it!" and Jonathan's reluctant acquiescence, followed by fumbling sounds around the doorknob and lock, and finally the door opened and Joshua came running into the room while

Jonathan retrieved the keys from the lock.

"Hi, Uncle Dick!" Joshua said brightly. "I unlocked the door all by myself!"

I glanced at Jonathan who gave me a slightly raised eyebrow but said nothing.

"Good for you!" I said, then knelt down. "Now, how's about a group hug?"

I scooped Joshua up in one arm, noting that he must weigh around 40 pounds or so, and was joined by Jonathan for a mutual hug. Jonathan gave an exaggerated grunt in response to Joshua's squeeze and, when we broke the hug, said: "You're getting pretty strong there, Joshua!" and the boy beamed.

While Jonathan was getting dressed, I took Joshua into the bathroom for a quick washcloth face-and-hands scrub and a hair combing, then led him into his bedroom where Jonathan had set out a clean Winnie the Pooh tee shirt and pair of pants.

Four year olds are pretty good at changing their own clothes, but haven't quite mastered all the fine points yet, such as the reasons for putting on one's pants before putting on the shoes.

We took Jonathan's car, which proved to be something of a challenge with me trying to hold the cake on my lap while Joshua decided he and Bunny should ride up front, too. After being assured he could ride in the front seat on the way home, he developed a sudden interest in traffic lights, wanting to know how they worked and who told them when to change color, etc.

We and the cake arrived in one piece, and found a parking place about half a block from Tim and Phil's apartment.

Phil greeted us at the door. We forewent our usual hugs, Phil apparently not wanting to confuse Joshua, to whom he extended his hand. "Hello, Joshua," he said, "I'm Phil." Joshua dropped Bunny on the floor, took Phil's hand without hesitation, and said "Hi."

* * *

The evening went remarkably well, and Tim endeared himself to Joshua by taking him over to the large, octagonal aquarium and introducing him to the fish. Joshua, of course, wanted to know all their names and, though unlike Jonathan, Tim and Phil had never found it necessary to name them, Tim quickly pointed from fish to fish, reciting the names of the Seven Dwarfs and the main characters from Bambi, which was fine with Joshua.

Their aquarium was about four times the size of Jonathan's and stood on a low table, which made it possible for Joshua to stand on the floor and put his nose against the glass and slap his palm against the sides to try to get the attention of the fish. Fortunately, it was also about four feet tall, which made it unlikely Joshua might decide to try to pet them.

"Be careful, Joshua," Jonathan said. "You're pretty strong and you might knock the tank over and hurt the fish." There was very little chance of that, of course, but it got Joshua to stop.

After Joshua and Tim were through greeting the fish, Phil fixed drinks for himself, Tim, and me, and Jonathan shared a bottle of ginger ale with Joshua.

Tim had made a pot roast which was, as always, delicious and with just a small amount of cutting of potatoes and a few larger pieces of meat into manageable sizes for Joshua, he did very well for himself. He and Jonathan got into a little game of "monkey see/monkey do"—Jonathan would spear a piece of potato with his fork, and Joshua would follow. When Jonathan wiped the corner of his mouth with a napkin, Joshua did the same. It soon evolved into Jonathan making exaggeratedly slow movements with his fork, and Joshua following suit. Joshua, of course, thought the whole thing was hysterically funny and soon dissolved into laughter. But it kept him occupied, and it wasn't until he'd pretty well finished most of the food on his plate that he began getting antsy. With Jonathan's okay, he scooted off his chair and, grabbing Bunny, wandered into the living room, toward the fish tank.

"Uh…" I began, but Phil cut me off.

"That's okay," he said. "He can't do any harm."

"Dream on," I said, grinning.

But Tim was sitting in a position that he could keep an eye on him, so I wasn't too concerned.

"He's a great kid," Tim said. "And I can sure see the family resemblance, Jonathan."

"Devastating good looks run in the family," Jonathan said with a grin, "and yeah, he really is a good kid. I think even Dick will agree on that one."

"Yeah," I admitted. "It hasn't been anywhere near what I was afraid it might be."

Jonathan gave me another one of his "significant" looks and raised an eyebrow, but didn't say anything.

After coffee and cake for the grown-ups and milk and cake for Joshua, we went into the living room to sit and talk for a few minutes. I could tell Joshua's clock was starting to run down when he wanted to get up on the couch between Jonathan and me and, after a minute or two of fidgeting and a lengthy if subdued conversation with Bunny, his eyelids became heavy. Despite valiant attempts to keep his eyes open, he began a slow list to port, ending up with his head against Jonathan's arm.

We left shortly afterwards, with Joshua waking up only briefly when I picked him up to carry him to the car. He put his arms around my neck and laid his head on my shoulder and I thought how maybe having a kid wouldn't be such a bad idea after all.

Watch it, Hardesty! a chorus of mind voices said firmly.

* * *

I'd mentioned to Jonathan on the way home about running up to Lake Verde to check out Jan Houston's story, and he thought it was a great idea, especially when I mentioned that we might take Joshua swimming.

"We'll have a picnic!" Jonathan enthused. "But we'll have

to buy Joshua a bathing suit—he doesn't have one with him."

"Can't he just wear a pair of shorts?" I asked.

"Would *you* just wear a pair of shorts?" he responded. "Joshua's four years old. He needs a real bathing suit."

So what I'd envisioned as a simple leave-the-house-after-breakfast drive turned into a go-grocery-shopping-and-swimsuit-hunt. We didn't even get everything into the car before eleven thirty.

When he learned we might be going swimming, Joshua immediately asked if we were going to take the fish with us and, upon being told 'no' launched a long series of questions as to why, whether we could bring home some new fish from the lake, if he could take along the fish food to feed the lake fish, etc., each answer being countered by "Why?"

* * *

It was a nice day, warm and sunny, and traffic was light. We didn't get to Lake Verde until quarter to one, during which time both Jonathan and Joshua dipped into the large cooler Jonathan had packed with sandwiches, fruit, soft drinks, chips, and several half-pints of milk. Joshua wanted the chips and a coke, but Jonathan convinced him to settle for an apple and a carton of milk until we got where we were going.

I decided to drive by the address Marty had given me first, so that when we did finally park we could just relax. It took awhile to find the road I was looking for, which proved to be the only road on and circling a small peninsula jutting out into the lake. Cottages and cabins lined the shore on this side of the lake, and the one I was looking for was just before the curve where the road turned and headed back to the mainland. I slowed down as we approached. There was a fairly long asphalt driveway with a new bright red convertible in front of the closed garage door; definitely not the car on the side road at Carlene's funeral. The owner's, maybe? I could see no one but, since we had all the windows down, I could hear a familiar sound from the lake-side of the house: a lawnmower. I noted that there were large sprays of fresh grass clippings on the driveway. If it was the owner's car, I imagined she was probably a little unhappy at having to mow the lawn herself, since she'd probably assumed Jan had done it when she was there last.

As we passed the house, I looked back to see Jan Houston coming around the side of the house pushing a mower. I quickly looked away and kept driving, and she didn't look up as we passed. Just as well.

So, that answered that question. From the amount of grass clippings on the driveway it appeared to me that the lawn probably hadn't been mowed in some time, which meant Jan Houston's story of having been at the cabin when Carlene was killed was most likely a lie. If she'd come up to mow now, and apparently with the owner or someone else with a red car—though I didn't see any signs of anyone else—it made me wonder just what the real story was between the two of them.

* * *

We drove to the other side of the lake which was mostly state-owned property with one large public beach. It was rather surprisingly uncrowded, but there were several kids Joshua's age running around—which didn't escape Joshua's attention.

We'd put on our bathing suits under our clothes before leaving the apartment, and while Jonathan got Joshua stripped down to his swim suit—a process not made materially easier by Joshua's fidgeting eagerness to get out and start playing—I carried the cooler, blanket, and towels to an area a bit removed from the main concentration of people.

As I was spreading out the blanket, I heard Jonathan call "Dick!" and turned just in time to see Joshua racing past me toward the water. I ran over and scooped him up.

"Whoa, Cowboy," I said as he struggled in my arms.

"I wanna go swimming!" he protested, squirming to get me to put him down.

Jonathan, who had been in the process of taking his own pants off when Joshua made his getaway, came up and took Joshua out of my arms, setting him down, but with a hand ready to grab should he try to make another break for it.

"Where do you think you're going?" Jonathan demanded.

"Swimming!" the boy replied.

"Well, just wait a second until Uncle Dick and I are ready."

Joshua was like a racehorse at the starting gate, so I said: "You go ahead. I'll get undressed and be right with you."

Joshua was off like a shot, with Jonathan close behind.

After I'd kicked off my shoes and was unbuckling my belt, I looked across the lake, seeing if I could spot the cabin—or even the peninsula—where I'd just seen Jan Houston, but the lake was just too big and meandering . I really was curious about her, and the possibility of her having had anything whatever to do with Carlene's death. Having a few words with a distraught mourner at a funeral doesn't exactly paint a fully rounded portrait of who that person might be under other circumstances. But after our brief encounter at the cemetery, I knew getting to talk to her again would be something of a problem. Still....

I felt a small, wet, sand-coated hand pulling on my arm.

"Uncle Dick!" Joshua said. "Uncle Jonathan says for you to hurry up!"

I looked out into the water to see Jonathan standing waist-deep, hands on his hips, staring in our direction. The sun was glinting on the water behind him, and I thought yet again of just how damned lucky I was.

Having performed his messenger duties, Joshua raced off toward Jonathan, only to make a sudden detour directly for the water. He stopped just at the water's edge and bent over to examine something of obviously great interest. I finished stripping down to my bathing suit, put my wallet and my keys in my shoes, and hurried over to see what had gotten his attention. It was a small, very dead catfish. Joshua had picked up a nearby stick and was tentatively poking at it.

"It stinks!" he said as I walked up. "How come it's dead?" I shrugged. "Fish die," I said.

"Do fish go to heaven?" he asked, dropping the stick but still staring at the fish.

"I'm not sure," I said.

He apparently pondered his question, then nodded firmly, not looking at me.

"They do," he pronounced. "Jesus loves fish."

"Come on," I said, "Uncle Jonathan's waiting."

* * *

Joshua slept all the way home, and Jonathan napped. It had been a fun but exhausting day. There hadn't been as much suntan lotion in the bottle as we'd thought, so most of it went to basting Joshua regularly. I could feel the heat on my shoulders as I drove, and knew I'd probably be a lobster red by morning. We didn't get back to the apartment until about six and ordered a pizza for dinner. There was a message on the machine from Samuel and Sheryl, telling Joshua how much they missed him. They confirmed that they'd be flying back to the mainland on Wednesday and should be here late Friday or early Saturday.

I had suspected that Joshua's long nap would merely recharge his batteries and turn bedtime into a major skirmish, which it did—complete with an Oscar-caliber tantrum and flood of tears calculated to melt even the most icy of hearts, and culminated by that absolutely sure-fire winner: "I want my mommy!" When that didn't work, he fell back on a variety of stalling tactics and frequent use of Jonathan logic. ("I don't want to take a bath! I just *went* swimming!") We—make that Jonathan—finally got him to bed by telling him that he could stay up all night if he wanted to, but that we were going to go into his bedroom and read Bunny a story and this would be his only chance.

* * *

As we were getting ready for bed, Jonathan suggested taking Joshua to Sunday School at the M.C.C. Apparently Samuel and Sheryl were regular churchgoers, and Jonathan felt he should keep up the tradition for Joshua's sake. As a practicing Agnostic who feels uncomfortable with any kind of organized religion no matter how nondenominational, I said I thought it was a good idea, but that I'd let the two of them go by themselves while I stayed home and read the paper.

Sunday morning, while Joshua "helped" Jonathan make breakfast by putting the silverware and napkins on the table and pushing the "on" and "off" switch on the blender to mix the eggs—Bob and Mario called, inviting us over for a barbecue that afternoon, and we readily agreed.

When Jonathan and Joshua went off to church, leaving me to my newspaper, I was able to enjoy probably a full ten minutes of complete relaxation before my mind started throwing in random thoughts like tossing dirty socks into the laundry hamper. I'd noticed how the amount of dirty clothes in the hamper had seemed to multiply like rabbits since Joshua had been in the house. Thinking how quiet it was without Joshua led me to wondering how Kelly was doing, which dragged in Jan Houston and Carlene and Estelle and Bonnie Bronson, Roy D'Angelo and the guy who was seen abandoning the van that had killed Carlene, and...

Aw, come on, Hardesty! It's Sunday, *fer chrissake!*

* * *

By the time we got to Mario and Bob's, I'd pretty much wrestled my work-thoughts back into their cages and was able to enjoy the rest of the day. We introduced Joshua to Bob and Mario, and they introduced all of us—but especially Joshua—to the two most recent additions to their household: Butch and Pancake, two young kittens someone had left in a box in the alley behind Venture, the bar Mario managed. That pretty much took care of entertaining Joshua for the time we were there. I was at first a little concerned he might unintentionally hurt them, but he'd been raised around small animals and was very careful with them.

"Where did you get their names?" Jonathan asked as we sat in the back yard watching Bob putter with the grill.

Mario grinned. "Well, when I first went to pick them up out of the box, one of them hissed at me and swatted me with both paws. I named him Butch on the spot, though it turns out he's a she. Pancake's a boy, and Bob named him the morning after I brought them home. He was trying to fix breakfast and Pancake somehow got on the counter and knocked over a canister of flour. Scared the shit out of the poor thing—he shot halfway across the room in one bound, and then left a trail of flour cat-paw prints up the stairs and into our bedroom, where we found him hiding under the bed."

I could read Jonathan's mind as he watched Joshua lying on the grass on his stomach, playing with the kittens.

"Don't even think about it!" I said.

"What?" he asked with open-eyed innocence, but his grin gave him away.

* * *

Okay. Monday. New day, new week. Now what do I do? Which trail of breadcrumbs to try to follow first? It would have been one thing had Carlene been shot, or stabbed, or, well...*obviously* murdered. But I *still* didn't know for sure that Carlene's death was not an accident. Neither did the police, of course, which is why it was largely up to me to find out.

I wished I knew how to get in touch with Roy D'Angelo, or even his mother. They might be able to point me in some sort of direction. The more I thought of Jan Houston, the less likely I was to consider her a number-one suspect, despite having caught her in the lie about where she was the day Carlene was killed.

My gut still told me there was some sort of connection between Carlene's death and that of Frank Santorini, about whom there was no question that he'd been murdered. Bonnie Bronson's name kept weaving its way in and out of my "look into it" list of things to do. But for the moment, I decided to concentrate on Roy D'Angelo and, by extension, his mother.

After I'd had my coffee, read the paper, and done the crossword puzzle, I called Beth Erickson, Carlene's sister. I didn't know if she had a day job, but if she wasn't home, perhaps she had a machine.

The phone was answered on the second ring by a very young voice I recognized immediately. "Who's this?" the voice demanded.

"Hi, Kelly, it's Dick." I doubted very much that he had the slightest idea who I was, but at least he had a name. "Is your Aunt Beth home?"

Just then I heard a voice in the background saying "Kelly, you're not supposed to answer the phone, remember?"

"But I know how!"

"I know you do, dear, but we'll talk about it later." Then the sound of the phone changing hands and then a very tentative: "Hello?"

"Beth, hi," I said. "This is Dick Hardesty. I'm sorry to bother you, but I had a few questions you might help me with."

"About Carlene?" she asked. "I really appreciate your taking so much interest in us, Dick, and I have to admit I'm a bit puzzled as to why."

I realized then that she had no idea Carlene's death may not have been a simple hit-and-run or that I had been hired to investigate the possibility.

"Well," I said, "this may sound a little strange, but as a private investigator I have a rather suspicious nature. And when I heard about Roy D'Angelo trying to get custody of Kelly within days of Carlene's death.... Please understand I'm not saying there's necessarily any connection between the two events, and

I'm certainly not trying to drum up business, but I'd just feel better if I could rule out the possibility, however remote. While I didn't know Carlene well, she was a neighbor and Jonathan and I cared about her and Kelly."

"That's very kind of you," she said. "But Mr. O'Banyon's office has agreed to handle it for us, and we have every confidence in him." There was a pause. "What was it you wanted to ask me?" she said.

"I was wondering if you might possibly have Roy D'Angelo's address or phone number?"

There was a slight pause, then: "No, I'm afraid not. It may be on the legal papers, but I sent them to Mr. O'Banyon's office the minute I got them."

"But as far as you know, he's still living in the Louisville area?" I asked.

Another pause. "As far as I know. But he didn't live in Louisville proper, I don't think. Saint Matthews comes to mind. I remember Carlene telling me he was living in a house his mother owned there. Why do you..." There was a sudden pause, then. "I know they haven't found the driver of the van yet, but surely you're not implying it wasn't an accident or that Roy might have...."

Not wanting to get her rushing off in directions she really didn't need to go, I interrupted her. "As I said," I...uh...said, "there is really nothing other than the probably coincidental timing of Carlene's death and Roy's showing up that might lead me to think that Roy was involved in any way, but for my own peace of mind, I'd like to follow through on it."

"Well," she said, "again, I do appreciate your concern, and thank you for everything you've done."

"And thank you for your help," I replied. "Please tell Kelly that Joshua, Jonathan, and I said hello."

"I will. Goodbye for now, then."

And we hung up.

* * *

It had been about 5 years since Carlene had moved from the Louisville area, and I had absolutely no idea if Roy D'Angelo was still even in Kentucky, let alone still living in his mother's house in Saint Matthews, but I thought I'd give it a try. I called long-distance information first for Louisville—no Roy D'Angelo listed—and then for Saint Matthews, where I lucked out. I wrote the number down, thanked the operator, and hung up. Not expecting that he'd be home—if, indeed, I even had the right Roy D'Angelo—I dialed the number. Carlene had told me he was a stock-car racer, but whether he was still doing it or, if so, if that was a full-time job or not I had no idea.

The phone was answered after three rings, by a woman's: "Hello?"

"Is Roy D'Angelo in?" I asked.

"No," she said. "He's at the shop."

I didn't ask what kind of shop it might be, so I just said: "Do you know what time he'll be home?"

"When he gets here, I expect," she said with mild disinterest. "Who's calling?"

I gave her my name, phone number, and where I was calling from.

"This about his kid?" she asked, again in a slightly distracted tone.

"Indirectly," I said, not wanting to go into more detail. "Would you like to have him call me, or should I call back and try to catch him later?"

"I'll give him your number," she said.

I thanked her and hung up.

* * *

I was just getting ready to leave the office for the day when the phone rang.

Picking up the phone, I said: "Hardesty Investigations."

"Hardesty *what?*" the male voice demanded. The sound of a car engine revving up in the background nearly drowned him out.

"Hardesty Investigations," I repeated, instantly irked. God, I wish I'd been blessed with patience rather than devastating good looks!

Uh huh, my mind voice said.

"Some guy named Dick Hardesty called my house this morning and wanted me to call him. That's you?"

"That's me," I replied. Since Roy D'Angelo was the only one I'd left a message to call me that day, I felt fairly confident in adding: "Thanks for returning the call, Mr. D'Angelo."

"So what's this all about? Are you working for the woman who's got my kid?" More loud engine noises. Either he kept a hot rod in his living room, or he was calling from a garage. I waited until it was quiet enough to make myself heard, then said: "No, I'm not."

"Then what do you want?" he demanded. "And what does it have to do with my kid?"

Mr. Personality, I thought. *He and Jan Houston would make a great couple if she weren't gay.*

"I'm looking into Carlene's death," I said.

"What the hell for? It was an accident. Who *are* you working for?"

"Who I'm working for doesn't matter. *Why* does. My client suspects the 'accident' wasn't, in fact, an accident, and I'm trying to find out if that suspicion might have basis in fact."

"That's no skin off my nose one way or the other," he said. "If it wasn't an accident, it was probably one of her dyke girlfriends." His voice was suddenly drowned out by the roar of the revving engine, which was muffled when Roy apparently put his hand over the mouthpiece of the phone and yelled: "Turn the fuckin' thing off a minute, will ya?"

There was abrupt silence, then: "So what do you want from me?"

Good question, I thought, but forged ahead anyway. "I was wondering when and how you first learned you had a son, and when you decided to file for custody."

"Not that it's any of your damned business, but Angelina told me. She read it in the paper."

"Angelina?" I asked, thoroughly confused. "…and she read what in the paper?"

"Angelina's my mother, and she read about Carlene's getting killed and that she had a kid."

He calls his mother Angelina? I thought. *Angelina D'Angelo? Now there's a name for you!*

"So what made you decide to file for custody?" I asked.

"He's my kid, and I didn't even know he existed! She's dead, so now he's mine."

He made it sound as though Kelly was a used car.

"I'm sorry," I said, "but I'd gotten the impression that you didn't want kids."

"Who told you that?" he demanded, then continued without waiting for an answer. "He's mine, and I want him."

"Are you still driving stock cars?" I asked.

"Yeah, so what's that got to do with anything?"

"Just curious. We have a track here: Elmsley Raceway. Are you familiar with it?"

"Yeah," he said. "It's on the circuit. So what?"

"Nothing," I replied. "Have you raced here recently?"

There was a pause, then the click of the receiver being hung up.

I guess Jonathan isn't the only one who could use a little work on his subtlety.

* * *

I must say, having Joshua around certainly helped take my mind off work. When I got home, Jonathan and Joshua had apparently just gotten in. Jonathan was in the kitchen unpacking a bag of groceries, and Joshua was busily transporting everything from his toy box in his bedroom, where we'd moved it, back into the living room. I went to the kitchen to exchange hugs with Jonathan and to fix my Manhattan. Upon reentering the living room, I had to put down my drink immediately to give Joshua his hug, too. I noticed he had a band-aid on one index finger.

"What did you do to your finger?" I asked, which set him off on a long story of his injury, which had a beginning, a middle, and an end, though not necessarily in that order, and there was something in there about Indians. I gathered it had been a paper cut, but the kid had a great future as an adventure writer.

During dinner, he ratcheted-up his usual every-three-minutes question about when his mom and dad were coming home to every two minutes, and I began to realize that I was really going to miss him. And any illusions I might have had about Joshua's visit toning down Jonathan's enthusiasm about having a kid had gone out the window about two days after Joshua arrived. Jonathan had been having a ball playing "uncle," and he was a natural at it. But I knew that the minute Joshua was gone, he'd probably start dropping Jonathan-subtle hints about our finding some way to get a kid of our own. And while Joshua had been a lot easier to have around than I'd imagined, I still was a long, long way from taking that next step.

* * *

Tuesday morning, my morning office ritual was interrupted by frequent mental replays of my conversation with Roy D'Angelo. I knew I was trying to tell me something and I finally zeroed in on it: Elmsley Raceway. The fact that he'd hung up on me when I asked if he'd raced there recently pretty clearly told me that yes, he had. And I wanted to know just how recently that was—though I could hazard a pretty good guess.

The raceway held stock car races every Friday and Saturday night, and while I wasn't much of a racing fan myself, I did remember frequently seeing ads in the paper. Out of curiosity I checked to see if there might be an ad in the paper I'd just been reading. There wasn't, but then I seemed to recall the ads usually ran Wednesday through Saturday. I didn't remember, though, if they ever said anything about who was racing.

I could run down to the library and look through past editions, but thought I'd try just calling the track first. I looked up the number and dialed. After thirteen rings, I hung up. It was unlikely that anyone was there. Elmsley Raceway was located in Vernon, one of the city's less affluent suburbs, and I'd been to the track once. Not exactly the Indianapolis 500, so I assumed they probably didn't have someone there full time. Still, I waited about half an hour and called again. Nothing.

So the library it was.

* * *

I like libraries. They remind me in an odd way of cemeteries—very calm, very peaceful—and I am almost palpably aware of being surrounded by the spirits and words of people long since gone, but who have much to tell those who will listen.

I checked out the papers for the Wednesday through Saturday of the week leading to the Monday of Carlene's death. Sure enough, in the sports section, which I seldom even look at, there was a quarter page ad for Elmsley Raceway's weekend races. At the bottom of the ad were two rows of small pictures of participating drivers in or standing by their cars, with their names—undoubtedly to encourage their fans to come out and root for them. And in the bottom row, third picture from the right, was one Roy D'Angelo, standing beside a car door with a large 38 painted on it and holding a racing helmet. I had to squint to try to see what he looked like, but couldn't tell much: just that he seemed to be relatively short in relation to the car, had medium-long hair and wasn't a bad looking guy, in a definitely Bubba sort of way.

Well, I didn't think I'd be able to recognize him on the street just from that photo, but I had a better idea of what he looked like than I'd had before. And it confirmed the fact that he had been in town at least through Sunday of that week. Carlene had been killed on Monday.

Gentlemen, start your engines.

CHAPTER 7

With Roy D'Angelo now firmly planted in the Suspects column, it occurred to me that I really should make an effort to either rule Jan Houston out entirely or consider her and D'Angelo equal possibilities. In an ideal world, it's always better to have just one suspect to concentrate on but I've seldom had that luxury.

So…get in touch with Beth and see if she'd be willing to let Jan see Kelly on some sort of scheduled basis. I really could understand Jan's position, and I couldn't imagine how I might react under similar circumstances. Problem there was that if Jan had indeed had something to do with Carlene's death, would it be fair to Kelly to let her back into his life?

This was Tuesday, and Samuel and Sheryl would be picking Joshua up at the end of the week. Maybe Jonathan and I could take a drive up to Carrington on Sunday and see if I might arrange to talk with Jan Houston. I knew Jonathan would probably be pretty down about having Joshua gone, so a little distraction might be in order. And maybe we could stop by and see Jared if he was there. I made a note to call Jared when I got home.

* * *

When I returned to the office, I tried the number for Elmsley Raceway again—obviously they weren't open on weekdays, but I've never been one to take "no" for an answer. To my surprise, the phone was answered on the first ring.

"Elmsley Raceway." Definitely a male.

"Hi," I said. "I'm glad I found someone in."

"Just doing some paperwork," the guy said. "We aren't officially open. What can I do for you?"

Yeah, what? I hadn't actually expected anyone to be there.

"Ah, I was wondering how far in advance you know who'll be racing on a certain date."

There was a slight pause, then: "Depends. Mostly the circuit guys set it up a month in advance. Locals can sign in right up to race night. Why? You a racer?"

"No," I said, "but I'm a big fan of Roy D'Angelo. I missed him when he was here a couple of weeks ago, and wondered if you might know when he'll be here again."

Another pause. "Hold a second, let me look. He travels around with about four other drivers, and they're pretty consistent." There was the sound of ruffling paper, then: "Looks like he's signed up for the 10th —two weeks from this coming Friday."

"Great! Thanks," I said. "I appreciate it."

"No problem," he said, and hung up.

Well, the trip to the library hadn't been a total waste. At least now I had a rough idea of what he looked like, and knew his car was #38. Maybe Jonathan and I could go out for a night at the races, and I could arrange to talk to D'Angelo afterwards.

* * *

When I got home, Jonathan and Joshua were in the kitchen, and Joshua was helping to set the table. We were using the Melmac dishes, so Joshua was in charge of not only the silverware but the plates, which he took particular pains to place in exactly the right position as he saw it. Apparently he had been practicing counting at day-care, and as Jonathan handed him each piece of silverware, Joshua would count it aloud. When the table was set, he wandered over to the fish tank and began counting the fish. He did very well up to "8" or so, but then things got a little tricky.

Shortly after dinner, Samuel and Sheryl called to tell Jonathan they were catching an early morning flight back to the mainland and would be on the road the minute they could get their car. Jonathan handed the phone to Joshua, who was overjoyed to hear his folks and set off on a detailed account of what he'd been doing, that we had gone swimming, what all he was learning at "school," etc. and he probably would still be talking to them had Samuel not asked him to have Jonathan back on the line, too. Both Sheryl and Samuel took turns reassuring Joshua how much they loved him and what a good boy he was, and how anxious they were to see him.

I called Jared while Jonathan was giving Joshua his bath and told him we were tentatively planning on taking a drive to Carrington on Sunday, if he'd be home. He said that Jake was coming up for the weekend, and they'd be delighted to see us. We made rough plans to have a barbecue early Sunday evening.

Bath over, jammies on, and the promise of story-time luring him to bed, it still took Joshua forever to settle down, and it took two stories before he finally went to sleep.

* * *

I called Happy Day during "nap time" on Wednesday to talk with Estelle Bronson and let her know what was going on: that there still was no definite indication that Carlene's death had been other than an accident, but that I planned to talk with Carlene's ex over the weekend, and that I'd be talking with Kelly's father when he came back to town in two weeks. I also promised that I would keep following up with the police to see if they had learned anything new. I told her that if, after I'd talked with Jan and Roy D'Angelo again, I found nothing to indicate their involvement, we should discuss whether I should just discontinue further investigation.

Wednesday being school night for Jonathan meant that I would be fully responsible for looking after Joshua, including putting him to bed—a prospect I viewed with some minor trepidation, since Jonathan wouldn't get out of school until nine. My experience with four year old boys had until recently been limited to when I was four myself, two or three infinities ago.

But I guessed I'd do what most adults do in dealing with children: wing it.

I called Jonathan's work and, on being told he was out on a job, left a message to have him call me. I figured we could save some time by going out to eat before Jonathan had to leave for school, and then I could take Joshua down to The Central to find him another children's book—maybe another one illustrated by Catherine Tunderew, since he got such a kick out of her pictures. Then by the time we got home it would be almost time for him to go to bed.

Good plan, Hardesty, one of my mind voices said approvingly, and I modestly had to agree.

* * *

All went according to plan…more or less. We went to Cap'n Rooney's Fish Shack for dinner, which Joshua loved because he could eat everything with his hands, and except for knocking over a bottle of the malt vinegar used with the chips (it had a squirt cap which reduced the spillage to a minimum), was very well behaved. Much of his good behavior was due, I'm sure, to his fascination with the huge fish tank in the center of the room. (He reported, after a careful count, that there were "seventy-twelve" fish in the tank.)

We'd brought both cars to the restaurant, since it was on the way to Jonathan's class. Joshua had ridden with Jonathan but, after switching Bunny from Jonathan's car to mine, Jonathan left, and Joshua and I were on our own. He insisted on sitting in the front seat with me, with Bunny on his lap, and carried on a running monologue largely having to do with his folks coming back and everything they were going to do when they got home…including, apparently, buying Joshua a tractor for him to drive to school, and….

We parked about a block from Bennington Books and, after a slightly heated debate on whether or not Bunny should come with us, we walked to the store—Joshua taking great pains to hop over every crack in the sidewalk. I suspect it had something to do with the fact that I had a four-year-old boy in tow, but I swear I've never been cruised so much in the space of one block in my life. My crotch was equal parts delighted and frustrated.

And I soon realized, on entering the children's section of the store, the naivete of my assessment of the task of buying a small boy a children's book. He wanted them all. Every one. But only after taking each one down from the shelf and looking through it. And upon being instructed to put the book back, it inevitably went back to the wrong place.

I was specifically looking for covers in Catherine Tunderew's style. I'd pick a book off the shelf to look at it, and Joshua would run across the aisle to grab another one and bring it over.

"This is a good one!" he'd say, handing it to me. I'd put back the one I'd just picked up to look at Joshua's offering, and he'd be off to grab another.

A very attractive young clerk came over and asked if we needed help.

"Yours?" he asked with a very...uh...friendly...smile, indicating Joshua.

I returned the smile. "Just on loan," I said. "We're looking for something illustrated by Catherine Tunderew—we got *The Popsicle Tree* last time we were in, and he loved it." I didn't add that Jonathan and I did too.

"Sure," he said. "We've got one right over here."

I interrupted Joshua in mid grab for another book and ushered him in front of me as we followed the clerk.

We ended in a compromise. Rather than the one I'd intended to buy and the 30 or so Joshua picked out, we got three: *Lemon Pizza*, *The Littlest Tractor*, and *Bunny Tales*.

* * *

By the time we got home, it was time to get Joshua ready for bed. With three new books to read, he was surprisingly cooperative. After we got him washed up and his teeth brushed—he did a pretty good job at each—I let him put on his pj's by himself. The bottoms were no problem, but he got a little tangled in the top and ended up with it being on backwards, but the situation was soon remedied and he ran into the living room to pick up the bag with the books with one hand and grab Bunny with the other, took them into his room and hopped onto the bed.

"Where's uncle Jonathan?" he wanted to know.

"He's at school," I explained for probably the fourth time in the course of the evening. "But we can start without him, okay?"

"Okay," he said.

"Which one shall we read?" I asked, taking the books out of the bag.

"All of them!" he said.

I very much doubted he'd last through more than one, if that (considering the time devoted to looking at the pictures and discussing the various elements and the characters, and any train-of-thought associations he made with them).

"Okay," I said. "But which one shall we start with?"

He reached over and grabbed the top book, *The Littlest Tractor*. "This one," he said.

While Bunny remained attentive throughout, Joshua started "resting his eyes" just about the point where the littlest tractor had to brave a storm to go get a needed part to repair Grandpa Thresher.

I carefully got out of bed, slowly slid one of the pillows out from behind his head so he could lie more normally, collected the books, and left the room.

I was watching TV when Jonathan came in, and we sat on the couch awhile talking about our day. As much as Jonathan enjoyed his college classes, he resented missing out on one of our few remaining nights with Joshua. He got a kick out of my relating our bookstore adventures—especially the part about my being conned into buying not one but three books.

"He's not dumb, that's for sure," Jonathan said, grinning. "He knows a patsy when he sees one."

"Thanks," I replied.

We watched part of the 10 o'clock news, then went to bed.

At 10:30 the phone rang.

"Damn!" I said. "I'll get it!"

I hoped out of bed, threw my robe on, and raced for the phone, hoping it hadn't awakened Joshua.

"Hello?" I said as softly as I could, carrying the phone into the living room.

"Is Jonathan there?" a male voice I didn't recognize asked.

Puzzled and mildly irked, I said: "Yeah. He's in bed."

"This is his dad," the voice said, and I detected something in his voice that I did not like.

"I'll get him for you," I said, laying the phone on the coffee table.

I hurried into the bedroom and told Jonathan, who looked startled and quickly got out of bed to go to the phone. Something told me to follow him.

Jonathan picked up the phone. "Hi, Dad," he said. "What's up?"

His face went totally ashen and he pressed his lips tightly together to stiffle the sound people sometimes make when they're punched full-force in the stomach.

He stood there, then began to tremble, and the tremble became a Richter Scale 7.0 shaking. He unconsciously lowered the phone, and I moved forward to take it from his hand with one hand and circle his shoulders with my free arm.

Jonathan was making no sound…just shaking uncontrollably.

"Mr. Quinlan," I said, putting the phone to my ear. "This is Dick. Can you tell me what's wrong?"

But I knew.

Samuel and Sheryl's car had been hit head-on by an out-of-control semi trailer which had swerved across the median and into their lane of traffic, somewhere near the Nevada border. They'd died instantly.

CHAPTER 8

If I could leave several pages blank here, I would. What can I possibly say? Time compressed as violently as the front end of a car hit by a semi trailer. What should have been easily identifiable and describable parts and pieces of time became an inseparable, unrecognizable, melded mass of events, thoughts, emotions, and memories.

I do remember a few things clearly, and I'll try to make some sense of the rest of it: Jonathan's father had been notified of the accident by the Nevada State Police. Arrangements would be made for the return of the bodies to Wisconsin pending the family's instructions.

Neither Jonathan nor I slept one moment. I'd taken Jonathan back to bed after hanging up from his father with the promise that Jonathan would call him in the morning. Jonathan still had not made a sound since that first muffled grunt. Without a sound he took off his robe and got under the covers, as did I. I'd said nothing, either, of course.

Jonathan just lay there on his back, his arms at his side, his eyes looking at the ceiling. When I moved closer to him and reached an arm around his shoulder, he began making soft gasping sounds which, just as his trembling had become shaking, increased in volume and intensity until he threw himself against me, buried his face in my shoulder, and gave a long, terrifying wail which, if not muffled by my shoulder, would undoubtedly have awakened the entire building. I'd heard a wail like it only once before in my entire life, and I had hoped I would never hear another.

* * *

I got up in the morning, got dressed without showering, and somehow got Joshua up, dressed, fed, and ready for school.

Don't ask me how. I knew he could sense something was wrong, but had no idea what, and did not know what or how to ask. He played with his cereal and kept looking at me out of the corner of his eye, but said very little. I did my best to act normal, and explained that Uncle Jonathan was really tired this morning and didn't feel well, and that I would be taking him to school. I had to leave my own thoughts and feelings totally out of the equation.

When I took him into Happy Day, I spoke to Bonnie and explained to her what had happened. Her reaction mirrored her vocalized expression of sincere regret, and I explained that at the moment everything was up in the air, but that I hoped to have more to tell her when I picked Joshua up that afternoon.

* * *

Jonathan was on the phone when I returned to the apartment. His eyes were puffy and he looked as though something had been drained out of him—which, of course, it had. His voice was calm. I went quickly over to him and kissed him on the forehead. He looked up and gave me a very weak smile, then went back to his conversation. I gathered he was talking with one of his sisters. I went into the kitchen to make coffee.

* * *

Of course I didn't even think of going to work. I didn't give one single thought to the case or to anything else except Jonathan and Joshua.

By the time I left the apartment to pick Joshua up from day-care, Jonathan had been on the phone much of the day. He'd called his work and explained the situation, and his boss told him to take all the time he needed.

The double funeral was set for Monday in Cranston. Sheryl had been an only child, and her parents were both dead, so all the arrangements fell on the Quinlans, mainly Jonathan's dad and the one sister who lived in the area. Jonathan's two out-of-state sisters would be returning home for the funeral, and he spoke with both of them during the day.

The biggest decision of the day was made by Jonathan: he would not be taking Joshua with him when he returned to Wisconsin for the funeral. He was adamant about not putting a four year old boy through the trauma of seeing both his parents buried, and while one of his sisters felt strongly that Joshua should be there, Jonathan remained firm. He told her that when it was determined who might become Joshua's guardian, he would bring the boy back at that time.

We didn't really even talk much about my looking after Joshua while Jonathan was gone. Jonathan asked me, as a matter of courtesy, if I minded, and of course I couldn't object. I think we both simply took it for granted. He would fly to Milwaukee Saturday to catch a connecting flight to Rhinelander, where his father would pick him up. He would return Tuesday.

Between phone calls, we talked a bit about what to tell Joshua, and how to explain to him that his mom and dad would not be coming to take him home.

I was amazed by Jonathan's control. Every time either of us would mention Joshua, the tears would well up in his eyes—and we both tried very hard not to mention Samuel or Sheryl at all. Jonathan would grieve for his brother and sister-in-law in his own time and in his own way, but right now Joshua was the only thing either of us could afford to think about.

* * *

I arrived a few minutes early at Happy Day to update the sisters. I asked if Joshua could keep going there until we knew what was going to happen, and they said 'of course.' Though I spoke to each of the sisters separately, neither Bonnie nor Estelle mentioned Carlene or Kelly or my investigation, and I very much appreciated their discretion.

I gave Joshua a piggy-back ride from the porch to the car, and let him ride in the front seat with me, reaching into the back seat for Bunny.

Joshua was not his usual chatterbox self on the way back home. Instead he sat with Bunny in his lap and talked quietly to him about whatever it is that four year old boys talk about to their favorite toy.

Realizing I was being much too quiet myself, I asked him about what he had done at school.

"We played games and painted and read stories," he said. "But everybody's sad."

Oh-oh.

"Really?" I asked. "Do you know why?" I was certainly hoping neither of the sisters had said anything to give him a clue.

"Because my mommy and daddy are coming to take me home."

*Oh, **shit!*** I found myself swallowing hard and blinking my eyes to clear the mist I felt forming there, and not a single one of my mind voices had a comment.

"You like it there at Happy Day, don't you?" I asked.

"Yeah. It's fun."

He went back to conversing with Bunny, and I kept my eyes on the road.

I'd told Jonathan I'd stopped at the store to pick up a few things for dinner and to give him a little more time for himself. I really dreaded what I knew was coming when Jonathan told Joshua, and I hoped he would be able to pull it off.

"How about you and me making dinner tonight, Joshua?" I asked, letting him carry the shopping basket. "What shall we make?"

I already knew the answer, but he reaffirmed it without hesitation: "Hot dogs and macaroni and cheese!"

"Good choice," I said.

* * *

When we got to the apartment, Jonathan was sitting on the couch in the living room. My Manhattan, his Coke, and a jelly-jar glass of soda for Joshua were on the coffee table in front of him. He had dark circles under his eyes and looked haggard, but he got up to come over and scoop Joshua up for our evening hug.

"Hi, Joshua," he said with a smile that tried very hard to make it and may have fooled Joshua, but not me. "How's my big boy?"

"We got hot dogs and macaroni and cheese for dinner!" Joshua announced. "I'm going to help Uncle Dick make supper!"

"That's great!" Jonathan said, setting Joshua down and giving me another very tight hug.

We made it through dinner somehow, Joshua telling us about a fire engine that had gone down the alley behind Happy Day and how he had waved at the firemen and they had waved back and that after his dad bought him a tractor, he was going to ask for a fire truck, and....

With every mention of Samuel and Sheryl, Jonathan would almost visibly wince, and he had to wipe his eyes several times. I'm not sure what my own reactions were, I was so focused on Jonathan.

When we had finished dinner—neither Jonathan nor I ate very much—Jonathan said: "Let's go into the living room, Joshua. I've got something to tell you."

My stomach was in knots as Joshua slid off his chair and ran into the living room to join Bunny, whom he'd left reading a magazine. As Jonathan got up I said: "Do you want to talk to him alone?"

He shook his head. "No," he said, "I need you."

I got up and followed him into the living room.

"Let's sit here on the couch," Jonathan said. "You can bring Bunny."

Joshua scooted up between us and looked up at Jonathan expectantly.

"Is it a surprise?" Joshua asked. "Are mommy and daddy

here?"

Jonathan took a deep, slow breath and put one arm around the boy's shoulder.

"I got a message from your mommy and daddy while you were at school," he began, his voice astoundingly steady and calm. "They were on their way here when Jesus asked them to come see him. They didn't want to go, but you know they teach you in Sunday school that when Jesus asks you to do something, you really should do it."

I couldn't take my eyes off Jonathan's face, and I had never loved him more than I did at that terrible moment.

"Jesus chose your mommy and daddy to come help him in Heaven because he knows what a very strong and brave boy you are," he said.

"So when are they coming home?" Joshua asked. "Tomorrow?"

Jonathan's chin trembled, just for an instant, as he shook his head.

"No," he said, "they'll have to stay with Jesus as long as he needs them."

Joshua started to cry, and it took every ounce of willpower I had to keep from joining him. I could not comprehend what Jonathan must have been feeling. But he took Joshua's chin in one hand and turned his face so that they were looking directly at one another.

"But they wanted me to tell you something, and I want you to listen very carefully and…" his voice faltered for a nanosecond "…never, ever forget it, no matter what. They want you to always remember that they love you more than anything else in the whole world, and though you won't be able to see them except when you're asleep, they'll always be with you and watching over you."

Oh, God, please let him make it, I thought.

Joshua threw himself against Jonathan and buried his head in his side, sobbing loudly as only a heartbroken little boy can sob. I was fighting like hell not to lose it myself, and Jonathan hugged Joshua to him, his lips clamped together to hold in any sound as his head nodded slowly up and down and he clenched his eyes shut, the tears running down his face.

I moved closer to them both and pulled Jonathan's head against my shoulder as he shook in silent sobs.

* * *

Enough.

* * *

Joshua stayed home from day-care on Friday. Jonathan and I slept on top of the covers of Joshua's bed in shifts on Thursday and Friday night so he wouldn't wake up alone—Jonathan had wanted to spend the entire night with him, but I made him go into our room around midnight so he would have some time for himself. I wanted to be with Jonathan, of course, but knew he had to have some time to be alone.

Both days were something of a bad-hangover blur: Jonathan quiet and withdrawn when Joshua wasn't needing his attention; Joshua sleepy and cross and petulant and defiant, throwing his toys around. Thursday afternoon I took Joshua to a nearby city park, hoping—with only partial success—that the swings and slides and teeter-totters would distract him.

Friday we went to pick up Jonathan's tickets and stopped at the bank for some cash. We had some travelers' checks left over from our trip to New York and I insisted Jonathan take them along, just in case. We'd explained to Joshua that Uncle Jonathan had to go away for just a few days to take care of some things, but that he would be home when Joshua got home from "school" on Tuesday, which set off a major outburst.

"No!" Joshua said, hitting Jonathan on the legs with both fists.

"It'll only be a few days," Jonathan said.

"No!" Joshua repeated frantically. "That's what mommy and

daddy said, and Jesus won't let them come back!"

Jonathan knelt down beside him. "It's all right," he said softly. "Jesus wants me to take care of you. He won't ask me to go to heaven, too."

* * *

We had discussed it, so while Jonathan was packing, I called our local florist and asked them to deliver a large circle of white and red roses with a gold silk banner across the middle saying "Mommy and Daddy" to the funeral home for the service. I also ordered a small circle of brown and white chrysanthemums with a card from me.

Going to the airport—we got there in plenty of time for Joshua to explore the terminal and stare out the windows at the planes coming and going—provided a welcome if temporary distraction, though he wanted to know if one of the planes could take him to heaven to be with his mom and dad.

Jonathan was quiet and probably a bit nervous about flying alone, though the purpose of the trip far overshadowed any such mild concern.

Joshua was relatively fine up until the time they called Jonathan's flight and we had to leave him at the gate. As Jonathan hugged us both, Joshua refused to let go of his neck and began crying uncontrollably. Jonathan gently pried Joshua's arms loose, and passed him to me, leading to a major tantrum which included a lot of squirming and kicking. But I held him tightly, one arm across his back, the other keeping his legs from kicking, as Jonathan gave me a sad little smile and a wave, and disappeared into the passageway.

* * *

Okay. Three days alone with a four-year-old boy who knows his life has changed dramatically but doesn't fully understand why or how, being taken care of by a gay adult who, with the exception of the past few weeks, had had no experience and very little contact with kids of any age since he was a kid himself. But I did the best I could. He did seem to need quite a bit of physical reassurance in the form of sitting close to me in the car or on the couch watching TV, roughhousing during our before-dinner playtime and the like.

And luckily, children seem to be remarkably resilient. There is so much going on in their world, so much to do and see and learn, they don't—well, at least Joshua didn't—tend to remain in any one state for extraordinarily long. So while Joshua had alternate periods of being surly, crying, combative, or needy, none of them lasted for any inordinate amount of time. Mostly I just tried to be there when I sensed he needed me—which, at the beginning, was a surprising amount of the time—and let him be himself when he didn't. Reading the cues as to which direction to take wasn't easy.

We (mostly I) had, of course, called all our friends to let them know what had happened and they all immediately expressed their concern and offered any help they could give. When Phil and Tim heard that Joshua would not be going back for the funeral, they offered to take care of him so that I could go back with Jonathan. It was very kind of them, but of course we couldn't even consider it. They all asked if they could or should come over, but we explained that partly because of our concerns for Joshua, and Jonathan's Saturday return to Wisconsin, it would probably be better to wait until his return.

Just as Joshua and I walked in the door upon returning from the airport, Tim and Phil called, asking if we would like to join them for a picnic in Riverside Park, which was about equidistant from their apartment and ours and just coincidentally had a large children's play area. I recognized Tim's fine handiwork immediately, that the whole thing was for our—mostly Joshua's—benefit.

I asked Joshua if he'd like to go to a picnic with Uncle Tim and Uncle Phil, and he immediately brightened and said "Sure!"

Thank God for friends!

* * *

Thanks to the distraction of the picnic, the rest of the day and evening passed with only minor temper tantrums, fits of crying (Joshua, not me), and demands that his mother and father and Uncle Jonathan come home. I didn't take it personally, of course, and when his bedtime finally came, he had deigned to let me read him a story. However, when I sensed he was asleep and moved to get up from the bed, he woke up, not wanting me to leave him alone, so I kicked off my shoes and slept on top of the covers again, fully clothed.

Jonathan had called earlier to tell us that he had arrived safely (we had not told Joshua where he was going—just "away"). He sounded drained and exhausted, but said everything was going as well as could be expected. His entire family—what was left of it—was getting together for dinner on Sunday before visitation at the church. Apparently he and at least one of his sisters had gotten into a heated argument over whether to have open caskets or not, and he never did say who had won. Then he talked for a moment privately with Joshua, assuring him that he was fine, and that he would bring him back a present.

* * *

Sunday morning Bob and Mario called just after breakfast and fish-feeding time (Joshua had wanted to give them some of his cereal but was talked out of it without a major outburst) to see how we were doing, and shortly thereafter Jared called from Carrington, asking if we'd like to come up for a visit as I'd originally intended before the bottom dropped out. He had a friend with a horse ranch just outside of town, and thought Joshua might like to go and see them.

"Hey, Joshua," I called toward his bedroom, where he'd been playing with some of his toys, "how would you like to go see some horses!"

He came running out of the bedroom carrying G.I. Joe.

"Yeah!" he said. "I like horses!"

So I confirmed with Jared, asking what time we should be there, and for specific directions to his house, since this would be my first visit.

Carrington is about an hour's drive, and we left in plenty of time. Joshua was pretty much his old self, probably in anticipation of seeing the horses. He insisted on bringing his cowboy doll and G.I. Joe as well as the ever-present Bunny, and I told him he would have to ride in the back seat to keep them all company.

It had occurred to me to bring Jan Houston's address and, even though I wouldn't have the time to try to contact her, at least I'd know where she lived if I decided to come up when Jonathan got back.

* * *

Carrington's a typical small college town, its skyline dominated by church spires and the imposingly fortress-like sandstone tower of Marymount's administration building. We pulled in to a gas station so Joshua could make a quick pit stop and I could ask for directions to Jan Houston's street, which turned out to be the next cross-street we came to.

It obviously wasn't one of the more fashionable streets in town (if indeed there were any), but it wasn't exactly Cannery Row, either. Small houses, small lots, most beginning to show their age.

I recognized the car before I saw the address. The same red convertible that had been at the cottage at the lake—the one I assumed belonged to the woman who owned the cabin. The garage door was open, and I could see it was empty. So where, I wondered, was Jan's car? And were she and the cabin owner an item now?

As we were approaching the house with the red convertible—the address checked out as being Jan Houston's—the front door of the house opened and Jan came out...alone. I slowed down a bit—just enough to take a look at the license number—but kept driving, looking in my rear view mirror as we passed. Jan walked directly to the car and got in the driver's seat.

It's her *car?* my mind asked. *What happened to the junker from the cemetery?* And from the way Carlene had talked about Jan's total lack of frugality, I wondered how she managed to come up with the money for a new car. Had she suddenly come into money?

Insurance money, maybe? my mind asked.

Aha! And I was right back on the case. Part of me felt just a bit guilty, but it was a positive sign, I guess.

Jan had pulled out of the driveway and was coming up behind us. I flicked on my left turn signal and made a turn onto the next street. Jan kept straight (no pun) ahead. I'm sure she didn't recognize me.

We found our way to Jared's, a comfortable-looking 1930's style bungalow on a street bordering the college campus. I recognized Jared's car parked in the double driveway, and beside it was a new pickup truck with *Sundgaard Construction* painted on the side, which told me Jake was up for what was apparently becoming a more or less regular weekend visit.

There was room behind Jared's car to park, and I got out and opened the back door for Joshua, who was trying to pick up Bunny, G.I. Joe, and Cowboy at the same time, apparently planning to bring them all with him into the house.

"Why don't we just bring one for now?" I suggested. "We can come get the others in a little while."

Too excited at the prospect of seeing the horses to put up too much of a resistance, he opted for Cowboy, and we went to the front door of the house and knocked. It was Jake who answered, in his full Nordic-god splendor. He pushed open the screen door to let us in.

"Hi, Dick," he said as we shook hands. Then he looked down at Joshua, who was standing slightly behind me, clutching Cowboy in his folded arms. Jake smiled and said: "And I'll bet you're Joshua, right?"

Joshua looked down at Cowboy and nodded.

"Jared's out in the yard," Jake said, gesturing for us to follow him as he led us through the living room, dining room, and kitchen, and out onto the back porch. Jared was on a large bricked patio that covered about a quarter of the totally-fenced-in yard. He'd apparently just finished putting charcoal in the large, wheeled grill.

"I figured maybe we could have hamburgers when we got back from the farm," he said, coming over to greet us. We exchanged a hug, and Jared smiled down at Joshua.

"Hi, Josh," he said.

The boy looked up at him solemnly and said, very firmly, "I'm not Josh. I'm Joshua."

Jared's grin broadened and he extended his hand. "Well, then, I'm glad to meet you, Joshua."

Joshua looked quickly to me and, when I nodded, he took Jared's hand and shook it.

Jake asked Joshua if he'd like a glass of lemonade—he would—and the adults sat on the patio talking while Joshua wandered around the yard.

* * *

The trip to the "farm"—actually a riding stable run by the husband of an instructor at Marymount—definitely brought Joshua back to his usual effervescent self, and when the owner offered to take him on a ride on one of the horses, Joshua was almost beside himself with excitement.

However, any illusions I may have had about Joshua's putting things behind them was shattered when, on the way back to the city, he said: "I'm going to ask my daddy to buy me a horse when we get back home!"

Sigh.

* * *

We didn't get back to the apartment until nearly seven, having joined Jared and Jake for an impromptu barbecue in Jared's back yard.

Joshua was pretty tuckered out and took his bath without complaint. I let him play in the living room for a little while in his pj's, then took him into his bedroom for story time. He was asleep within minutes, and did not wake up when I got up and left the room, leaving his door open just a crack so I could hear if he called.

I stayed in the living room near the phone, watching TV until around 9:45, when Jonathan called. He still sounded tired and depressed, but said everything had gone as well as could be expected under the circumstances, and the open-casket/closed-casket controversy had been resolved with a compromise: they remained closed unless someone specifically asked to see the bodies, at which point one of Jonathan's brothers-in-law would do the honors while Jonathan turned away until the caskets were again closed. Luckily, very few people had requested it. Seeing the caskets closed, most people assumed they were supposed to remain closed.

Dinner had been a somber affair, not surprisingly, and they'd all gone out to a local restaurant rather than have any of the sisters or other relatives have to go to the trouble of preparing one for the entire family.

The issue of Joshua had been skirted by mutual consent, though it was decided that after the funeral Monday, everyone would gather at Jonathan's dad's house to discuss the situation. Apparently there was a will at the family lawyer's office, but no one had looked at it yet. The lawyer was to bring it to the meeting after the funeral.

* * *

Monday was a pretty good day, if the word "good" can be used under the circumstances. Well, I learned a few things, and it passed fairly rapidly. I woke up around 6, went quickly to the shower, got dressed, had a cup of coffee, and then went in to get Joshua up and ready for "school." He was anxious to tell everybody about his adventures with the horses, and only mentioned his parents three or four times—always in the present tense.

I walked with him into Happy Day and exchanged a few casual words with Bonnie Bronson—neither of us mentioning Jonathan or Joshua's situation.

Joshua, of course, had dashed off to be with one of his friends, and I managed to catch his eye and wave before leaving. He left his friend and came running back to me.

"Where are you going?" he asked, looking anxious.

"I have to go to work," I said, putting my hand on his head and tousling his hair. "I'll be back to pick you up after school."

"Promise?" he asked.

I bent over and picked him up. "I promise," I said. "Now how about a hug?"

He gave me a quick arms-around-the-neck squeeze, and I set him down. "I'll see you later, then," I said. He stood there looking at me for just a moment, then turned around and ran back to his friend.

* * *

On the way to the office I kept thinking about Jan Houston's new car and the probability that she might have taken out an insurance policy on Carlene's life—and if so, when. On the one hand, it was logical for gays and lesbians—not having the same legal rights as straights—to name their partner as beneficiary of their life insurance policy, and it's possible that's what Jan and Carlene did. But I'd have imagined that any policy Carlene might have had would have Kelly as her beneficiary. Well, I'd check it out.

* * *

Though I'd only been away from the office for... what?... three days, it seemed like a lot longer. But by the time I'd gone through my coffee/newspaper/crossword puzzle ritual, I was back on track.

I called Beth Erickson, not really expecting her to be home, but she was. I asked her if Carlene had had any life insurance, and she said "Unfortunately, no"—Carlene was not really old enough for the intimations of mortality which generally prompt the taking out of life insurance, even though she had Kelly to support and care for. Beth sounded rather unhappy about it, particularly because Carlene had worked for an insurance company in both Louisville and Cincinnati for three or four years.

I asked about Kelly—not mentioning Joshua or the death of his parents—and was told he was doing very well, and enrolled in a new day-care center which he liked.

I also asked if she had heard from Jan, and she again said "no."

"Would you consider letting her see Kelly occasionally?" I asked.

"We might," Beth said. "Jan and I have never really gotten along, and she was the reason Carlene left. Still, I know she cares for Kelly and can imagine how she must feel. But she's never asked, and it's not my place, under the circumstances, to offer."

She was right, of course, but I thought it was quite possible that Jan never asked because she was sure Beth would say "no." But perhaps now I might have a wedge to get Jan Houston to talk to me.

* * *

I picked Joshua up at 4:30 and at his insistence gave him a piggy-back ride to the car, where I merely had to ask: "So what did you do today?" to get a detailed if disjointed verbal journey through his day—real and imagined. But it was good to see him returning to his normal self and I'd found that, though it took quite a bit of concentration at times to follow his meanderings, they were really pretty much worth the effort.

I really didn't feel much like cooking, so we stopped at a Cap'n Rooney's Fish Shack so Joshua could see the fish while we ate dinner.

I'd deliberately tried not to think about Jonathan during the day. When I did, I realized how rough it must be for him and since there was nothing I could do to help him through it....

The evening went fairly well, though as time passed I found myself getting more and more anxious to hear from Jonathan. And every time I'd look at Joshua, I'd feel oddly sad for him thinking of him having to go to a new home. With relatives, true, but still never the same.

I made some popcorn and Joshua intermittently played on the floor and came to sit beside me to watch a TV special on elephants.

Bath, story time—*Bunny Tales*, which I had to take great pains to read to Bunny, too—and Joshua was set for the night.

I returned to the living room and alternated my attention between the TV and the telephone. The late news was just starting when the phone rang. I grabbed it halfway through the first ring.

"Hi, Babe," I said, keeping my voice down. "How are you doing?"

"I'm okay," he said, but his voice said otherwise.

"How did the funeral go?" I prompted after a moment's silence from his end.

"It was...fine, I guess. I don't remember most of it."

Another long silence.

"And did you decide who would be taking care of Joshua?" I asked gently.

A third pause, then a simple: "Me."

CHAPTER 9

"What do you mean, *you*?" I managed to ask.

"That's what Samuel and Sheryl wanted. It's in their will. They want me to be his guardian. And no one else could take him anyway. My dad's too old and he works too much, and my sisters have enough to do to manage their own families.

"They want me to move back here with Joshua..."

My first, terrible thought was: *He's leaving me!* and I was literally ill.

"... but I told them 'no.' I have a good job, and he's in day-care, and I can find an apartment..."

"What in hell are you talking about?" I demanded, probably a lot more harshly than I intended. "What about us?"

I could tell he was crying, though he tried hard not to let me know.

"I know I've teased you about us having a kid," he said, "but I know you don't want one, and now I realize I just can't do that to you—change your life so completely."

I didn't know what to say, but I said it anyway. "Jonathan, Jonathan! *You* changed my life completely. I'd never be the same without you. Joshua is a part of you—and I want him to be a part of both of us!"

I said that? Dick Hardesty actually said that?

Jonathan dropped all pretext that he wasn't crying.

After reassuring each other that he didn't want to leave and I didn't want him to, we managed to get through the rest of the call, which mainly concerned logistics. He didn't know what of Joshua's things to bring back with him, or what of Samuel and Sheryl's personal things he should set aside for Joshua when he got older, or....

I finally suggested that he just bring some of Joshua's clothes and a few toys back with him, and simply close the house up—his dad and local sister could look after it—until next spring, when we could drive out there and see about everything else. The house and everything Samuel and Sheryl owned, of course, was willed to Joshua under Jonathan's guardianship.

We confirmed that he would be taking the first connecting flight from Rhinelander and would be home around three o'clock, in time to pick Joshua up at Happy Day. I'd of course meet him at the airport.

We exchanged "I love you"s and hung up.

* * *

I didn't sleep much that night, realizing the truth of that old saying: Today is the first day of the rest of your life. I didn't feel I was being melodramatic when it dawned on me that my life—*our* lives—had been changed forever.

Tuesday morning was a repeat of Monday, but it had new significance in the realization that now Monday and Tuesday mornings were going to be repeated every day for the next foreseeable number of years.

The first thing Joshua wanted to know when he got up was if Uncle Jonathan was back yet. I told him no, but that he would be at school to pick him up that afternoon. Getting dressed, he asked again. Same question, same answer. Joshua wanted to wear his Winnie the Pooh pullover shirt, and insisted on putting it on himself. He didn't get tangled up in the arms this time, but he did manage to get it on backwards.

Get used to it, Hardesty.

* * *

At the office I got to thinking again about insurance—partly because it was on my mind now in regard to Joshua, and partly because Jan Houston's red convertible popped into my head. If Jan did buy her car with insurance money she got from Carlene's death, that begged the question of how. Did Carlene have a policy her sister Beth didn't know about? Again, if she did, the beneficiary would most certainly have been Kelly, not Jan. And if Jan had taken out a policy on Carlene, that would be very odd indeed. And depending on when the policy had been taken out....

Jan and Carlene had both been working for...what was the name of the company...Indemnity Mutual, I think it was, when they first got together. How could I find out if there was a policy, and if so, what company issued it—which would clue me in as to how recently it was issued.

I pulled the license plate number of the red convertible out of my billfold and called Bil Dunham at the DMV again, asking him for verification of ownership and who held the title.

He returned my call half an hour later, saying the vehicle was in the name of Janice Maureen Houston, and she held clear title—which strongly indicated she'd paid cash! Since my mind often knows things before I do, I found myself asking for Jan's date of birth from her driver's license and wrote it down.

Following the same hunch, I called Information for the phone number of Indemnity Mutual's Carrington office—having no idea, of course, if they even had an office there. Luck was with me, and I was given a number.

Flying totally blind, I dialed the number, hoping my luck would hold. I guess I figured that since both Jan and Carlene had worked for Indemnity Mutual, it might be logical that any insurance they had might have been placed through them.

"Good Morning, Bolger Insurance," the young female voice said.

"Good Morning," I replied in my best confident Butch voice. "I wonder if you might help me? I..."

"I'm sorry, sir," she interrupted, "but Mr. Bolger is not in the office at the moment, and I am temporarily replacing his secretary, who is on maternity leave."

"Well, this is a rather simple question," I said. "My sister recently died and she had told me she had a life insurance policy with Indemnity Mutual, but we've been unable to find the paperwork. Could you just check for the policy number so I can request it from the main office?"

She appeared hesitant. "I…I'm not sure I am allowed to give out that information, sir."

Damn, I thought, but kept going. "I'm sure it's no problem. My entire family has been insured through this company for years." I hoped she wouldn't look too closely at the non-sequitur aspect of that last statement. "Her name is Carlene Jane DeNuncio; her address in Carrington was 2016 Blythe Drive. I'd really appreciate it," I added as warmly as possible. Luckily, I'd remembered her middle name from the minister's saying it several times at the funeral.

There was a slight pause, then: "That name does sound familiar. Just a moment, sir. We've just gotten a new computer system, and it may take me a moment."

"That's fine…I can wait. Thank you."

Fingers crossed.

A very long silence, in which I could hear what sounded vaguely like typing.

Finally: "I'm sorry, sir, I can't find anything on it."

"Ah," I said, "that's very strange." I paused for effect, then said, feigning a light-bulb moment: "Oh, of course!! The policy was taken out in her name by her partner, Jan—Janice Marureen Houston, same address. I can give you her social security number if it will help."

I did, and she went back to her computer.

Another long delay, then: "Yes, sir. Now I remember. The policy was issued from this office—I remember because it was the first claim I processed when I started here, about a month ago. Your sister did have a policy, but it was under the name of Jan Houston, who was the sole beneficiary."

"It was issued from your office, you said?"

"Yes. It had Mr. Bolger's signature, I remember."

"Aha," I said. "I see. Well, I very much appreciate your help."

"If you'd care to hold a moment," she said, "I see Mr. Bolger just driving up now. He might be able to give you some more information."

"Thank you very much," I said, "but I think I have what I need. Have a nice day." And I hung up.

I hadn't asked the amount of the policy, but it didn't really matter…it was enough to buy a new car. And if it was taken out from the Carrington office, that meant it had to have been within the last year.

Next step: to have a little talk with Jan Houston.

* * *

But not right then. It was getting close to lunch time, and I was already getting antsy to pick Jonathan up at the airport. I puttered around the office for awhile, then went downstairs to the café in the lobby for a ham-and-turkey club with an order of potato salad and a large coke. Actually, for some reason, I felt like walking down to Hughie's, the local hustler bar about two blocks from work, for a dark beer. I hadn't been there for a long time, and had no idea where the urge had come from, but I resisted it. Probably just another subconscious reminder that the past was past.

I guess I'd been subconsciously resisting giving any thought to just how strong an impact Samuel and Sheryl's deaths would have on my life—well, *our* lives, of course. I didn't mean that to sound like I was making it all about me. Samuel and Sheryl were dead, and my heart ached for Jonathan's grief. But the fact was that I was sort of on the far side of the equation in dealing with their deaths. Dealing with Joshua's entrance into our lives was another matter entirely. It wasn't that I didn't think I'd be able to cope with having a four year old boy around all the time. I realized I was already getting more attached to Joshua than I thought I would, and even more than I probably should. But Joshua was Jonathan's blood relative, and I really didn't have any idea of how that might affect my relationship with Jonathan.

And now with Jonathan coming home, a whole new and different set of dynamics would be put into place—plus dealing with Jonathan's grief to boot.

Well, we'd just have to wait and see.

* * *

Jonathan's flight was ten minutes late getting in and I was standing as close to the door as I could get when the passengers started coming off. Jonathan was in the second wave of disembarking passengers and we spotted each other at the same time. Neither of us smiled, and he just walked directly over to me and put his arms around me without a word. I didn't know hat to say, myself, so we just hugged until it became obvious we were interrupting the traffic flow. We broke the hug and Jonathan readjusted his bookbag on his shoulder.

He looked a little pale, and had obviously lost some weight, though he'd not been gone all that long.

"I missed you," we both said in unison, as we headed toward the baggage area.

In addition to his bookbag and the one carrying case he had with him, there was another very large, older model Samsonite suitcase and a slightly smaller cloth bag.

"I brought most of his clothes," Jonathan explained as I picked up the largest suitcase and smaller bag. "And a couple of toys dad and Sarah said were his favorites—I figure we can always get him more toys, but I wanted him to have some things he's familiar with."

We had just enough time to swing by home and bring everything inside. Jonathan suggested we put them in our room, then we could take our time putting them away where they were going to go. We didn't talk all that much in the car. I felt a little awkward in that I wasn't sure what to say and what not to, so I just drove with one hand and held his hand with the other most of the way. I didn't want to pressure him, and I knew he'd tell me whatever he wanted to tell me when he got around to it.

It was odd, in a way; he was Jonathan, but something was

different. He wasn't the same Jonathan I knew so well, but how could he be? No quick smiles, no joking around, no spontaneous laughter. I hoped this was all just part of the healing process and not a permanent change.

We arrived at Happy Day just in time. We passed a few of the parents and their kids on the sidewalk, and as we opened the gate to enter the yard I could see Joshua standing behind the screen door, his hands and nose pressed against the mesh. When he saw Jonathan, he stepped back from the screen and began hopping up and down, his face in a huge grin. Jonathan took the porch steps three at a time and hurried to the door. Opening it, he scooped Joshua up, raising him over his head, then lowered him to give him a big hug.

"Did you bring me a present?" Joshua asked.

And so began our new life.

* * *

Though I suggested that Jonathan might want to take a day or two off before returning to work, he insisted on going in the next day. And before he and Joshua left Wednesday morning, Jonathan reminded me that he had class Wednesday night. He was obviously bound and determined to get his life back as quickly as possible, and while I admired him for it, I was a little worried about him trying a bit too hard. But I decided that getting life back on track was a logical and worthy goal, and the first thing I did upon arriving at the office was to dig out Jan Houston's work phone number.

I'd debated on whether to contact the police with the information about the insurance policy Jan had taken out on Carlene's life. I had no idea what if anything the police were doing as follow up to Carlene's death, or if there was any sort of investigation going on. Chances are, there wasn't. It was mysterious, yes: why the driver of the van that killed Carlene was apparently never found. But it was a male driver, and since I'm sure the police knew Carlene was lesbian.... And Jan had an alibi for the day Carlene died, flimsy though it was. I just wondered if the Carrington police had the time or the experience—not to mention the willingness—to launch a full-scale investigation.

So I decided, before making any unnecessary waves, to try to approach Jan directly. I knew she'd be reluctant—which was probably a gross understatement—to talk to me, but I had to try. I'd use my conversation with Beth about the possibility of Jan's seeing Kelly on a regular basis as a wedge to open the door. If it worked, fine. If it didn't, I'd at least tried.

I waited until a little after nine, then called.

"Parker Precision Products," the female voice announced.

I asked to speak to Jan Houston and was asked who was calling, and I gave her my name hoping Jan wouldn't remember it.

She did. After a pause for the transfer to be made, Jan's voice came on, low, quiet, and no-nonsense.

"I told you to leave me alone!"

"I wouldn't be calling if it weren't important," I said.

"Yeah, I'll bet. To me or to you?" she said.

"To both of us, actually," I replied. "I wanted to talk to you a little about Kelly and ask you a few questions about Carlene." Not waiting for a reply, I forged ahead. "I've got to come up to Carrington today on business," I lied, "and wondered if you could meet me for lunch."

"I bring my lunch," she said.

"That's okay," I said, feeling rather like I were trying to reel in a fish. "Is there a park nearby? I can pick up something and we could eat there."

There was a long pause, then: "What did you want to say about Kelly?" she asked, still trying to get off the hook.

"I don't want to tie you up on the phone too long," I said. "I know you're busy. So can we meet?"

A sigh. "I…I suppose. Scarletti Park's about a block away. I can meet you there at noon, near the sundial in the middle of the park."

"Great!" I said. "I'll meet you there. And thanks."

I glanced at my watch as we hung up, and saw I'd need to hurry if I was going to make it to Carrington on time. I made a quick call to Evergreens just to leave a message for Jonathan as to where I was going in case he might try to call me.

I next called down to the diner in the lobby to ask for a pastrami on rye, a bag of chips, and a large coke to go, and also asked for a large cup of crushed ice. I had a small cooler in the trunk of the car, and figured the ice would keep the food fresh for the drive.

Just as I was walking out the door, the phone rang, and I debated on whether to answer it or not—not much of a debate, though, since I think I'm genetically incapable of ignoring a ringing phone.

It was Phil, calling to ask about Jonathan. They'd hesitated to call the apartment until they thought Jonathan was up to talking, and I thanked him and assured him it would be okay.

"Oh," he said, "Tim and I were talking, and any night you and Jonathan might want to get out for just the two of you, let us know. We'll be happy to look after Joshua."

"Thanks, Phil," I said, meaning it sincerely. "That would be great! We'd really appreciate it."

"Just give a call," Phil said. "I start shooting for Spartan's new line of underwear next Tuesday, but until then I don't think we have anything scheduled. Maybe this weekend, if you feel like it."

I thanked him again, profusely, then told him I had to run up to Carrington, and we ended the call.

* * *

Scarletti Park was a pleasant one-block square of the kind usually seen in front of old courthouses on movie back lots. I parked near two grey painted cannons, vintage WWI, flanking a granite column with a list of the town's military dead. Lots of trees. Very pleasant. No fountain, but a large sunken sundial in the exact center of the park. I got there just a few minutes before noon and found an empty bench near the sundial. I wasn't quite sure which direction Jan Houston would be approaching from, but I was pretty sure she'd spot me if I didn't see her first.

I didn't have long to wait. About seven minutes after the hour, I saw her cross the street and enter the park. I was a little surprised to see her wearing a very attractive grey dress.

You were expecting maybe Levi's and a motorcycle jacket? a mind-voice asked, and I felt immediately embarrassed for falling into the Lesbian Stereotype trap.

She came directly over and sat down beside me, not really looking at me.

"So what about Kelly?" she asked in lieu of any form of greeting.

"Have you spoken at all to Beth Erickson?" I asked.

She opened her brown paper bag and looked into it. "No. She hates my guts. There's no way she'd let me see Kelly."

I picked up my cooler and set it on the bench beside me. "So you haven't even asked?"

She shook her head, taking a large plum out of the bag and biting into it, reaching up quickly with one index finger to catch a trickle of juice.

"Well, I suggest you do ask," I said. "I've spoken with Beth and she appreciates the position you're in. I'm sure she would be amenable to working out some sort of visit schedule."

She looked at me for the first time. "I don't want a visit schedule. I want Kelly."

"And there's no way in hell you're going to get him, and you know it," I said. "The law sucks when it comes to situations like this, but it's the way it is. Your best chance to be a part of Kelly's life is to play it cool. Take it one step at a time."

She sighed and stared into her paper bag again, as if it held a crystal ball only she could see.

"God, I miss him!" she said.

"I know you do," I said. "So call her."

She gave an almost imperceptible nod of her head. "I will," she said, then looked directly at me. "So what else?" she asked.

"There's a possibility someone may have killed Carlene," I said.

She just looked at me. "Of course someone killed her. She was hit by a car."

"I mean there's a possibility her death was not an accident, that someone wanted her dead."

Her expression never changed. "Are you serious?" she asked. I nodded.

"And you think *I* did it?" she asked. "You're out of your mind. I was at a friend's cabin at Lake Verde."

"Mowing the lawn?" I asked, and saw a flicker of...something... anger?... in her eyes.

"Yes," she snapped. "Mowing the damned lawn! Are you spying on me?"

I shrugged. "Well, I am a private investigator. And I like your new car, by the way."

Her expression had gradually transformed from calm to fury, her eyes narrowing almost to slits.

"What the hell is *that* supposed to mean?" she demanded.

It doesn't take a slide rule and a caliper to figure that one out, lady, I thought.

"Probably nothing," I said.

"You're damned right, 'nothing!' I told you before I could never do that to Kelly!"

"But you did take out a policy on Carlene's life, didn't you?" I asked.

We'd both given up any attempt at trying to eat lunch.

"So what if I did?" she said...it wasn't really a question. "I got it for Kelly. I didn't know Carlene was going to leave me, and I sure as hell didn't know she was going to get herself killed."

"Then why didn't you put Kelly as beneficiary?"

She was silent a moment, then shrugged, and some of the anger seemed to leave her.

"I suppose I was afraid that what *did* happen might happen," she said. "I wanted to be able to take care of Kelly if anything happened to Carlene, but Kelly's just a kid, and if I put the policy in his name there might some sort of problem with my using it for him. And when Carlene's sister took Kelly and I realized I'd lost him, I figured the money was mine."

There were a few logical threads in there, I had to admit. Still....

I was suddenly aware Jan was staring at me.

"So just what makes you think it wasn't an accident that killed Carlene?"

My turn to shrug. "Too many loose ends," I said. "If they'd caught the driver of the van, the whole question might have been moot, but they didn't. And since they didn't...."

"What about that what's-her-name woman? Bronson?" Jan asked.

Bronson? How in hell would she know Estelle Bronson had been seeing Carlene? I wondered. So I asked.

"How do you know Estelle Bronson?"

She looked puzzled. "I don't. I just talked to her on the phone. But her name wasn't Estelle."

Bonnie?

"How did that come about?" I asked

"She called me one night out of the blue. Told me Carlene was sneaking around with her sister and she didn't like it one bit. She wanted to know my side of the story, and I told her it was none of her business, but she said she wanted to protect her sister. That's how I found out where Carlene lived."

Well, that was something of a non-sequitur, going from "wanting to protect her sister" to telling Jan where Carlene lived, but I let it pass. I suspected Jan might be leaving out a few of the details, but I didn't want to call her on it at the moment.

I did ask, though, when she'd gotten the call.

"I don't know," Jan replied. "Probably the Thursday or Friday before...well, before. My phone hadn't been disconnected yet.

Damn phone company!"

She looked at her watch—which looked pretty new to me—and said: "I've got to be getting back to work. Did you get what you wanted?"

I nodded. "I think so," I said, and resisted adding, "for the moment." But then I had another thought. "Oh," I added: "one more thing. I understand you knew Roy D'Angelo, is that right?"

I could almost feel the hostility which suddenly radiated from her like the heat from opening a furnace door.

"What if I did?" she said, defensively.

"I was just curious as to how you knew him," I said.

She glared at me and got up from the bench, turning toward me. "That's none of your damned business! I never want to hear that son of a bitch's name again!"

I was really taken aback by the ferocity of her reaction. "Sorry," I said. "I didn't mean to hit a raw nerve."

She took a deep breath, and I could see her forcing herself to relax. "Well, you did," she said, then paused. "So you'll get off my back, right?"

"Sorry again," I said, getting up. "I didn't think I was on it. But you'll call Beth Erickson?"

She was already walking away, but turned her head slightly back toward me and said: "I'll call."

* * *

I got back into town in plenty of time to take a detour to The Central and stop at Reef Dwellers, the fish store Jonathan liked so much, and bought him one he had had his eye on for some time but resisted buying because of the cost. I figured it might be a good—and distracting—welcome home present. I also bought two very small, brilliant-blue what I call "darters"—I could never remember their technical names—for Joshua. He'd been very good about helping me feed Jonathan's fish while he was away, and since we still had Jonathan's original fish bowl, I thought Joshua would enjoy having some fish of his very own. Besides, I knew I couldn't walk in with a present for Jonathan without getting one for Joshua, too.

I got home in time to put Jonathan's fish in with the others—I knew Jonathan would spot it immediately—and dug out and filled the smaller bowl with water. I didn't put the darters in right away until the tap water temperature had a chance to equalize to the room.

I heard Joshua's footsteps running down the hall, then the rattling of the knob.

"Hold your horses, Joshua," Jonathan's voice said, and I heard the sound of the key in the lock.

Joshua, carrying Bunny by one ear, ran into the room as though the devil were after him, and raced into his bedroom. Jonathan, looking very tired, managed a small smile and came over to give me a hug, resting his head on my shoulder.

"Bad day?" I asked, somewhat foolishly.

He nodded his head against my neck, then backed away and gave me a quick kiss.

"I'll survive," he said, as Joshua came back into the living room, his arms loaded with more toys than I would have thought he could carry.

"Let's play!" he announced, dropping everything at once and sitting down next to the pile.

"In a second, Joshua," I said. "Why don't you come see what I got you today?"

He scrambled to his feet and ran over, looking up at me. "What?" he asked eagerly.

"I got both you and Uncle Jonathan something to celebrate his coming home," I said, taking Jonathan's hand. "It's in the kitchen."

By the time I'd reached the second syllable of "kitchen," Joshua was halfway there.

"Definitely track team material," Jonathan observed, following me.

* * *

They both liked their gifts, though Jonathan protested (weakly) that I'd spent too much on just one fish. Joshua immediately named his two darters "Blue" and "Fishie" and insisted on feeding them immediately. I was very glad we'd established the ritual of either Jonathan or I sprinkling the food into Joshua's hand first, or he would surely have dumped the entire cannister into the bowl. "That's not enough!" he complained, and even after having it explained to him that they were very little fish and didn't eat much, he was unconvinced. We made certain to put the cannister in a cupboard well out of his reach.

It was Jonathan's class night, and he insisted that he go. "I don't want to start falling behind," he said. I knew, too, that keeping busy was a way he had of letting reality filter in rather than letting himself be swept away by it.

A new Italian place had opened up about three blocks away from the apartment, so I suggested we try it rather than attempting to cook anything at home.

Oh, and a suggestion: when a four year old boy wants spaghetti in an Italian restaurant and you offer to cut it up for him and he says "no"...cut it up for him anyway. It was partly Jonathan's fault, of course, for demonstrating how to suck up a long strand. By the time Joshua was done, his face was covered in spaghetti sauce from his hairline to his chin. Normally, Jonathan would have stepped in long before it got that far, but I realized he was still dealing with a lot of things inside and, messy as Joshua managed to get himself, it wasn't anything a washcloth couldn't cure.

We'd taken Jonathan's car to the restaurant, and since dinner took slightly longer than we'd planned, I told him just to go on to school and Joshua and I would walk back home. Joshua was all for the idea, since he'd seen a small park with swings along the way. Kids may not remember where they left their shoes, but they can remember every park with swings and a slide within a two mile radius.

* * *

Okay, back to business.

I was debating, Thursday morning at the office, what direction to take next in the case. My meeting with Jan Houston hadn't taken her completely off the hook, but my gut told me she probably was not directly involved in Carlene's death. But talking with her definitely made me want to speak to Bonnie Bronson, and I was trying to figure out exactly how to approach her when the phone rang.

"Hardesty Investigations," I said, picking it up on the second ring.

"Dick: Marty. I have some news on the van that killed the DeNuncio woman. We were able to get fourteen separate sets of readable prints. Only one came up with anything in the N.C.I.C. files, but it's got potential: a thumb print belonging to one Eddie Styles."

"Great!" I said. "Who's Eddie Styles?"

"I'd never heard of him, either," Marty said. "Apparently he's not from around here."

Interesting, I thought. "So where is he from?"

Marty sighed. "Kentucky, apparently, but it seems from his rap sheet he moves around a lot. His rap sheet starts in Kentucky, when he was 17, and where he served time there for racketeering; he was an enforcer for a couple of big-time bookies, then he apparently branched out from there. He's served time in Pennsylvania and New Mexico as well as Kentucky, but trying to track his between-jail time isn't very successful. No known permanent address."

"What's his 'specialty,' if he has one?" I asked.

There was a slight pause and the sound of shuffling paper. "Appears he's mostly a free-lance enforcer. Mostly aggravated assault, battery, racketeering."

"No murder charges?"

"Umm," Marty said, obviously scanning his records, "two arrests, one for multiple homicide. No convictions. He's got several outstanding warrants, but he's pretty elusive. No idea what he was doing in our neck of the woods."

I shook my head. "Well, I hope the answer to that one's not as obvious as I'm afraid it might be."

"A connection between Carlene DeNuncio's death and Eddie Style's fingerprint, which might have been there for a long time before the accident, is kind of a stretch, isn't it?" Marty asked.

"A very long one," I admitted. "But a possibility."

"We'll find out," Marty said. "If Eddie Styles is anywhere in the area, we'll get him, and when we do we'll be able to find out just how much of a stretch it was."

"Thanks, Marty," I said, and we hung up after exchanging goodbyes.

What neither Marty nor I said, but I'm sure were both thinking, was that Eddie Styles was undoubtedly long gone from local law enforcement's immediate jurisdiction.

CHAPTER 10

So if Eddie Styles had deliberately run down Carlene DeNuncio, who would/could have hired him? How could they even have either known of him or known how to contact him? Jan Houston? Very unlikely. She didn't come into the insurance money until after Carlene died, and it's unlikely hit men—an ironic term in this case—would do a job on a promise of being paid at some future time.

Interesting thought, "way out in left field" variety: might there have been some link between Eddie Styles and the murder of that detective who was following Carlene, Frank Santorini? From what I'd gathered, it wasn't inconceivable that Eddie Styles would be the kind of character Santorini may have known...and maybe even called upon from time to time. Yeah, but then why would Styles kill Santorini, if he did?

Stretch much further and you'll fall over, one of my mind voices cautioned.

Well, anything's possible.

So back to the fact that hit men cost money, and it's unlikely that Jan could have afforded it even if she wanted to. That brings us to Bonnie Benson: she could undoubtedly afford it, but why? Just to "protect" her sister? Again unlikely.

Which leaves Roy D'Angelo. But again, why? If he had enough money to hire a hit man, which seems highly unlikely, why wouldn't he just have spent it trying to get legal custody of Kelly? If that didn't work, *then* he could order a hit—if he would ever have considered it to begin with. So that, in turn, leaves us with whom? Roy's mother, Angelina? Talk about stretching! From what I knew of her relationship with Roy, I doubted that she would give her son carfare, let alone bankroll a hit man for him.

So that pretty much left Bonnie Bronson in the cross-hairs. Though there had been apparently no indication that the death of Estelle Bronson's previous erstwhile lover was anything other than accident, Carlene's addition to the list still struck me as possibly something other than just bad luck.

The thing to do was to talk to both Bonnie and Estelle again—I really needed a deeper understanding of their relationship, and how each one of them saw it. I wanted to tune in a little more closely to what was going on between them.

I decided to call Happy Day and try to set up a private meeting with whichever sister answered the phone. I realized it would be something of a juggling act either way, trying not to let each sister know I also wanted to talk to the other. I didn't think either of them would voluntarily tell the other, though if Bonnie suspected I wanted to talk to them both, she could probably wheedle it out of Estelle fairly easily.

"Happy Day Care Center." I recognized the voice but hadn't talked all that much with either of the sisters to remember whose voice was whose.

"Estelle?" I asked tentatively.

"No, this is Bonnie Bronson speaking. How can I help you?"

"Ah, Bonnie…yes. This is Dick Hardesty calling and I wonder if we might arrange to meet privately within the next day or two. I realize you're very busy, but I thought we might talk for a few minutes about the Carlene DeNuncio matter."

"And you have come up with concrete evidence that there *is* a 'Carlene DeNuncio matter,' then, I assume?" she asked. For some reason I got a quick mental picture of Queen Victoria saying: "We are not amused."

"I'm still not 100 percent certain," I admitted, "but it is looking more and more as if there is."

"I see," she said—her tone strongly implying that she did not. There was a pause before she continued, then: "Yes, I would like to hear what, if anything, you've found out, and how soon you are planning to draw this thing to a close."

I really couldn't blame her for being impatient: she was trying to look out for her sister, and the fact is that hiring a private investigator *is* something of a crap-shoot. There's almost never a timetable, and no time cards to look over at the end of the week, and I'm sure any private investigator so inclined could pad his bill quite easily.

Since I didn't want to commit myself to an end date just yet, I avoided her last statement by saying: "So when could we meet, then?"

There was a slight pause, during which I heard kids shouting and laughing in the background, then: "Estelle does our grocery shopping Saturday morning, and she has a few errands to run as well. We could meet here at, say, ten o'clock. I assume it will not take long."

Not one second longer than it has to, lady, I thought. If she was implying that it wouldn't take long because I didn't have much to tell her, she was pretty well right.

"Ten will be fine. Thank you, and I'll see you Saturday morning."

"Very well. Good-bye," and she hung up. I didn't take it personally, but I suspected I was not one of Bonnie Bronson's favorite people.

Obviously, I couldn't call back and hope to have Estelle answer the phone, so I gave Jonathan a call at work, asking him, if he got the chance to speak to Estelle alone while picking up Joshua, to have her call me.

* * *

That evening, Joshua brought home a drawing he had made at school, which Jonathan had immediately scotch-taped to the refrigerator door. As soon as I entered the apartment and we'd had our group hug, Joshua insisted I accompany him to the kitchen to see it. Actually, I was pretty impressed. There was a large animal that I assumed to be a horse with a small stick-like figure on top of it. In front of it were two larger figures, one with long hair.

"That's great, Joshua," I said, picking him up so he could touch it and point out details. "I'll bet that's you riding him, isn't it?" and Joshua nodded happily.

"That's Bill," he said, pointing to the horse. "My daddy's going to buy him for me when we get home."

I knew without asking that the two other figures were his mother and father, but lest I had any doubts, Joshua pointed to each of them in turn. "That's mommy," he said, "and that's daddy." I noted there was a large yellow blob over the horse's head with yellow lines coming out from it, and there was purple grass.

I gave him another hug. "Well it's a wonderful picture, Joshua, and you're a very good artist!"

I set him down and he went running off into the living room while Jonathan got out a glass for my Manhattan. I pulled him to me and gave him another hug, too. "How are you doing, Babe?" I asked, and he gave me a semi-sad smile.

"I'm okay," he said. "Every time I look at Joshua, I see Samuel and Sheryl, and that makes me feel better, somehow. I know part of them is still here and always will be."

He backed his head off my shoulder to look at me. "Does that make any sense?" he asked, and I pulled him closer again.

"It does," I said, "and I'm proud of you for being able to think of it like that."

We broke the hug and I fixed my Manhattan while Jonathan started dinner.

* * *

Jonathan had relayed my message to Estelle, and shortly before ten Friday morning, she called. When I explained I'd like to talk with her privately, she said: "I have grocery shopping and errands tomorrow morning, but one of them is in The Central and I could put that one off 'til last. I could meet you at Coffee & again around noon, if you'd like."

Juggle time, a mind voice observed.

"Well," I said, "I have a meeting in the morning, but I think I might be able to make it if it doesn't run too long. Or we could make it sometime early next week if you prefer."

There was no pause before she said: "I find it very hard to get away on weekdays, as you can imagine. And I am very curious to hear what you've learned. I'll arrange to be at Coffee & at noon, and if you're not there by quarter after, I'll assume you couldn't make it."

"Well if you're sure you don't mind…"

"Not at all," she said. "I have so little time for myself, I enjoy having a few minutes to just sit and have a cup of coffee."

"I'll do my best to be there," I said, and we exchanged good-byes and hung up.

* * *

Jonathan had been home, what…three days?…and it hadn't been exactly easy. We were both trying to get things back to normal, which of course was impossible, since our "normal" had never included a four-year-old boy. I decided what we really needed was a few hours just for the two of us, so on a whim I called Tim and Phil. I knew Tim would be at work, but Phil said he wasn't working until next week, so took a chance on his being home, and he was.

We talked for a minute or two about how things were going for each of the four of us, and I finally broached the subject: "I was wondering if you had any plans for tomorrow night?"

"Nope," Phil said. "We're going out to dinner tonight with some friends: Karl and Johann—I think you met them over here once—but tomorrow's a stay-at-home. Did you want us to look after Joshua?"

"You wouldn't mind?" I asked.

"Not at all," he said. "It'll be fun. He's a great kid."

"It'd be just for a few hours," I said. "I thought we'd go have dinner at Napoleon, just the two of us."

"That's a great idea," Phil said. "Joshua can have dinner with us."

I paused on that one. "Uh, are you sure? He can get a little wild if he thinks he can get away with it."

Phil laughed. "So can Tim," he said. "But I'm sure we can handle him."

I gave a sigh of relief. "Well, if you're sure. What time shall we bring him by?"

"How about six? We can have a drink and talk awhile before you go."

"Great!" I said. "We'll see you then. And thanks."

* * *

When I told Jonathan of my plan for Saturday, he was at first a little hesitant about imposing on Tim and Phil, but the idea of a partial evening with just the two of us overcame his objections. Joshua had spent enough time with Tim and Phil to feel comfortable around them, and he liked them. And he looked forward to the prospect of spending some time with their fish.

* * *

I left the apartment before ten Saturday morning for my meeting with Bonnie Bronson. The more I thought about her relationship with her sister Estelle the more curious I got. I reflected on the fact that it had been Bonnie who had told Jan Houston where Carlene lived, and wondered as to her motivation for doing so. Whatever it was, it probably wasn't good.

But again, as far as Bonnie Benson being a prime suspect, how then would Frank Santorini, the dead detective, fit into the picture? Bonnie would have had no reason to hire him…she knew where Carlene lived. To keep tabs on Carlene and Estelle? Unlikely.

And I realized that I'd never really given serious thought to there being any connection between Carlene's death and Santorini's. Considering Santorini's reputation, any number of people could have killed him. There *are* such things as coincidences, and I didn't want to go chasing after what I think the detective novels call "red herrings."

To play it safe, I stopped at a gas station close to Happy Day and called to be sure Estelle had left on her errands. (If Estelle answered, I'd pretend it was her I wanted to talk with, and verify our noon meeting.) But it was Bonnie who answered, and when she said Estelle had left shortly before, I told her I'd be right over.

She met me at the front door and I followed her through the house to the back porch, which had two comfortable padded lawn chairs and a small round table sitting in front of the kitchen window.

"It's such a nice day, I thought we might sit out here," she said. "Would you like a glass of iced tea?"

"If it's no trouble," I said. She motioned me to one of the chairs and turned back toward the door into the house.

I sat down and looked out over the large yard, smiling when I saw the sandbox and remembering Joshua's story of his battle with the monster who lived beneath it.

Bonnie returned with a tray holding two tall glasses of ice cubes and a pitcher of tea, which she set on the small table. When she'd poured the tea and sat down herself, we each took a sip before she said: "And what did you want to talk to me about?"

I was rather relived by her obvious desire to cut right to the chase.

"I understand you spoke with Jan Houston some time ago, and it was you who gave Jan Carlene's address here. I was curious as to why."

She set her glass on the small table and leaned back in her chair. "Why I called her, or why I gave her Ms DeNuncio's address?" she asked.

"Both, actually," I said.

"I was protecting my sister," she said simply.

I couldn't help but ask: "From what?"

She reached for her glass and took a long drink. "From probably being hurt. From herself," she said without looking at me.

I cocked my head. "I'm sorry," I said, "I don't follow."

"Estelle is…well, gullible…and naive. She's always followed her heart rather than her head, ever since she was a child."

Yeah, I thought, *but she's not a child anymore. You're not doing her any favors by treating her as if she can't look out for herself.*

"When I was much younger," Bonnie continued, "I found myself in a situation not unlike Estelle's, with a young woman not unlike Carlene DeNuncio. After falling hopelessly in love, I found out she was just out to use me and get whatever she could from me. I vowed it would never happen again, and that I would never let it happen to Estelle."

"So you called Jan Houston to…?" I left the question incomplete.

"To find out whatever I could about Ms DeNuncio from the person who was in a position to know her best, frankly," she said.

Surely she couldn't have expected a recently-dumped—for however valid a reason—and embittered ex lover to give her a glowing recommendation! And why give Jan Carlene's new address? But I said nothing and took another drink of my tea.

"I know what you're thinking," she said after a moment. "That I was trying to stand in the way of Estelle's happiness."

Well, not exactly, I thought, *but close.*

"But nothing could be further from the truth," she continued. "I love my sister, and I want her to be happy. I just don't want her to be hurt."

Well, that little statement could open the door to a very long philosophical debate, but I chose to leave it closed.

I decided to toss a pebble into the pond to see what sort of ripple it might create. "Have you ever heard of a man named Frank Santorini?" I asked.

She looked at me very strangely, then raised an eyebrow

and gave me an odd half-smile.

"I do read the newspapers," she said. "Why in the world would you ask me about him?"

Ooops. Tread carefully, Hardesty, I thought.

"Were you aware he had been following Carlene DeNuncio before she was killed?" I asked.

She took another long drink of her tea, which was now nearly gone.

"No," she said, putting her glass down and not looking at me. "I had no idea. Though if a detective was following her, it only supports my belief that I was right to suspect she was not who or what she presented herself to Estelle as being. Do you know why she was being followed?"

"I have no idea," I said, truthfully. And I wondered again exactly how much she knew of Estelle's relationships with other people.

"And exactly how much longer do you expect this to go on?" she asked.

I knew what she meant by the question.

"Not too much longer," I said. "I do have a few more people I need to talk to, but I'd say no more than two weeks."

She nodded. "Good. And I assume you will give Estelle a detailed accounting of your time? I don't mean to appear rude, but I'm sure you understand my concern."

"Of course," I said, and I did. I looked at my watch, then took another drink of my tea, finishing it. "Well, I should be going, before Estelle gets home" I said. "Thank you for talking with me."

"You're welcome," she said simply. We both got up and she led me back through the house to the front door.

* * *

I was on my second cup of coffee at Coffee & when Estelle came in. She came over and sat across from me at the small table—the booths were already filled.

"I hope I haven't kept you waiting," she said with a smile.

"Not at all," I assured her.

The waitress came over to refill my coffee and pour a cup for Estelle.

"Would you like to see a menu?" she asked Estelle. (I'd declined the offer earlier.)

"Coffee's fine," Estelle replied, and the waitress moved on to another table.

"So have you found anything?" Estelle asked, reaching for the sugar dispenser.

I took a sip of my coffee before answering. "Yes, no, and maybe," I said, and then proceeded to go over everything I'd done on the case—leaving out her sister's possible involvement—and that I planned to talk with Kelly's father when he came in to town next weekend. If nothing else developed between now and then, and if talking with Roy D'Angelo didn't give me a viable lead, I was pretty much afraid we'd run out of options unless or until the police found Eddie Styles.

She sat back in her chair and sighed heavily, looking into her coffee cup. "I understand," she said, then looked at me. "But there's still a chance?" she said.

"Of course," I replied, though I don't know how strongly I believed it. Then, hoping she wouldn't make any connections, I said: "So tell me about you and Bonnie. It's really great that you two are so close."

She looked into her coffee cup again, and nodded, giving me the distinct impression that she may have been thinking "Too close." But she didn't say it.

"Has Bonnie ever had a relationship?" I asked

She shook her head. "No," she said. "Just that one, when I was still in high school. Right after our parents died."

"I gather it wasn't long term?" I asked, and she shook her head again.

"Only a few months, and it was…well, it nearly destroyed Bonnie, I'm afraid."

"How so?" I asked. I knew exactly what she meant, but I

was hoping it might bring forth more information.

The waitress came over with a pot of coffee and refreshed both our cups, then moved off.

"Bonnie is a wonderful woman," Estelle began, "and no one could ask for a more caring sister. But she has never really had any…well, any *fun*. She's six years older than I, and our mother had a very difficult pregnancy with me, and nearly died. She was never really healthy after that. So Bonnie had the responsibility of raising me. Our father was always away on business. Both our parents loved us, and they did what they could, but it was difficult."

She paused while she added sugar to her coffee and emptied another small cup of cream into the mix. She appeared a little lost in her own thoughts, but I knew she'd continue when she was ready.

"Bonnie is very strong," she continued. "She's one of the strongest women I know, and I've always admired her for that. When our father died of a heart attack while I was a senior in high school, it sent our mother's health into a downward spiral from which she never recovered, and she died within six months of my father. Bonnie was a rock. She hid her grief as best she could—which was very, very well, though I could sense it in her—and devoted her efforts to comforting me, and handing all our parents' business affairs, and…well, you know."

I knew.

She looked out the window at the passing traffic on Beech, not really looking at anything in particular. Then, with a small jerk, she pulled herself back to the moment and gave me a quick glance and an equally quick smile.

"Sorry," she said. "Anyway, about eight months later, as I was getting ready to go off to college, Bonnie met someone…her name was Susan, and she was beautiful, and Bonnie actually fell in love. I really think that for the first time in her life, she was *happy*, and I was happy for her. So I went off to college: it was just to Mountjoy, up in Carrington, and I got totally caught up in being on my own for the first time. I'm afraid I didn't call home as much as I should have, and I deliberately didn't come home on weekends to give Bonnie and Susan time to spend together."

"So what happened?" I heard myself ask. I should have just waited for her to continue on her own, but you know me.

She put her cup down on the saucer and looked at me, again shaking her head.

"I honestly don't know!" she said. "Everything was wonderful, and Bonnie was a different person, and then suddenly, it was over! Bonnie would never tell me what happened, but it must have been terrible. I never saw or heard from Susan again, and Bonnie refused to even let me mention Susan's name." She sighed, heavily. "And Bonnie turned into a lesbian who hates women."

She saw my startled look.

"Oh, not on the outside," she amended. "We have a few lesbian friends, but Happy Day takes up so very much of our time. But as far as Bonnie's ever even trying to find another relationship...nothing. And while it hurts me to say so, she apparently projects her own experience onto me and any woman in whom I develop an interest. That's why I tried to keep my relationship with Carlene away from Bonnie. She's so afraid I'll be hurt like she was. She just doesn't understand...." Her voice trailed off.

It was my turn to shake my head in empathy. "Unfortunately, we can't always protect those we love from being hurt. It's just a part of life."

"I know," she said.

We sat in relative silence, finishing our coffee, and I finally excused myself. "I've really got to be getting home," I said.

"Of course," she said, a little sadly, I thought. "And so must I. I'm glad we had the chance to talk, and I hope you find out something from Kelly's father."

The waitress came by again with coffee, which I declined, but Estelle accepted. "Just half a cup, if you would," she said, then looked at me. "Oh, but please, don't let me keep you," she said. "I'll be leaving as soon as I finish this."

I felt a bit guilty, but realized she'd probably enjoy a little time by herself.

I got up, we exchanged goodbyes, and I left, first catching our waitress' eye and indicating I'd like the check. She met me at the cash register and I gave her money for the coffee and a tip, and left.

* * *

Joshua was having one of his hyperactive days—which, come to think of it, would probably apply to most of his days—and the apartment was strewn with toys, books and the various debris found in the wake of a 4-year-old whirlwind. When I came in, he was "helping" Jonathan water the plants, getting more on the floor than in the pots, and talking a blue streak. Jonathan gave me a weak smile, looking around the living room. "I thought I'd give him his head today," he said, "so he might have run out of steam by the time we go to Tim and Phil's."

"Good idea," I said.

They'd already had lunch, not being sure when I'd be home, but Jonathan had left me a sandwich and some potato salad in the refrigerator. We still had an afternoon of chores: groceries, laundry (lots of laundry), etc., so while Jonathan corralled Joshua into picking up his toys and books with the lure of going shopping for something for him to get for Tim and Phil, I sat in the kitchen and ate my lunch.

There was a new Laundromat on the edge of The Central that had a kids play area, so we went there, letting Joshua put the coins in the washers and press the "start" button before we let him lose in the play area. We'd chosen machines fairly close to it so we could keep a close eye on both him and the machines.

Supermarket shopping with a small child is an adventure, and I'm glad both Jonathan and I were there: I don't know how one adult can do it alone with a kid in tow. I was kept busy returning things that Joshua kept trying to put in the cart, including a huge box of Yummy-O's cereal, whose main ingredient, according to the small print on the box, was sugar. He reluctantly settled for Rice Krispies. And we did let him pick out the kind of fruit he wanted. In the bakery section, we bought half a dozen large chocolate chip cookies for him to take to Tim and Phil (he wanted to take them a huge three-tiered wedding cake he saw in the display case, but was talked out of it).

* * *

We—Jonathan, Joshua, Bunny, and I—arrived at Phil and Tim's just before six. Just as we got to the door I exchanged the bag of cookies for Bunny. Tim opened the door, and Joshua immediately thrust the bag at him.

"Here," he said. "These are cookies. Can we have one now?"

Phil came up behind Tim as we entered and Jonathan closed the door behind him. Tim handed Phil the bag of cookies and bent down to pick Joshua up and raise him over his head, then brought him down for a hug.

"Thank you, Joshua," Tim said. "Those are very special cookies, so let's save them for dessert, okay?"

Looking only mildly disappointed, Joshua nodded and Tim passed him to Phil for a hug, then exchanged hugs with Jonathan and me, an act Phil repeated after setting Joshua down. The minute Joshua's feet hit the floor, he was off to the fish tank.

Tim, Phil, Jonathan and I sat around talking and having a drink (tonic for Jonathan and Joshua, who was too busy talking to the fish to drink it). Phil asked how my current case...if it could be called that...was going, and I told them what I could.

"Have you got any plans for next Saturday?" I asked.

Phil and Tim looked at one another, then Tim shook his head. "Not that we know of," he said. "Why?"

"How would you like to join us for a night at the races?" I asked. "That way I could combine business with pleasure."

"Jeez," Tim said, "I haven't been out to Elmsley since I was a teenager. It sounds like fun." He turned to Phil. "Okay by you, Phil?"

Phil nodded. "Sure: I've never been there at all."

So we made it a tentative date and, after finishing our drinks, got up to leave.

Joshua came running over. "Are we going now?" he asked. "We haven't had our cookies yet!"

Jonathan got down on one knee and explained to him, for probably the fourth time, that he was going to have dinner with Uncle Tim and Uncle Phil all by himself, just like the big boy he was, while Uncle Jonathan and Uncle Dick went to a grown-up's place for dinner. "But we'll be back in plenty of time for your story."

"I want to go with you!" Joshua said, on the verge of tears.

Tim stepped over to him. "But what will we do with those cookies?" he asked. "And I've made you a meatloaf—you like meatloaf, don't you?"

Joshua reluctantly nodded.

Then it was Phil's turn: "And I thought you might help me feed the fish after dinner."

That did it.

* * *

Dinner at Napoleon was exactly what we both needed, but I, for one, hadn't realized just how much. We took our time, and splurged and had Chateaubriand and talked, and some of the old Jonathan peeked out from around the corners of his shell. It was good to see him. He even asked if maybe we could run home first before picking Joshua up so we could just chase each other around the apartment naked, and play a noisy, no-holds-barred game or two, but we both realized there wasn't time. But I was glad he was considering it.

We got back to Tim and Phil's around 9:30. Phil opened the door with his index finger to his lips, and we saw Tim sitting on the couch, watching TV, with Bunny on his lap, and Joshua, sound asleep, using Bunny as a pillow.

We thanked them both profusely (and quietly), and declined their offer to stay awhile, with thanks. Jonathan went over and picked Joshua up off the couch, and I took Bunny. Joshua woke up, sleepily, for just a moment, then put his arms around Jonathan's neck, laid his head on Jonathan's shoulder, and went back to sleep.

And our new little family went home.

CHAPTER 11

Sunday and the entire rest of the week went by quickly. I had a couple of fairly simple cases, the longest lasting all of three days.

With Saturday approaching, I began thinking more of Roy D'Angelo, and wondering when he might be coming into town.

I keep a city/suburbs map both in my car and at the office, so Thursday morning, after doing my coffee/newspaper/crossword puzzle routine, I got out both the map and the phone book and started looking up motels in Vernon and their proximity to Elmsley Raceway. Vernon is mostly industrial as opposed to residential, and there were only four motels, three of which were within half a mile of the track. I began to call each one, asking if Roy D'Angelo had a reservation for the weekend, and lucked out on the second call (The Twilight Inn). Apparently Roy stayed there whenever he was in town, because whomever it was I talked to mentioned that he "usually" checked in early Friday afternoon. I left a message asking him to call me when he got in—I had no reason to think that he would, if our last conversation was any indicator, but I didn't have anything to lose, and if he didn't, I'd still try to find a way to corral him after the race Saturday.

* * *

So needless to say I was quite surprised to answer the phone around 2:30 on Friday to hear: "This is Roy D'Angelo. What the hell do you want?"

I'm fine, thanks, Roy. And how are you? my mind voice asked.

"Thanks for calling. I really do want to talk to you about…"

"I told you, he's my kid and I want him!" he interrupted.

I paused a second before saying: "This isn't about Kelly. It's about Carlene and who killed her."

That got his attention.

"What the hell has that got to do with me?" he demanded.

Now, there are some people—most people, actually—with whom tact and diplomacy are very effective tools. And there are some people who can't even spell "tact" or "diplomacy", with whom no-nonsense monosyllables appear to work better. Roy D'Angelo, I sensed, was one of the latter. I hadn't had any intention of a confrontation, especially over the phone, but there was something about this joker's attitude that got me.

"Well look. Roy," I said, "this is the way it is: Carlene's death was no accident." I still didn't know that for an absolute fact, but what the hell? "The police know who was driving the van that killed her, but they haven't found him yet. The guy's a known hit man, so that means somebody wanted Carlene dead."

I paused a moment, but D'Angelo remained quiet, so I continued. "Now, I've been looking into the case, and I've come up with some pretty interesting facts which I'm going to be taking to the police. The only loose end right now is you."

"*Me?*" he said incredulously. "Why drag me into it? I haven't had any contact with that lesbo bitch for five years, and I sure as hell didn't have anything at all to do with her death!"

Other than the use of the pejoratives, I wondered how he knew Carlene was lesbian if he hadn't had any contact with her since their affair.

"Well, then, you shouldn't mind answering some questions for me. It would be nice, when I talk to the police, to be able to rule you out as a suspect and keep them from bothering you."

There was a long pause while he mulled that one over.

"What kind of questions?" he asked, finally.

"I'd just as soon not go into them over the phone," I said. "Could we get together privately either sometime today or tomorrow? I'll be coming out to the track for the races Saturday anyway, and maybe…"

"No, that won't work," he said. "I'm with my team, and we've got a lot of work to do before the race. But I suppose I can get away for a few minutes Sunday morning before I head back home. I can meet you at The Finish Line around noon."

I gathered The Finish Line was a bar probably not too far from the track…I could look up the address.

"Noon it is. See you there." I hung up without saying goodbye.

You think he'll actually show up? one of my mind-voices asked.

He'd better, I answered.

* * *

Having already made plans with Tim and Phil to join us at the races, I couldn't very well cancel just because I wouldn't be talking to Roy D'Angelo afterwards. It was probably just as well to meet him privately on Sunday, anyway.

If he shows up, the mind voice said.

You made your point, I replied. But I was fairly sure he would…if not because he wondered what I might have on him, then to keep me from siccing the police on him.

* * *

Actually, the races were kind of fun, and everyone had a good time: especially Joshua, even though he kept his hands over his ears a lot. He wasn't used to being in large, enthusiastic crowds, let alone the roar of the cars zooming. There were a couple of dramatic spin-outs and one major pile-up—caused, interestingly, by car #38: Roy D'Angelo's car, clipping another while attempting to pass. It didn't look accidental, but the crowd loved it. That delayed the race for about ten minutes while they hauled off four cars, but Roy went on to win one other heat.

I wished we were a little closer to the track so I could get a good look at Roy in person. But of course he was wearing his helmet anyway, so….

Phil, Tim, and I had a couple of beers during the races, so Jonathan drove while Joshua fell asleep in my lap. We didn't get back to the apartment until about 11:30. We managed to get Joshua to bed, which was an interesting experience in that, as he'd done when we'd left him with Tim and Phil the week before, Joshua managed to sleep through most of the changing into his pajamas ritual. It was rather like trying to undress and dress a very large rag doll.

When we went into our own room and closed the door, Jonathan moved a chair in front of it. He then came over to me with a wicked grin—God, it was good to have the old Jonathan back—and pushed me down on the bed.

"How about a game of The Race Car Driver and the Pit Chief?" he whispered, unbuckling my belt. "I think we both could use a lube job and an oil change."

Great idea, and he was right, as usual.

* * *

Ah, and another observation about having a four-year-old in your life: don't count on sleeping in on Sundays. Or ever. I woke to the gentle tapping of something soft on my nose, and opened my eyes to see it was Bunny, whom Joshua was using to subtly get my attention. The chair had been moved away from the door in the course of my trip to the bathroom in the middle of the night.

"We're hungry," Joshua announced in a semi-whisper.

"Why didn't you go wake up Uncle Jonathan?" I asked.

"He's sleeping," he said.

I resisted the temptation to point out that I had been sleeping, too, until he woke me.

"Okay," I said, speaking softly so as not to wake Jonathan. "You and Bunny go into the kitchen and I'll be right there."

"Okay," he said, and ran out the door. Luckily, I'd put my robe on the chair within reach of the bed, and I was able to slide out of bed and into the robe in practically one motion. Joshua had pulled a chair over to the counter and was in the process of opening the cupboard where the cereal was kept. He wasn't in danger of falling, so I said: "Okay, you get the cereal and I'll get the bowl."

"Two bowls!" Joshua insisted, taking down the box of Rice Krispies.

"I'll eat a little later," I said, "when Uncle Jonathan gets up."

"No," Joshua said, climbing down from the chair and taking the cereal box to the table, "…a bowl for me and a bowl for Bunny."

"Bunny doesn't eat Rice Krispies," I said.

He looked at me with mild exasperation. "He *pretend* does," he said.

So I got two bowls, two napkins, and two spoons. I drew the line at pouring milk in Bunny's bowl, however.

Jonathan got up shortly thereafter, and while he was making regular breakfast—pancakes and sausage—I retrieved the Sunday paper from the hall and sat down with Joshua and Bunny to read the funnies. He didn't understand most of them, of course—most funnies aren't really for kids, after all. But Joshua particularly enjoyed the ones with animals and he was pretty good at identifying them. And of course there were the usual endless questions, some of which because he wanted to know, and some of which because he just enjoyed asking questions.

* * *

Since I was going to be gone, Jonathan decided to take Joshua to 12:00 services at the M.C.C. I left the apartment for The Finish Line at around 11:15. According to the address in the phone book, it was within a block of the Twilight Inn, where Roy D'Angelo was staying.

The bar's parking lot was about a quarter full, mostly with trucks with flatbed trailers behind them, and most of them carrying cars with race numbers painted on the sides. The cars, with only two exceptions, displayed obvious evidence of their battles, like old prizefighters sporting out-of-shape noses and cauliflower ears.

I did not see #38 among them. Well, I was a little early, as usual.

The bar itself, I saw when I entered, was your usual windowless square box, fairly good sized, with metal posts holding up the flat roof, a pool table, several neon signs touting various beer brands, a small stage in one corner and an L-shaped bar running most of the way along the opposite wall. There was a faint smell of motor oil mixed with the usual stale-beer smell I associate with a lot of less-than-classy bars.

There were maybe 20 people in the room, most of them men, including the bartender, who wore a striped shirt usually seen on referees and the guys who wave the checkered flag at auto races. There were one or two patrons who made me fleetingly wish they were gay and I was single, but no one I recognized even vaguely.

I walked over to the bar and took an empty stool two places away from where a beer bottle stood on the bar, unattended. I ordered a beer and was just taking some money out of my wallet when I saw someone coming out of the bathroom. I couldn't be absolutely positive, but I thought it might be Roy D'Angelo. He came across the room and sat at the stool in front of the unattended beer.

He didn't look in my direction; just sat with his forearms on the bar, head down, looking at nothing in particular.

When I'd given the bartender my money and picked up my beer, I turned to the guy.

"Roy D'Angelo?" I asked.

He turned his head to look at me, expressionless.

"Yeah," he said. "You the p.i.?"

I nodded. Neither of us made any attempt to shake hands.

"I didn't see your car in the lot," I said for no particular reason.

"Mike's got the truck. He'll be by shortly to pick me up, then we're outta here. So let's make this quick."

Fine by me, I thought. I had no idea who 'Mike' might

be…probably his mechanic…but it didn't matter.

"So how did you know Carlene was a lesbian?" I asked. Quick he wanted it, quick he'd get it.

His scowled and eyes darted around the bar to see if anyone had heard the dreaded "L" word.

"I just knew," he said.

Nothing like a definitive answer, a bemused mind-voice said.

"Yeah, but I'm curious how you knew. Carlene didn't have her first lesbian experience until after she dumped you." I saw him flush.

"*She* dumped *me*?" he hissed, trying to keep his voice down. "No cunt *ever* ditched Roy D'Angelo! I don't get trapped, neither. She deliberately got pregnant. I gave her money for an abortion and told her I never wanted to see her sorry ass again!"

Uh-huh.

"So how did you find out she was lesbian?" I asked again.

He scowled again. "What the fuck difference does it make how I heard? I heard, okay?"

"Do you know a Jan Houston?" I asked.

"Never heard of her," he said. It was obviously a lie.

"She knows you," I said.

There was a pause, and he looked definitely uneasy.

"How?" he asked.

"She wouldn't tell me," I said. "But she knows you."

He took a long drink of his beer, then set the bottle back on the bar. "Well, I don't know *her* and I'd like to keep it that way."

I decided to switch track slightly. "So it was your mother who told you Carlene was dead, and that she had a son."

He nodded. "Yeah. So?"

"I understand you and your mother aren't exactly close," I said.

"We get along okay," he said, noncommitally. I was rather surprised he didn't ask me how I came across that bit of information.

"Ever heard of a Frank Santorini?" I asked.

He shook his head.

"How about Eddie Styles?"

There was a quick flash of something in his eyes—too quick for me to get an idea of what it might mean, before he said: "Never heard of him."

Like you never heard of Jan Houston? I wondered.

I skipped to another subject. "You make pretty good money on the race circuit?" I asked.

The scowl returned for the third time. "That's none of your damned business, but yeah, I do okay. What's that got to do with anything?"

I shrugged. "I was just thinking it must cost a bundle to hire an expensive Louisville lawyer to handle your custody suit."

"It's worth it to get my kid back," he said.

Again, I found the word "back" pretty ironic, since he never had Kelly to begin with, but I let it go.

"Is your mother still in town?" I asked.

He shrugged. "No idea. Why?"

"I was just curious," I said. "I was wondering how she feels about your filing for custody of Kelly."

He glared at me. "Look," he said, "I don't care how she feels about it! I'm my own man, and I don't need anybody's permission for anything!"

Well, that was a rather interesting non-sequitur, I thought.

"I wasn't suggesting that you did," I said. "Do you think your mother would be willing to talk to me, if she's still in town?"

"What the hell do you want to talk to her for?" he demanded.

"I was just curious as to how she could have been so sure Kelly was your kid, just reading about Carlene's death in the newspaper."

He looked toward the door, where a man was standing holding the door open and making a "come on" gesture in our direction. drained the rest of his beer and started to get up from his stool. "Knock yourself out," he said. "Mike's here. I gotta go."

"How can I reach her?" I asked, before he got away.

"If she's still here, she's staying with her sister, Mildred Collins." And he walked toward the door.

* * *

On the way home, I went over my not-totally-rewarding visit with Roy D'Angelo. He obviously wasn't the brightest button in the jar, and his personality certainly left a lot to be desired, but I still had the distinct impression that there was a lot more going on than he was telling me.

I admit I was a little surprised that he was willing to tell me how to get in touch with his mother; it was pretty clear that mother and son were something less than close. Maybe he'd given the information so casually because he knew his mother would be pissed at having someone questioning her about sore spots in her life. But I still wondered where/how Roy was coming up with the money for the custody suit. Again, I had no idea how much such a lawsuit might cost, but I was sure it was more than he had in his pennies jar.

Well, I would like to talk to his mother just to see what I could learn.

* * *

I checked the phone book at work first thing Monday morning for a Mildred Collins. There was more than a full page of Collins' in the book, but no "Mildred." Three "M. Collins'," though...two here in town and one in Karnak, one of the more upscale suburbs. I took a chance and decided to try the one in Karnak first. I always liked Egyptian city names—Karnak, Memphis, Thebes, Luxor—and besides, I'd gotten the impression that Angelina D'Angelo was rather well-off, financially. Maybe her sister was, too.

I picked up the phone and dialed.

It was answered on the second ring: "(*hech-hem*) Hello?"

I gathered from the sound of her voice that it was an older woman, and from the volume that she must be a little hard of hearing.

"Excuse me," I said, "but I'm looking for a Mildred Collins. Could you tell me if..."

"Just a minute," she said, "I'll get her."

"Is thi..." I started to ask, but she was gone.

A moment later: "Hello?" It seemed to be the same voice.

"Mildred Collins?" I asked, more than a little confused.

"Yes," she said, a faint hint of suspicion in her voice.

"I'm sorry to bother you Mrs. Collins," I said, assuming she was a Mrs., "but I'm trying to locate an Angelina D'Angelo."

"Well you were just talking to her," she said, the suspicion tinged with mild exasperation. "What is this about?"

I heard a voice in the background...I assumed the first woman to whom I'd talked...asking: "Who is it, Mildred?"

"I have no idea," Mildred said, followed by a question obviously directed to me. "Who is this?"

"My name is Dick Hardesty, ma'am, and..."

"It's somebody named Dick Hardesty," she said, obviously not to me.

"I don't know anybody named Hardesty," the away-from-phone voice said. "What does he want?"

Jeezus, lady, just get on the phone and I'll tell you myself!

"Could I speak with Mrs. D'Angelo directly?" I said, hoping I sounded a lot more polite than I felt. "It's in regards to her son, Roy."

"It's about Roy," the message-relayer said.

"What's he done now?" the off-phone voice said, obviously exasperated. "Oh, here, give me the phone!"

Finally!

There was a series of muffled sounds as the phone changed hands and then the formerly-off-phone voice saying: "(hech-hem) What about Roy?"

Start from scratch, Hardesty, a mind voice advised calmly. *And be nice!*

"Mrs. D'Angelo," I began, "my name is Dick Hardesty and I'm a private investigator. I'm working on a case on which Roy may have information…" I was lying through my teeth, but hoped she didn't know it.

"Well then, you take that up with Roy," she interrupted. "I don't want to get involved. (*hech-hem*)."

"I've spoken with Roy," I hastened to add, wondering if I'd caught her in the middle of eating something, "and there are a couple of questions I have that you might be able to help me with. It was Roy who told me how to get in touch with you."

"I'm sure he did," she said. "(*hech-hem*) He has been nothing but a thorn in my side since the day he was born. And after everything I did for him!"

I thought that's what mothers are for… to do things for their children, I mused. She made it sound as though it was a chore.

"Could I possibly talk with you in person?" I asked. "I promise I won't take up too much of your time."

There was a moment's silence, then: "Well, I don't know. I'm having my hair done this afternoon. (*hech-hem*) I suppose I could meet you afterwards."

"That would be fine," I said, thinking that "*hech-hem*" throat-clearing thing could get very old very fast. "Thank you. Where would you like to meet?"

"Andre does my hair when I'm here," she said. "Do you know of him?"

Uh, yeah, as a matter of fact, I did. I'd tricked with him a couple of times back in my single days, but he was a little too much in love with himself for my taste. He was now one of the city's top hairdressers with an exclusive shop on Brookhaven, on the edge of Decorator's Row.

"Yes," I said. "There's a coffee shop right next door, as I recall. I could meet you there. At what time?"

"(*hech-hem*) We should be through around three. My sister will be with me. We'll see you there, then."

We exchanged goodbyes and hung up. Neither of us had asked how we'd recognize the other, but I figured two late-middle-aged women with fresh hairdos wouldn't be too hard to spot.

I found it very interesting, however, that she did not ask exactly what about Roy I wanted to discuss. I suspected she knew it was either about Kelly or Carlene's death and didn't want to give away anything, even by asking. Obviously she knew Carlene was dead, and I'd not be surprised that the money for the lawyer had come from her, despite her apparent distance from her son. I also suspected she wanted to know what I knew.

* * *

Looking for a parking space, I passed both the coffee shop and Salon Andre before I found a spot. As I approached Andre's coming back toward the coffee shop, two ladies emerged from Salon Andre and turned toward the coffee shop. Though I was behind them and really couldn't see their faces, one was tall and very thin, wearing a black dress and what looked like a cone of intensely white cotton candy on her head. The other was slightly shorter and considerably heavier, with a brown dress and greying brown hair in a much less dramatic style. My money was on the cotton candy as being Angelina D'Angelo.

I caught up with them just as they entered the coffee shop and they were approaching the "Please Wait to Be Seated" lectern.

"Mrs. D'Angelo. Mrs. Collins?" I said, and they turned to look at me. I upped my bet. The more heavy set one had a pleasant face and smiled, if a little shyly. The cotton candy lady's thin face had a look of mild perpetual displeasure and merely raised a sculpted eyebrow in acknowledgment. If she'd been wearing heavy green makeup and a pointed black hat, she could have been Margaret Hamilton's understudy as Wicked Witch of the West. When I extended my hand, each of them took it somewhat hesitantly. Neither introduced herself.

The waitress came up, picked up three menus, and led us to a table at the back of the shop. She said she'd give us a minute, and left.

"Thank you for agreeing to meet me," I said after we'd been seated. Cotton candy merely nodded, and I had a hard time taking my eyes off that fascinating confection. A light behind her haloed clearly through the fluffed hair which was so white it had the hint of blue you see inside of a snow cave on a very bright day. I wondered how she could possibly sleep with it. And for someone with so fanciful a hairdo, her face gave the impression of someone who had spent a lifetime registering disapproval.

Fishing a pack of cigarettes out of her purse, she lit one—neither offering one to either her sister or me, or asking if anyone minded if she smoked.

"(hech-hem) About Roy," she said, exhaling a long, thin plume of smoke. Her tone clearly indicated she had no interest in wasting time.

"Yes…," I began, but the waitress' return cut me off. The ladies each ordered tea and a popover, and I opted for coffee and a piece of banana creme pie.

When she left, I continued: "I was a friend of Carlene DeNuncio and I have reason to believe that her death was not an accident."

Mildred Collins eyes widened and she looked quickly to her sister, who showed no reaction at all.

"And what might this have to do with Roy?" Mrs. D'Angelo asked.

"Well," I began, "The police know who was driving the van that killed her and are devoting all their efforts to finding him. However, I have reason to believe that someone else arranged the 'accident.' Rightly or wrongly, as the father of Carlene's son, Roy would be considered a logical suspect. So before I take my suspicions to the police, I'd like to be able to rule Roy out, if at all possible. And as his mother, you know him better than anyone. I was hoping you could give me some insight into his character and background."

She took another long drag of her cigarette, exhaled, and

then shrugged, noncommitally.

I pressed ahead. "I understand it was you who told Roy of Kelly, and of Carlene's death. I was wondering how you could be so sure Kelly was Roy's child?"

She looked at me with a slightly raised eyebrow. "I know Roy," she said, as though that were a definitive explanation. "I know Roy had been (*hech-hem*) seeing her about five years ago, and that he tossed her aside as he has tossed women aside all his life. I know she became (*hech-hem*) a lesbian shortly after."

And how might you know that? I wondered, at the same time mildly irked both by the throat-clearing and by the phrase 'she became a lesbian' as though it were a casual, spur of the moment decision on Carlene's part. I had to ask.

"And how did you find that out?" I asked.

She exchanged a quick glance with her sister, who up until this point had simply sat silently with the detached air of a cat on a windowsill. I couldn't decide if it was disinterest or total deference to her sister. Her only movement was her left thumb and index finger idly turning a bracelet on her right wrist.

"I have my ways," Mrs. D'Angelo said, cryptically.

The waitress brought our order and asked if there would be anything else. When we said 'no' she put the check beside my cup and left.

I suddenly wondered if Mrs. D'Angelo hadn't known about Kelly all along! How? She didn't strike me as the kind of person who would be above hiring a private investigator to check up on her son's girlfriends, but why would she have kept tabs on Carlene after Roy moved on to his next conquest? There's no way she could have known Carlene was pregnant. And if she knew about Kelly all this time, why didn't she tell Roy before?

And if she would hire a private investigator to keep tabs on Carlene, could Frank Santorini...?

Slow down, there, Hardesty, my mind cautioned. And it was right. I do have a tendency to run off into the woods without my bag of breadcrumbs and end up getting lost.

"Did Roy mention that we'd talked briefly on Sunday?" I asked.

She took a sip of her tea before answering. "No," she said. "I (*hech-hem*) wasn't even aware he was in town. He has a busy life. I have a busy life. Our schedules don't often coincide."

I read between the lines on that one fairly easily.

"What do you think of Roy's attempts to gain custody of Kelly?" I asked. I hoped she wasn't going to try to act like she didn't know about it, and she didn't.

"I think it's the first time in his life he has taken responsibility for his actions," she said. "(*hech-hem*) Perhaps there is hope for him yet."

I wondered how her sister could possibly listen to the endless throat-clearing without going absolutely crazy. I finished a bite of my pie before saying: "Well, no offense to Roy or his current girlfriend," I said, "but do you really think it fair to take Kelly from his aunt and her family?"

Her facial expression reflected her disdain. "What I think has nothing to do with it," she said. "The boy is Roy's. He belongs with Roy."

"Do you know a man named Eddie Styles, by any chance?" I asked.

I saw her sister shoot her a quick sideways glance, but her face maintained its impassivity.

"No," Mrs. D'Angelo said. "(*hech-hem*) Why?"

"Just curious," I said. I had a feeling I'd found out just about everything I was going to, and Mildred Collins total silence since we'd sat down was getting to me.

"That's a very nice bracelet," I said, in an attempt to have her say *something*.

"Thank you," she said with a quick smile. "It was a gift from my daughter."

Again I was surprised at how much alike the sisters sounded. The same inflections, the same slight accent…southern? If I had my eyes closed there's no way I could tell them apart…except for the throat-clearing. And did I detect a hint of disapproval on Mrs. D'Angelo's face? Apparently she had expected her sister to be seen and not heard.

"Ah, you have a daughter," I said, trying to see if a bit of small talk might get her to say...and possibly reveal ...something. "Does she live near you?"

She looked at me a little strangely, but as she was opening her mouth to speak, Mrs. D'Angelo took a quick sip of her tea and said: "(*hech-hem*) Mildred, we're running late. We have to get going." For exactly what they were running late she did not say, and the slightly puzzled expression on Mrs. Collins' face clearly showed she obviously didn't know either. Mrs. D'Angelo gave me a cursory glance and said: "Thank you for the tea, and I trust you won't need to contact me further."

Mrs. Collins took a quick bite from her almost untouched popover, and washed it down with a swig of tea, without looking at her sister. Maybe it was just me, but I got the definite feeling that it was somehow an act of very passive defiance.

I rose when they did and extended my hand to each of them, admittedly partly because I sensed it made Mrs. D'Angelo uncomfortable.

"Thank you again for meeting with me," I said as Mrs. D'Angelo bent to pick up her purse beside her chair.

"You're welcome," she said without smiling. And the two women turned and left.

Well, that was interesting, I thought, and sat down to finish my pie.

CHAPTER 12

Angelina D'Angelo came across to me as being a pretty cold fish who wasn't particularly fond of her own son. But that she was apparently willing to bankroll his attempt to gain custody of Kelly indicated that there might be a spark of maternal warmth in there somewhere. And I suspected their personalities had a lot more in common than either of them might choose to admit.

And Roy...now there was another mystery. His motivation for wanting custody of Kelly was pretty darned vague. He definitely did not strike me as the fatherly type. But then it might be a simple case of, as he himself said: "He's mine, and I want him." I'm sure he probably gave no thought whatsoever to what he would *do* with Kelly if he did get him. No, the more I thought it over, the more convinced I was that Roy wanted Kelly as some sort of key to his mother's bank vault. Exactly how I wasn't sure, but...

Perhaps, as Mrs. D'Angelo had said, she still had hopes—unrealistic as they may be—that Roy might straighten out, and she might be financing the custody suit to that end. But if he did win custody of Kelly, it would in effect put the kid in the position of a guinea pig in an experiment.

I suddenly thought again of Jan Houston. She and Roy knew—and apparently detested—each other, though neither of them would say why. Carlene had implied their animosity predated Carlene's pregnancy. Did Roy know Carlene had hooked up with Jan? A lot I *didn't* know, and wanted to.

I decided to give Jan Houston a call, ostensibly to see if she might have contacted Beth Erickson about being allowed to see Kelly, but primarily to see if she might give me some indication of her problem with Roy. I didn't want to bother her at work, so decided to wait until I got home.

Just as I was getting ready to leave the office, the phone

rang.

"Hardesty Investigations," I said.

"Mr. Hardesty, this is Bonnie Bronson." Her voice made it quite clear I probably wasn't going to like what she had to say—and I hoped it wasn't anything to do with Joshua.

"Yes, Ms Bronson, What can I do for you?"

"I think this 'investigation' has gone on quite long enough," she said, coldly. "You've obviously found nothing, and are rather desperately looking into areas which not only have nothing to do with Ms DeNuncio's death, but are by no stretch of the imagination any of your business!"

Estelle! I thought. Obviously, however and for whatever reason, Estelle had told her of our meeting at Coffee &. *Why in the hell would she do that?* I wondered.

"I'm very sorry you feel that way, Ms. Bronson," I said, "but as I told you before, since it was your sister who hired me, it should be she who determines when the investigation should end. I have come on a few new leads, but I assure you as I have assured your sister that if they do not go anywhere, I will consider the matter closed."

"I will give you one more week," she said, "and then I will seek legal counsel on my sister's behalf."

Wow, lady! I thought: *What the hell is your problem?*

"I understand," I said, though of course I didn't. "Again, I will consider the matter closed the moment your sister tells me to. And it goes without saying I sincerely hope that your displeasure with me won't be reflected on Joshua in any way."

"Of course not!" she said. "He has nothing to do with this and we would never be so petty as to involve him in a personal disagreement between us."

"I very much appreciate that," I said.

"As long as we understand one another," she said. "Good-bye."

And she hung up.

Oh, great!

* * *

We'd rather quickly settled into an at-home routine: Jonathan and Joshua usually got home shortly before I did, and Jonathan would have my evening Manhattan ready. We'd have our group hug, and I'd play with Joshua while Jonathan fixed dinner. Then more playtime for Joshua while Jonathan tried to study for his Wednesday night class. Joshua's bath time was around 8:00, then bed and story time. One of the things Jonathan had brought back from Wisconsin was an 8x10 framed photo of Samuel, Sheila, and Joshua as a baby, and every night Joshua would say his prayers and kiss the picture, which we kept on the bedside table.

Okay, okay...I know a lot of single gay guys' eyes start glazing over with boredom at the very idea of such an overdose of "Leave It to Beaver" domesticity, and before I met Jonathan, I was certainly one of them. But I *had* met Jonathan, and Joshua was now in our lives, and that's the way it was. And while, to be honest, I sometimes wished I were still out there cruising the bars and picking up tricks, when I weighed that period against now, now always won.

As to Joshua, he still hadn't fully adjusted to the fact that his parents weren't coming back for him, and he talked about them often, always in the present tense. Every now and then when he'd get angry with us, he'd start crying and calling for his mother or his dad (interestingly, which one he called on seemed to depend on the cause of his anger), and he had occasional nightmares about someone coming and carrying him or his folks away, but all in all he was making as good an adjustment as we could have hoped for.

* * *

Around 7:30, I looked up Jan Houston's number and dialed it, hoping it hadn't been disconnected again. It hadn't, and was answered on the fourth ring.

"Hello?" I recognized Jan's voice at once.

"Jan, this is Dick Hardesty," I said. "I don't mean to bother you, but I was wondering if you'd called Beth Erickson about Kelly."

The usual hostility was absent from her voice when she said: "Yes, I did, and I owe you. I got to spend some time with him this past Sunday, and next weekend he's coming to my company picnic with me."

"That's great!" I said. I really was glad for her.

"Of course Beth doesn't completely trust me yet, and I can't say I blame her, really. But Kelly was almost as glad to see me as I was to see him. He kept asking me where...his other mommy...was. That nearly broke my heart."

"I can well imagine," I said, thinking of Joshua's asking about his mom and dad. "You do know that Roy D'Angelo is trying to get custody of Kelly, don't you?"

The anger immediately returned to her voice. "Yes, I knew. But no way in hell that bastard's going to get Kelly!" she said. "Beth's family has hired the best lawyer in the state!"

So, I thought but did not say, *apparently has Roy.*

Well, I'd sort of pried the door open. Now to step in. "I remember your saying you knew Roy, and I gather you're not overly fond of him. I was wondering about exactly how you know him, and why you dislike him so. Without him, there wouldn't be any Kelly."

The anger was still there when she said: "Like I said, I owe you. But that doesn't mean I want you prying around in my private life. So just drop it."

"Well," I said, "I'm afraid that once I really want to know something, I usually manage to find out somehow. Maybe from Roy."

"Not if you know what's good for you," she said.

Why, Jan, one of my mind voices asked with mock surprise, *was that some sort of threat?* Not a very bright move from someone who still hadn't totally dropped off my suspects list.

"Jan," I said, "I'm not out to cause you grief, believe me. But I am out to find out who killed Carlene and why, and if that involves prying into places I probably shouldn't, I'm sorry."

"Well you damned well should be!" she said emphatically. "I had nothing to do with Car...*her*...death, and my life sure as hell has nothing to do with it—and it's none of your damned business. Now if you're through, I've got things to do."

"Sure," I said. "I..." But she'd hung up, leaving me to ponder the fact that even now Jan Houston could not or would not say her ex-lover's name.

Why do people insist on making things so hard for themselves? If she'd just come up with some sort of even remotely plausible story and not acted like an exposed nerve end, I might have just accepted it and moved on. But I was hooked now, and determined to find out what the hell she was covering up—whether it had anything to do with the case or not.

* * *

We'd gotten a notice in our mailbox from the building's owner telling us that the city would start repaving the alley that same day, which would mean the entrance to the garage would be blocked and that we'd have to park on the street until at least Thursday. Then. on my way to work, I discovered they'd begun major road work on the main route between home and my office. The detour added between ten and fifteen minutes to my driving time, depending on whether, as usually happened, I got held up by a commuter train that crossed the detour route and was one of the reasons I would not normally go that way. To add to the fun, the detour also involved going over a series of steep San Francisco-like hills known as "The Hump." I kind of enjoyed it, actually...rather like being on my own little roller coaster...but it was a real challenge for people without automatic transmissions.

* * *

As I sat waiting for the train to pass—I suspected the engineer just sat there, down the line, waiting for me—I continued, as I'd done since I left the apartment, thinking about Carlene DeNuncio and the entire case-that-might-not-be-a case. I'd been pretty successful in getting about everybody involved: Roy D'Angelo, his mother, Jan Houston, and now Bonnie Bronson.

Well, if I wanted everyone to love me, I sure as hell picked the wrong profession.

Once at the office, the day passed fairly quickly with paperwork and reports and minor routine chores.

Around 1:30 the phone rang.

"Hardesty Investigations."

"Mr. Hardesty, this is Estelle Bronson," the voice said.

Ah, here comes the ax, I thought.

"Yes, Ms Bronson," I said. "What can I do for you?"

I was afraid I knew.

"I'm sorry to bother you at work," she said, "but Joshua isn't feeling well, and we were wondering if you could come and pick him up? I tried calling Mr. Quinlan, but couldn't reach him."

"Of course!" I said, more than a little surprised by how concerned I was. "I'll be over shortly. Do you think I should call a doctor?"

I'd never dealt with a sick kid before.

"Oh, no," she said. "I'm sure that won't be necessary. There's some sort of 24-hour bug going around, and I'm afraid Joshua isn't the first of our children to get it. But we do feel he'd be better off at home."

"Thank you," I said. "I'll be over as soon as I can get there."

I made a quick call to Evergreens to leave a message for Jonathan telling him what was going on, and then left the office.

* * *

Estelle met me at the door, and took me immediately into the "nap room" to the left of the entry. Joshua was curled up, asleep, on one of the mats, a thin blanket over him. I knelt down beside him, removed the blanket, and picked him up. He didn't seem at all surprised to see me.

"I don't feel good," he said. "I want my mommy!"

The poor kid really looked unwell, and I felt bad for him. My mom always used to say she could tell when I wasn't feeling well by looking in my eyes. I could tell the same thing by looking into Joshua's.

"That's okay, Joshua," I said. "We'll get you home now."

Bonnie Bronson appeared in the doorway of the main playroom, where the other kids were doing various kid things involving a minimum of noise.

"Ms. Bronson," I said by way of acknowledgment, and she merely nodded, then looked pointedly from Estelle to me. Estelle merely lowered her head, then led me to the door.

"I'm sure he'll be better tomorrow," she said as she opened the door for me.

"Thank you," I said again, and carried Joshua to the car. I looked back toward the house as I was opening the driver's side door after depositing Joshua in the back seat, and saw the two sisters standing behind the screen door, watching. Well, Estelle was watching me. Bonnie was watching Estelle.

* * *

I don't know how real parents do it, but I'm very glad we skipped the diaper changing stage. A vomiting four-year old is plenty bad enough! Poor Joshua threw up twice on the way home, and once when we got inside—luckily I had enough advance warning to get him to the toilet bowl in time.

As I was cleaning him up, I reflected on my earlier thoughts about single life as opposed to family domesticity, and the single life didn't look so bad.

I managed to get him into his pajamas and into bed. He wanted me to read to him, and I got about three pages into *The Littlest Tractor* before he fell asleep. I had to clean the car, but I didn't dare leave him alone. But the minute Jonathan walked in the door, after a brief hug, I grabbed a roll of paper towels and the spray cleaner, and was out the door.

Though I'd had to park on the street (as had Jonathan, but I couldn't spot his car anywhere), I'd arrived home in time to find a spot fairly close to the apartment. God knows how far away Jonathan had to park.

* * *

By morning, Joshua seemed to be pretty much back to normal, though when I took his temperature he still had something of a fever, so Jonathan called work to say he wouldn't be in. ("It's been pretty slow this week," he reassured me, "and we finished that big job yesterday.") Then he called Happy Day to tell them he'd be keeping Joshua home for the day.

I left for work a few minutes early, hoping I could avoid the commuter train this time. Everything was fine until I reached the top of the hill leading down to the railroad crossing at the very bottom. There was a fair amount of traffic ahead of me and I saw the damned crossing lights start flashing as the gates started coming down. Damn it!

I started applying the brakes to slow down, and the pedal went all the way to the floor!

Shit! I started pumping the brakes and nothing happened, except that I continued to pick up speed. I tried shifting down, which didn't do much, then pulled the emergency brake. Nothing! I was rapidly coming up on the car in front of me. Thank God no cars were coming up the hill, so I swung over into the other lane, missing the car in front by just feet.

Great! Now what? I'm going faster and faster down a steep hill, headed straight for a railroad crossing with an approaching train! *Shit!* I shut off the engine and tried to jam the gears into reverse! Nothing but a loud screeching, grinding sound. I glanced at the speedometer. 45 and rising. I could cut across the street and go up over the curb, but there was nothing to slow me down except houses and trees, neither of which seemed like a wise option.

Then I saw the small cemetery paralleling the railroad tracks and surrounded with a hedgerow fence. With luck, the hedge would slow me down without totally destroying the car; but if it didn't slow me down enough, I'd go right onto the tracks and into the side of the train!

Laying the heel of my hand on the horn...*what the hell good is* that *supposed to do?* my mind voices wanted to know, rightfully... *Let the train know you're coming?* I pulled the wheel to the left, watched the cars of the passing train coming closer and closer, bounced roughly over the curb, and into the hedgerow. I heard the loud hissing and scraping of the branches on the car, then a large, solid thunk as the front end hit something very solid, stopping the car. I was ten feet from the end of the hedgerow and 40 feet from the railroad tracks, where the last car of the train was just passing.

Thank you, God!

* * *

Somebody gave me a ride about four blocks to the nearest phone, where I called for a wrecker and for Jonathan to come get me. I was just thankful that he and Joshua hadn't been in the car with me.

After making the calls, I walked back to my car, where two patrol cars were waiting. I explained what had happened, and that I'd called for a wrecker. Seemingly reassured that I wasn't either drunk or on drugs, one of the cops still wanted to give me a ticket for reckless driving and/or for operating a motor vehicle in an unsafe manner. Apparently he'd already met his ticket quota for the month, since I managed to talk him out of it.

About fifteen minutes later, the tow truck arrived and, after both cops directed traffic while the wrecker backed up to my car, the ticket-prone cop got in his squad car and drove off. Just as the truck hooked up to the car, Jonathan pulled up on the other side of the street, with Joshua and Bunny staring out the back window at the scene. Seeing no cars coming, Jonathan made a U-turn...*not the wisest of moves, Jonathan,* I thought... and pulled up behind the squad car.

"My ride," I explained lamely to the cop, and he just nodded. *Whew!*

I hurried over to the car and got in.

"Are you okay?" Jonathan asked, as he'd already asked on the phone, and I again assured him I was. His face reflected his concern.

"Why is your car in the bushes?" Joshua asked.

The wrecker was now winching the much-the-worse-for-wear car out of the tangle of flattened and broken hedgerow. The front end had sustained quite a bit of damage, and the paint was badly scraped, but it looked reparable. At least I hoped it was.

When the car was totally winched to the wrecker, the cop again directed traffic while it pulled out into the street. Jonathan pulled around the squad car and followed it as I waved a thanks to the cop.

"You're *sure* you're all right?" Jonathan asked for the third time.

"I'm sure," I said, aware that Joshua and Bunny were trying to climb through the space between the front bucket seats to get up front with us.

"Leave Bunny back there," I told him, and he did, then climbed up onto my lap.

"And how are *you* feeling, Joshua?" I asked, putting my arms around his waist both as potential protection from a sudden stop and to keep his inevitable squirming to a minimum.

He looked at me, his face taking on a wide-eyed look of utmost solemnity, and said: "I've been very, very sick!" nodding his head slowly up and down in confirmation.

"But you're better now," I said, and Joshua looked to Jonathan, who grinned and nodded.

"Yes," Joshua said, reassured, "I'm better now."

We followed the tow truck to the garage, and the owner told me he'd get to it as soon as he could. I gave him my home and office numbers, and the number of my insurance man, and asked him to call me as soon as he knew anything—especially about what might have caused the brakes to fail. I knew I'd had them checked as part of my last tune-up.

I was tempted to just not bother going in to work, but I had to finish up a research assignment for one of my lawyer clients, so had Jonathan drive me to work. I told him I'd catch the bus home.

It was nearly 9:30 by the time I got to the office, and the light on my answering machine was blinking. I walked over and pressed "Play."

"Mr. Hardesty," the immediately recognizable voice said, "this is Estelle Bronson. I've been giving a great deal of thought to the matter, and since you've come up with nothing to indicate Carlene's death was anything but an accident, I think we should consider the issue closed. Please send me a bill for your services, and thank you very much for indulging me."

No "Good-bye". No "Give me a call if you have any questions." Nothing. But I got the definite impression that while Estelle was saying the words, Bonnie had put them in her mouth and was probably standing right behind her when she said them.

Great! So here I was with no client and a wrecked car, all in the space of two hours. Estelle had perhaps been technically correct in my not having come up with any solid evidence that Carlene's death was not an accident, but I'd bet my bottom dollar that it wasn't.

Well, it was her nickel, and I couldn't afford the time or money to pursue the case any further on my own…especially now that Joshua had entered the picture. I always hated to leave a case dangling, but I had no choice.

I left the office and went to the Hall of Records to do the research I needed.

* * *

Rather than go directly home from the Hall of Records, I stopped by the office to drop off the materials I'd collected and to make a few notes to myself for typing a report up in the morning. Once again, the light on my answering machine was blinking.

There were two messages: the first from the garage where my car had been taken. Well, they didn't waste much time, obviously. "Mr. Hardesty, call Otto at Otto's Auto Repair right away, please."

The second was from Jonathan.

"Dick, it's Jonathan," he began. I never understood why he always felt it necessary to tell me who he was—I was pretty sure I could recognize his voice by this time. "…The guy at the garage wants you to call him right away."

So I did.

I asked for Otto and there was a long pause until the owner's voice came on.

"Hello?"

"Otto, this is Dick Hardesty returning your call. What did you find out?"

"Uh, yeah, Mr. Hardesty," he said, sounding a little hesitantly. "This might be a strange question, but do you have any enemies?"

That one struck me as peculiar, to say the least. "Yeah," I said finally, "I'm sure I've got a couple. Why?" I didn't have an immediate idea of what he was getting at, but I was pretty sure I wasn't going to like it.

"Well," he said, "I just thought you might want to make a police report."

"On what?" I asked. "They took a report at the scene."

"Yeah, but did they know somebody cut your brake fluid hoses?" he asked.

(HAPTER 13

My first reaction was surprise, which quickly segued into a mild shock. No one had ever seriously tried to kill me before—and I had to assume cutting someone's brake hoses had to be considered serious. *Nothing gets by you, does it, Hardesty?* a mind voice observed. And if whoever did it knew I would be going down that hill toward a train track, I'd say it was pretty damned serious.

My second reaction was anger, which blossomed into near fury. What if Jonathan and or Joshua had been in the car with me and those bushes hadn't been there? If anyone has a grudge against me, they can take their best shot...but they'd damned well better keep everyone else out of it, especially people I care about.

If whoever had done this had just left well enough alone, I'd have put the whole matter behind me. I'd just resigned myself to the fact that with no client paying the bills, I'd simply have to let it drop. Ah, but that was before it became *really* personal, and I had very little doubt that when I found whoever was responsible for the brakes, I'd also find who killed—or was responsible for killing—Carlene DeNuncio.

I wanted a cigarette, and that alone told me I was more shaken up than I thought. I hadn't had a cigarette, or wanted one, in literally years.

I put in a call to Marty Gresham at police headquarters, just to let him know what was going on, but he wasn't in the office, so I just decided to try again in the morning.

I closed up the office, and walked to the bus stop.

* * *

I wasn't really aware of the ride home—almost missed my stop, as a matter of fact—for thinking about who might have cut my brake lines, and why. Well, the 'why' was fairly obvious: someone suspected I knew more than, in fact, I did know and didn't want me to find out any more. As to who that "someone" might be, though....

Bonnie Bronson? She'd always been a sort of peripheral suspect as far as I was concerned, and she had obviously talked Estelle into firing me. So why not let it go at that?

Well, maybe she was covering her ass with Estelle and anyone else who might follow up on my movements/activities prior to my demise, had the attempt to kill me succeeded. I still wasn't certain about the relationship between the two sisters, but it struck me that Estelle might be a tad suspicious of her sister if I suddenly turned up dead. I couldn't really picture Bonnie with a pair of clippers cutting the lines herself—she didn't strike me as the mechanical type. But if Eddie Styles was still around somewhere, she—or Jan Houston—could have had him do it for her. Roy D'Angelo could easily have done it himself, but it was highly unlikely he was still in town.

Jan Houston hadn't been too happy with me when I last talked to her. Actually, I wouldn't be surprised if Jan knew her way around an engine. Had I asked her if she by any chance knew Eddie Styles? I don't think so, but I would.

I remembered mentioning him to both Roy D'Angelo and his mother, and getting some sort of vibes from them which I hadn't followed up on. I'd make a point to do that now.

* * *

I was a little concerned, when I got off the bus and was walking to the apartment, to see Jonathan's car parked on the street, then remembered that it was his school night and he probably didn't want to take the time to put it in the garage and then take it out again. Though it was about three doors past our building, I walked over to it and looked underneath for any signs of pooled liquid. There wasn't any, of course. I checked his tires while I was at it. All seemed to be well.

Better paranoid than sorry.

Joshua was obviously feeling much better. Just about every book and toy he owned were scattered around the living room when I got home. I was quite sure he'd been playing his 'I've been very, very sick' card with Jonathan, who otherwise would have seen to it that at least most of the toys were put away before he got out more.

Joshua was doing his little dance-of-impatience when I came in, demanding a cookie before dinner.

"It'll spoil your appetite," Jonathan was saying over his shoulder as he took ice cubes out of the freezer for my Manhattan.

"No it won't!" Joshua insisted. "I'm hungry."

"We'll be eating in a little while," Jonathan said.

"I'm hungry now!" the boy insisted, and Jonathan relented, taking out a wrapped piece of sliced American cheese and, laying the ice cube tray on the counter, peeled the wrapper and handed it to Joshua.

"That's not a cookie!" the boy said.

"Yes, it is," Jonathan replied. "It's a cheese cookie. Do you want it or not?"

With a look of resigned nobility, Joshua took the slice of cheese.

They obviously hadn't noticed my entrance, but when they did, both came over for our group hug.

"What did the garage man want?" Jonathan asked as I set Joshua down to finish his slice of cheese.

"Nothing much," I lied, and he gave me a raised eyebrow look.

"Uh-huh," he said. "So what did he want?"

Shit! I didn't want to lie to him, but I didn't want to worry him, either. Still, he had a right to know.

"Well," I said, "he claims somebody cut my brake lines— probably just some local random vandalism. I'm really going to have to start keeping it in the garage."

"Jeez!" Jonathan said, obviously distressed as I feared he

would be. "You could have been killed! And what if Joshua had been with you? Did you report it to the police?"

I shook my head. "No, but I will in the morning. Let's just be sure you keep your car in the garage tonight as soon as you get home—I gather they're through working on the alley."

From the look on his face, I could tell he didn't believe my 'random vandalism' theory, but he didn't say anything, probably because *he* didn't want to worry *me* in case I bought into it.

* * *

I took Jonathan's car in the morning, dropping Joshua off at Happy Day and Jonathan at Evergreens. Since I parked in a guarded lot at work, I wasn't too concerned that anything would happen to it, even if whoever was out to get me was aware I was driving it, a thought I realized had more than a little paranoia in it.

Though I was still a little shaken by the idea that someone might really have tried to kill me, it didn't keep me from my coffee/paper/crossword puzzle routine first thing when I got to the office. That done, I typed up my report on the previous day's research, put everything in an envelope, and decided to hand deliver it to the lawyer's office. It was a fair distance, but I could walk it.

...and save having to take the car out of it's nice, safe lot? a mind-voice asked.

Of course not! I mentally replied. *I need the exercise.*

Sure.

I spent the time on the walk over and back to think about the case, which was now not Estelle Bronson's case but mine. I realized I had no fewer than four people pissed off at me, and every one of them was, I had no doubt, capable of acting on their displeasure. But attempted murder? If I were to rank them in order, I'd probably put Roy D'Angelo at the top of the list, Jan Houston right below him, Bonnie Bronson next, and Angelina D'Angelo at the bottom. But it was a pretty flimsy list, at best, and of the four on it, only two were really likely: Roy and Jan, because they each had by far the strongest motivation: Kelly. Bonnie Bronson...well, I still wasn't perfectly clear on her motivation; killing someone is a tad extreme a method to "protect" a sister. And Angelina D'Angelo...well, motherly love and wanting to have her grandson be with her son might be a motive, except that she didn't strike me as the kind of mom who would go too far out of her way to help a son she obviously didn't get along with in the first place.

But I've learned that logic is not a necessary component of motivation.

So Roy wanted Kelly. Why? I've seen guppies with a stronger paternal instinct than I sensed in this guy. And having a kid would certainly put a crimp in his lifestyle. Probably he saw Kelly as a way to oil his way into his mother's good graces—and her checkbook. And Angelina D'Angelo certainly did not strike me as the grand-motherly type.

I decided I'd really like to have a talk with Mildred Collins. I wasn't really quite sure why, but perhaps she could give me a third-party insight into Angelina and Roy. I'd have to think about exactly how to get to her without letting Angelina know. I'd sensed that Mildred was to Angelina as Estelle was to Bonnie, somewhat—in other words, under the thumbs of their sisters.

In the meantime, though, I thought it best to give Marty Gresham a call at police headquarters, just to let him know what was going on. Part of me—the "I'm a big boy and can take car of myself" part—hated running to anyone else with my problems, but then attempted murder is a bit more than a "problem".

"Officer Gresham," the familiar voice said when I was transferred to his extension.

"Marty, hi, it's Dick Hardesty."

He sounded surprised. "Dick! Small world! I was going to give you a call."

For some reason my crotch was very happy to hear that. So what if Marty was irredeemably straight? So what if I'm happily involved? Fantasies are fantasies, and my crotch has a mind of its own.

"What's up?" I asked.

"I think we might have a lead on Eddie Styles," Marty said. "We think he might be back in town."

"Well, talk about small worlds," I said, and told him about my recent close encounter with the commuter train.

Marty was quiet for a moment when I'd finished, then said: "I guess that pretty much resolves any question of whether or not the DeNuncio woman's death was more than a hit-and-run." There was another pause, then: "I think I'd better talk to Lieutenant Richman about intensifying our investigation. To be honest with you, our preliminary investigation really didn't indicate even a remote connection between her and Styles. From what we know of Styles, his services don't come cheap, and the only one close to Ms. DeNuncio we considered was her ex roommate. We found out the roommate had taken an insurance policy out on Ms DeNuncio, but it wasn't all that big a policy and she accounted for all of it."

We talked for a few more minutes, then hung up.

That the police had looked into Jan closely enough to find out about the insurance, or had questioned her about what she'd done with it was all news to me. Not that the police were obligated in any way to let me know everything they were doing, but it would have been nice to know. Whereas I'd been assuming that the insurance money might have been enough to hire Styles, I now doubted very much that Jan could have afforded it. So unless she had another source of income I didn't know about....

I realize, too, that sometimes I tend to hang some pretty heavy assumptions on some very weak strings. How would Jan even have known about Styles in the first place? How would Bonnie? I mean, the yellow pages don't usually carry a "Hit Men" listing. But there was something Marty had told me about Styles when he first entered the picture....What was it?

Oh, yeah. Styles' rap sheet went back to when he was 17...in

Kentucky…and he had served time in prison there. Jan met Carlene in Kentucky. A bit of a stretch right there, but I probably hooked subconsciously onto the Kentucky link. But then again, the D'Angelos were from Kentucky, too! Jan knew Roy—I still wasn't sure how, but I'd find out. And Roy's father had a rather shady past, and…

And, and, and to the end of recorded time, one of my mind voices said wearily.

I pulled myself back to reality and reached for the phone, hoping I remembered Mildred Collins' number, and hoping Angelina didn't answer the phone. I wasn't at all sure I could tell them apart. Well, if there was any throat-clearing, I'd know.

"Mrs. Collins?" I asked in response to a "Hello?"

"Yes. Who is this?"

"This is Dick Hardesty calling." I assumed she'd remember me, but didn't want to take any chances. "We met the other day at lunch. I'm sorry not to have recognized your voice, but you and your sister sound so very much alike."

"Oh, yes," she said. "Everyone says that. Just a moment, I'll go call Angelina."

"No," I hastened to say before she put the phone down, "it was you I wanted to talk to. Do you have a moment?"

Her voice reflected her hesitation. "Well, I don't know, Mr. Hardesty," she said. "Angelina is out on the patio, reading, and I just came in to fix our lunch. What is it you wanted? Are you sure you wouldn't like to speak to Angelina?"

"Actually, I did want to talk with you," I said. "I'm trying to understand the relationship between Mrs. D'Angelo and Roy."

"Why?" she asked.

Good question, I thought. *Now let's try for a good answer.*

"Well, as I explained at lunch," I said, "I'd like to be able to tell the police that I doubt Roy had anything to do with Carlene's death, but I'm afraid I didn't get all that much assurance on that point from Mrs. D'Angelo. I gather there is some tension between her and Roy."

There was a significant pause, then: "Yes, I think you might say that. I fear our entire family is somewhat dysfunctional."

Can I assume you're including yourself? I wondered.

"Angelina can be very…difficult…at times," she said. "She has her own agendas in life. Roy inherited many of Angelina's traits."

I was getting the distinct impression that, like with the Bronsons, there was a lot more going on beneath the surface of her relationship with her sister than Mildred Collins cared to make known. Being an only child, I never did really understand the dynamics between siblings, but I suspected that both the Bronsons and Mildred and Angelina probably weren't typical examples.

"What do you think of Roy's seeking custody of Carlene DeNuncio's son?" I asked.

There was a very long pause, then: "I…I…I really can't talk about that," she said, sounding mildly flustered.

I decided to push it. "I'm sorry," I said. "I don't understand. Is there some reason why?"

Another pause. "It…it's not that I can't, it's that I really don't want to. And I really must go fix lunch now."

"Of course," I said. "I'll let you go. But I was wondering, since I still have several questions, if I could give you my work number and perhaps you might call me when you have time."

To be honest, I was a little surprised when she said: "Let me get a pencil."

I heard the phone being set down, and when she returned I gave her my number.

There was a slight pause while she apparently wrote it down, then: "I really must go now."

And she hung up.

Well, that was an intriguing conversation, I thought. *And I'd say it was pretty much a dysfunctional family, all right.* And while I didn't have a conscious clue as to what that was all about, somewhere in the far corners of my mind I could hear whispers.

Daughters. Agendas. Abandoned. Roy D'Angelo. Jan Houston. Carlene said…

Oh, the hell with it! When they got louder, I'd listen to them. I went to lunch.

* * *

As usual, it didn't work. The whispers were there for a reason, and trying to ignore them was pointless. So I just left them as much to themselves as I could. But I kept coming back to something Carlene had said at one time about…about being abandoned.

Jan Houston! Carlene had said Jan's mother had abandoned her when she was very young.

Yeah, that was rough. But what did that have to do with what was going on now?

Jan had been raised by an aunt.

Okay, so…?

Oh, come on, Hardesty! my mind voice said, disgustedly. *Surely you're not trying to make a link between Jan and the D'Angelos? You've done some pretty illogical stretching in the past, but…!*

Well, why not? There *was* a link between Jan and Roy D'Angelo: she really hated him, though from what I knew of Roy, there could have had any number of reasons for that. And true, Jan had never given me any indication that she even knew who Angelina D'Angelo was, but then the woman's name had never come up when I talked to her. So…?

Well, there was one way to find out.

* * *

I didn't want to try to reach Jan at work, so made a mental note to call her from home.

The afternoon passed, and I left the office early enough to swing by and pick up Jonathan before going to Happy Day for Joshua. Not particularly wanting to see either of the Bronson sisters at the moment, I waited in the car while Jonathan went in to get him. He was gone what seemed like a very long time, and when he came out with Joshua, he did not look happy.

"Something wrong?" I asked after Jonathan had put Joshua

in the back seat and gotten in the front seat beside me.

"We'll talk about it later," he said.

I didn't think I liked the sound of that. And when Joshua wanted to get in the front seat with us, Jonathan firmly told him 'no.'

I had no idea of what was going on, but didn't want to step into anything until I knew more about it.

When we got home, Jonathan told Joshua to go play in his room while Jonathan and I talked about grown-up things. I followed Jonathan into the kitchen and fixed my Manhattan, opened a can of Coke for him, then joined him at the kitchen table.

"Okay," I said. "What's the problem?"

"He got into a fight today with another boy," Jonathan said.

"He's four years old," I said. "How much of a fight could it have been?"

Jonathan scowled at me. "That's not the point!" he said. "He gave the boy a bloody nose!"

"So what was it all about?" I asked.

He took a long drink of his Coke before replying: "Apparently the other boy said something about the fact that while every other kid there has a mother or a father, Joshua didn't, and Joshua just lit into him! I'm not going to have him turning into a bully!"

"That hardly sounds like being a bully to me," I said.

"You're defending him?" Jonathan asked, obviously not pleased.

"No, I'm not defending him," I said. "He shouldn't have hit the kid, but I can understand why he did. He's four years old! He doesn't know how else to react."

"Well he'd damned well better learn," Jonathan said firmly.

The fact that Jonathan seldom swore underscored the intensity of his feelings. There had been a couple of previous occasions when Jonathan and I didn't agree on how to handle Joshua's behavior, and I usually deferred to Jonathan, since Joshua was his blood relation. But as time went on and it began to sink in that Joshua was going to be a permanent part of both our lives, I'd been a little less hesitant about putting my own opinions forward. I still tried to do it diplomatically.

I reached across the table and took Jonathan's hand. "And he will learn," I said. "We just have to strike a balance between over-reacting and under-reacting. What did the Bronsons say? Were they upset?"

"Well, they certainly weren't happy about it, but Bonnie said she would talk with the boy's mother and try to explain what happened. I'm just worried that if it happens again, they might try to throw Joshua out. Then what would we do?"

I smiled...I hoped reassuringly. "I don't think that's likely to happen," I said. "The Bronsons have had a lot more experience dealing with kids squabbling than we have."

I was surprised to have a sudden thought that I hoped Bonnie Bronson was not involved in Carlene's death, because if she were, Happy Day might have to close. A pretty odd thought, and a pretty big sea change from the old nobody-to-worry-about-but-me Dick Hardesty.

When Jonathan didn't say anything, I continued. "So what do you want to do about this?"

He took another swig of his Coke. "What do *you* suggest?" he asked, and I was pleased that he was acknowledging that it was something we both were part of.

"I suppose we should start out with a talk with Joshua," I said, and Jonathan nodded.

"And an apology to the other boy," he added.

"Definitely," I said.

And another crisis resolved—at least for the moment.

* * *

After dinner we took the opportunity of a communal dishwashing/drying to talk with Joshua about how big boys were expected to behave when challenged, and I gained new respect for the art of parenting. Later, I dug out and called Jan

Houston's number, hoping she'd be home. Again, I had no idea when I picked up the phone exactly what I was going to say if she was there, but I'd become fairly good at winging it over the years.

The phone rang three times when I heard it being picked up, followed by Jan's voice: "Hello?"

"Jan, this is Dick Hardesty," I said, "I..."

She cut me off before I could finish the sentence. "What do you want now? Why can't you just leave me the hell alone?"

"Well, I'm still trying to find out why Carlene was killed."

"How many times do I have to tell you I don't know anything at all about it?" she said, a little wearily, I thought.

"Because like it or not, you're a central figure in the whole thing," I said.

Silence.

"Tell me," I continued, "when you lived in Louisville, did you ever know a man named Eddie Styles?"

Her voice was heavy with suspicion when she said: "Eddie Styles? Where did you hear that name?"

"Someone I know in Louisville was mentioning it," I lied.

"So why ask me if I know him? Do you have any idea how many people live in Louisville?"

"A lot, I'm sure," I said. "But you do know him, don't you?" Actually, I had no idea whether she did or not. If she did it was a pretty small world, but I didn't really have anything to lose.

So imagine my surprise when, after yet another pause, she said: "Yes, I know—knew—him. I haven't seen or talked to him since I was a kid. What does he have to do with anything?"

I reminded myself to go out and buy a fistful of lottery tickets!

"Do you know what Eddie Styles does for a living?" I asked.

"How should I know?" she demanded. "I said I haven't seen or talked to him since I was a kid."

Time to drop the bombshell. "Then you didn't know he was driving the van that killed Carlene?" I asked.

Utter silence. I waited for a full 30 seconds, then said:

"Hello? You still there?"

"I…" long pause. "…Yes, I'm here. What are you saying? What are you trying to tell me? It can't be the same Eddie Styles! That's impossible. I…"

"Can I ask how you know…knew…him?" I said.

"He's my godfather," she said.

CHAPTER 14

What do they call it? *Deus ex machina*? Something from so far out of left field you're left shaking your head wondering where in the hell *that* came from!

How did I ever associate Eddie Styles and Jan Houston in the first place? Because they were both from Kentucky? So were several million other people. Both from Louisville? Okay, that narrows it down to only about...what?...950,000?

Yeah, but while I've never really been quite sure how or why my mind comes up with the things it does, more often than not it turns out to have a reason. It seems to be pretty good at putting tiny pierces of a puzzle together, even if I'm not sure of the connection at the time.

And Louisville was a definite link between Carlene and Jan and Roy. So maybe the *deus* wasn't totally *ex machina*.

That Jan Houston *did* know Eddy Styles of course could be seen as practically an admission that she was behind Carlene's death. But if she was, why would she admit to even knowing who Eddie Styles was? She didn't have to, and I'd have had a heck of a time trying to find it out on my own. But maybe she thought I knew more than I did, and was admitting to knowing him to throw me off track. And maybe the Easter Bunny lays colored eggs.

Before I'd hung up on my call to Jan Houston, she had said again that she had never had much contact with her godfather and hadn't seen or heard from him in years, had no idea how to reach him, where he lived or what he did for a living, or even that he was still alive. She didn't even know why he had been named as her godfather. Obviously, he'd been a friend of her parents...maybe through Jan's father having been involved in gambling.

And the revelation of her knowing Eddie Styles had so disconcerted me I hadn't even mentioned the D'Angelos.

And there was something else…another piece to the puzzle, relating to the D'Angelos…*come on, mind, give it up!*…Roy's dad?…auto repair shops and…?…*bookies!* Carlene said Roy's dad was a bookie! So was Jan's dad! A link there? Eddie Styles could have known them both? Even in a city the size of Louisville, it's pretty likely that most of the shady characters know one another.

Put two and two together, Hardesty, a mind voice urged.

Jan and Roy are brother and sister? I asked myself incredulously.

Uh, no, my mind responded. *I don't think you have to go quite that far. Nobody's even so much as suggested that Jan had a brother.*

But she could! I thought.

Yes, she could. And the Easter Bunny really might lay colored eggs. But 'could' and 'do' are two different words. Don't try too hard to make them interchangeable.

Granted—a racetrack town like Louisville was bound to have more than one bookie. Well, Jan at least knew Roy, somehow, and actively disliked him. There had to be a reason.

Okay, so there was a more-than-possible chance that Eddie Styles was some sort of link between Jan's family and Roy's… which meant that Roy might well know Eddie Styles too, and that if Jan Houston didn't hire Eddie to kill Carlene, maybe Roy D'Angelo did!

Roy had denied knowing Eddie when I'd asked him about it, but I'd doubted his answer when he gave it, and I doubted it even more now. Same with Angelina.

So what to do? Well, the bull-in-the-china-shop approach might work. One thing I've learned is that if you have some sort of title (like "private investigator") and sound like you know what you're talking about, most people tend to accept that you do. And with people from families as dysfunctional as Roy D'Angelo's seemed to be, that might be a definite advantage. Considering the apparent strain between his mother and him and his mother and his aunt, he probably couldn't really be sure how much I might have learned from talking with them all. I'd call him in the morning.

* * *

I suddenly was aware that Joshua was bouncing Bunny up and down on my lap, obviously trying to get my attention.

"Come on!" Joshua said impatiently. "It's time to read a story!"

I was surprised to see him standing there in his pajamas, hair still damp from his bath; his face freshly scrubbed to that fantastic little-kid shine. I looked up at Jonathan and he just returned the look with a grin and a slow shake of his head.

"You've been away," he said.

I realized he was right. I hate it when I do that.

When we got Joshua into bed, he announced that tonight *he* was going to read to *us*! When I asked him which of his books he was going to read, he pulled *The Popsicle Tree* out from under his pillow. I could definitely see a bit of collusion going on here; Jonathan sat there with a barely-repressed smile.

We all sat propped up with pillows against the headboard, Bunny on Jonathan's lap. With great fanfare, Joshua opened the book and began to read. Considering the number of times he'd had the book read to him, it wasn't surprising he knew most of it by heart, and he did a very convincing job of it, getting off track only occasionally as something in one of the pictures would catch his eye and he would stop to point at it and make some sort of stream-of-consciousness observation about it. But then Jonathan would cue him with a few words from whatever page we were on, and Joshua picked it right up.

It was sort of an improvisational rendition, not word for word, of course, and there were numerous chunks of the story out of order, but it was all there, and I was delighted that he so loved books at such an early age. And Joshua, of course, was very proud of himself as well he should have been.

When he'd finished, Jonathan and I each gave him a big

hug and told him what a smart boy he was.

"Now *you* read one," Joshua said.

Knowing he wouldn't go to sleep until we did, Jonathan got off the bed to get *The Littlest Tractor*. Joshua was out like a light after ten pages, and we got up and left the room. After we'd turned out the lights in the living room and kitchen and gone into our bedroom, Jonathan slipped his arm around my waist, his face in a huge mischievous grin, and said: "Hey, Farmer Jones: feel like plowing the south 40?"

As a matter of fact, I did.

* * *

At the office in the morning, after my coffee / paper /crossword puzzle routine, I thought of Roy D'Angelo. On the grounds that I really had very little to lose, I looked up his Saint Matthews phone number I'd written on an index card and dialed, not expecting him to be home. He wasn't, nor was his girlfriend. But I left a message on his machine to have him call me, collect—to save him the excuse of "I ain't gonna spend my money to call anybody long distance" and I was hoping he'd be curious enough to return the call to find out what I knew.

The phone ringing pulled me out of my reverie.

It was my insurance agent with some definitely not-good news. He'd just heard from the owner of the garage where I'd taken the car, and apparently the damage was a lot more extensive than was first thought: the frame had been bent, and the rear axle cracked. Plus it would need a lot of body work to get out the dents, then would need a new paint job, and...

"We're willing to consider it totaled," the agent said. "Considering the age of the car, you'd be just as far ahead to use the money to put a down payment on another one."

Great. Just great! I thought, looking out the window for an approaching plague of locusts.

Well, at least it took my mind off the case for a while.

But not for that long. The phone rang again about ten

minutes after the insurance agent called. *Well,* I thought with a flash of hope, *at least maybe it's a paying client.*

Wrong again.

"Mr. Hardesty," the vaguely familiar female voice said, "this is Mildred Collins, and I do think we should talk."

* * *

Well, surprise, surprise! I thought. When I'd given her my phone number, it was more or less an afterthought, and I never seriously thought I'd hear from her. But...

"Of course," I said. "When would be convenient for you?"

"Any time at all," she said. Then, as if sensing my unspoken question, she added: "Angelina was unexpectedly called back to Louisville. She left this morning."

"Would you like to join me for lunch?" I asked. "We really didn't have much of a chance to talk the last time."

She gave a quiet laugh. "That would be nice," she said. "I really don't get out much. And why don't we meet at the same place? I'd never been there before, but the popover was delicious—what little of it I was able to eat before Angelina rushed us off."

"That's fine," I said. "About 12:30?"

"I'll see you there," she said, and hung up.

I didn't muse this time. Musing is a quiet, almost lazy process. My mind was going much too fast for that.

Okay, so what's going on here? my mind wanted to know. So did I. Obviously she had a reason—I hesitated to call it a "motive"—but I didn't have a clue as to what it might be. From what little I'd seen and subsequently conjectured about Angelina D'Angelo and her sister, it just might be some sort of payback time for Mildred Collins—though payback for exactly what, other than Angelina's obvious dominance over her, I again had no idea. And why had Angelina suddenly up and taken off for Louisville? Was that the sort of thing she did all the time? Well, once again, I'd find out.

* * *

I was just finishing my first cup of coffee at the restaurant when I saw Mildred Collins walk in. I waved to catch her attention, and she came right over and took the chair opposite me.

"Thank you for coming," I said, and she smiled.

"It's my pleasure, really," she said. "As I told you, I don't usually have the opportunity to get out nearly as much as I'd like. And now I'll be able to see my daughter again."

I somehow suspected that was more than a non-sequitur. "I'm sorry?" I said. "I'm afraid I don't follow."

She smiled again. "My daughter will not come near me when Angelina is visiting," she said, picking up the menu the waitress had left by her plate.

"That's too bad," I said, hoping she'd shed a little more light on the subject.

She nodded, studying the menu and not looking up. "Most of my friends are the same way, and I now have very few friends left, I'm sorry to say. Angelina is something of a dark cloud at a picnic."

The waitress came with coffee for Mildred and a refill for me. "Are you ready to order?" she asked, as Mildred put down her menu.

"It must be difficult for you," I said when we were alone. "I'm curious as to why you don't have a talk with your sister, if she is a problem for you."

She added sugar and cream to her coffee before speaking. "Because," she said with a small shrug, "she is my sister, and without me, she really would have no one. I couldn't abandon her."

"I admire you for that," I said, honestly.

She smiled again. "It's not an application for sainthood," she said. "It is merely the way things are."

"Well, I'm really glad you agreed to talk with me," I said, "but to be honest, I'm a bit curious as to why you did."

"There are several reasons, I suppose," she said. "For one, I sensed a certain empathy in you, and that you would be willing to listen to an old woman ramble on without passing judgment. I don't really have anyone with whom I can discuss certain things, and sometimes an empathetic stranger can provide an outlet."

The arrival of the waitress with our food paused the conversation

Squeezing a slice of lemon over her cod, she resumed talking.

"Please don't misunderstand me, Mr. Hardesty," she said. "I do love my sister. Really. But we couldn't be more different. Angelina always sees the glass as being half empty, and I see it as being half full. I'm early to bed and early to rise, Angelina's a night person, staying up until two or three A.M., then sleeping until 10 or later."

She sighed. "She is in many ways a very difficult woman to be around for long periods of time. Many of the things she does, and the way she does them, are, I know, rude, thoughtless, spiteful. But I long ago recognized that they are not conscious choices. That's simply the way Angelina is. I understand her actions, but I don't excuse them."

We each took several bites of food before she picked up where she'd left off:

"Being the oldest, Angelina was the apple of our father's eye. She is very much like him in many ways, which may be the reason he favored her so. She could do no wrong, so she never learned otherwise. They both had wills of iron and both, once they decided upon something, let nothing stand in the way until they achieved it. I always found it fascinating that she and our father never fought. She was smart enough to know that she would not win. As I told you, Roy shares many of her traits, but he never acquiesced to her as she did to our father, and as a result they have never gotten along.

"Ever since we were children, Angelina has operated on the principle that what is mine is hers, and what is hers is hers. I don't think she's ever given a moment's thought to it—it's just the way it is and has always been. After my husband died, and my daughter was grown, I gathered together enough fortitude to try to construct my own life. I left Louisville and moved here." She sighed. "But I should have realized that just moving away wouldn't make any difference. Angelina spends several months a year here—she refers to it as her 'summer home,' though she comes and goes throughout the year, often with little or no advance notification."

"I was wondering," I said, after taking another forkful of casserole, "if there might be something wrong at home that she would leave so suddenly. I gather you weren't expecting it?"

She dabbed the corner of her mouth with her napkin. "No, I wasn't expecting it," she said, "but that's hardly unusual behavior for Angelina. She had a phone call last night, and right afterwards she called the airport. I have no idea who called. Angelina doesn't feel it necessary to confide such things to me."

We ate in silence for a minute or two while I sorted through my thoughts.

"I'm still very curious," I said, "about not only why Roy might take such a sudden interest in a son he apparently never even knew he had, and where he might have gotten the money to hire a top lawyer to press his custody suit."

Mildred looked at me over the rim of her coffee cup as she took a sip, then lowered the cup to its saucer. "I'm afraid I would have no way of knowing for sure," she said. "Roy's…antipathy… toward Angelina spills over onto me. Guilt by association, no doubt. We really aren't close. To be honest, I was very surprised to hear that he was filing for custody. He definitely never struck me as the fatherly type. But I support him in his efforts. Kelly is his son, and he should be in his father's custody. I'm sure the Ericksons are fine people, but Roy *is* his father. And as to where he got the money…well, that's not too difficult to figure out. I would expect Angelina gave it to him."

"And why might she do that?" I asked. "I had the definite impression that she totally disapproved of Roy."

She smiled a Mona Lisa smile. "Angelina totally disapproves of almost everyone," she said. "But as in everything she does, she would have her reasons."

"Can you imagine what her reasons might be in this instance?"

She carefully cut open her popover and lathered butter into the concave interior of one half.

"Of course," she said, lifting the buttered half to her mouth. "She wants Kelly."

* * *

Whoa!, I thought.

As I sat there, momentarily speechless, Mildred savored her popover.

"She wants Kelly?" I finally said.

Mildred nodded, taking another sip of her coffee. "Yes," she said. "I think she looks on it as a second chance to have the kind of son she feels Roy should have been."

My mind was trying to catch and sort out the thoughts that came tumbling to the surface. "So she is, in effect, buying herself a new son?"

Mildred gave me a very small smile. "She can afford it," she said.

So that was it! Roy didn't want Kelly: Angelina did! He'd get custody, and then just turn Kelly over to her—undoubtedly being well paid to do so.

As if reading my thoughts, Mildred said: "But Angelina is far from stupid—nor, contrary to appearances, is Roy. It would be impossible to prove. Roy will be, for purposes of the custody proceedings, the perfect father. He will, as they say nowadays, 'get his act together.' I imagine he will probably even marry the woman with whom he is living, to reinforce the 'loving family' image. But Angelina, you can have no doubt, will be the primary influence in Kelly's rearing, and it is highly unlikely, given Roy's desire for money and Angelina's considerable wealth, that Roy will put up much resistance to whatever she might want to do with Kelly."

"But the courts would never allow that to happen," I heard myself saying, realizing even as I said it that Angelina's intentions would be impossible to prove and would therefore have no effect on the custody suit.

Mildred merely gave an almost imperceptible shrug.

It was all coming together, now!

"Do you remember when we met the other day," I said, "I asked if Mrs. D'Angelo knew a man named Eddie Styles?"

"Yes," she said, "I remember, and I'm afraid she wasn't being quite truthful. I'd say she simply did not recall, but Angelina remembers everything…and everyone. We both knew an Eddie Styles in Louisville. Not well, but we had some social contacts through our husbands and our father. I understand he had a rather disreputable reputation, but he was always quite pleasant when I saw him. Our husbands and father knew him much better than we did."

"And Roy knew him?" I asked.

"Yes, I assume so. As I said, Mr. Styles was fairly close to Angelina's husband—both her husbands, now that I think of it. Roy must have known him. Why do you ask?"

"Were you aware that Eddie Styles was driving the van that killed Carlene DeNuncio?" I said.

She was in the process of picking up her coffee cup, but put it down abruptly. It made a rather loud "click" as it made contact with the saucer. Her eyes opened wide and she looked directly at me. "Why, no, I didn't," she said, her brows furrowed. "Are you sure? How could it possibly have been him? What would he be doing here? And why would he have done such a thing?"

Good questions, lady, I thought.

But before I could say anything, she said: "Surely you're not implying …Angelina…?"

"Or Roy," I added.

She shook her head strongly. "No! Impossible! I know both Angelina and Roy are capable of a many things, but this? Never. There has to be another explanation!"

Well, I realized there was one.

"Do you know a Jan Houston?" I asked.

She looked at me.

"Of course I do!" she said. "I thought you knew. She's my daughter."

CHAPTER 15

Uh, no...I didn't *know,* I thought as I mentally picked myself up off the floor—though I certainly *should* have at least guessed. The evidence was there: the unconnected pieces of a jigsaw puzzle, but all there. Carlene had told me about Jan's having been abandoned by her mother and being dumped on an aunt: Angelina D'Angelo was her real mother! Angelina had dumped Jan on Mildred, who raised her as her own! So Jan and Roy D'Angelo *were* brother and sister—well, half-brother/sister: no wonder Jan hated Roy—and from what Mildred had inferred, Angelina as well.

Good Lord, what a mess!

"No, I didn't know," I repeated aloud, hoping not too much time had passed between the dropping of the bomb and my response. "Then you knew Carlene, too," I said.

A look of sadness crossed her face. "Not very well, I'm afraid," she said. "When I moved here, Jan stayed in Louisville—that's where she met Carlene, and then they moved to Cincinnati, and Kelly was born. I didn't have a chance to see her very often."

"And then they moved here. You must have been pleased," I said.

The look of sadness returned, and she dropped her eyes to the table. "I was," she said. "They moved to Carrington because Carlene wanted to be near her sister. I was hoping to see them often, but..." Her voice trailed off.

"But?" I prompted.

She took a deep breath. "But since Roy was Kelly's father, and since Angelina comes and goes between here and Louisville and I never know when she'll be here or not, Jan...well, she preferred to keep her distance. It broke my heart not to be able to spend as much time as I wanted with her or Kelly, whom I came to consider as being my grandson."

She looked up at me. "I know," she said, anticipating a reaction to her referring to Kelly as her grandson, "but in a way I do feel he *is* my grandson. Jan has been a part of his life from the moment he was born, and she adores him. He calls her 'Mommy Jan.'"

"And how did you feel when they broke up?" I asked.

"I was devastated for Jan," she said. "But technically and legally Kelly is Carlene's son, not Jan's, and Jan has no legal rights when it comes to him." She sighed. "Things that can't be changed must be accepted. At least now I get to see her every now and again…when Angelina isn't here, of course."

I had to ask: "Did Angelina know about Kelly—and that he is Roy's son—before Carlene's death?"

Finishing the last of her popover, she shook her head. "Oh, no! I didn't know myself for quite some time, and when I found out I, of course, would never tell Angelina. I may feel like a grandmother but I can assure you that Angelina would not. I really, after all these years, don't know how Angelina's mind works, and sometimes it's best not to find out. I didn't dare tell her about Kelly because I couldn't bear the thought that for whatever reason she might decide to try to take Kelly away from Jan…and his mother, of course."

"But that's what she's attempting to do now, I gather," I said.

She dabbed her mouth with her napkin, then said: "Yes, but Jan doesn't have Kelly now, either, does she?"

That struck me as just a bit odd, but I let it pass.

I was positive that Mildred must be aware I knew Jan was not her real daughter, but neither of us mentioned it. We just more or less small talked through the last few minutes of lunch. My mind, as well as my stomach, was full and needed time to digest everything.

We finished our lunch, exchanged "thank you"s, and went our separate ways.

* * *

There was a lot to digest, and I was still going over everything Mildred Collins had said when I arrived back at the office. I'd just sat down at my desk when the phone rang.

"Hardesty Investigations," I said, picking up on the second ring.

"I have a collect call for Dick Hardesty from Roy D'Angelo," the operator's professionally disinterested voice announced. "Will you accept the charges?"

"Yes," I said, and heard a slight "click."

"What the hell do you want now?" Roy's voice demanded.

"Thanks for calling," I said. "I just thought I'd let you know what's going on with my investigation into Carlene's death."

"Why?" he asked. "I told you before, I didn't have anything to do with it, and it's none of my concern."

I'm sure his butch/bully attitude was very effective in third grade, but I wasn't buying it.

"Well," I said, "As soon as I can put a couple of more pieces of the puzzle together, I'll turn what I know over to go to the police, and it occurred to me that with a custody hearing coming up, you would probably want to make sure you're not being considered a murder suspect. I need you to convince me you aren't involved."

Of course one of the classic stupid moves in crime fiction, movies, and TV is for someone to tell a suspected murderer that they're going to go to the police. It's like painting a bulls-eye on your forehead. And somebody had already tried to kill me. I do some really dumb things sometimes.

But it was the only way I could think of to get something out of him, one way or the other.

"And how the hell am I supposed to do that?" he demanded.

"We can start by your being honest with me. You said you didn't know Eddie Styles. You do."

There was a slight pause, then: "Yeah, so I know who he is. I knew him when I was a kid. So what?"

"And you didn't tell me Jan Houston is your half sister."

"Again, so what?" he asked. "You never asked, and it's none

of your business anyway. What's that got to do with anything?"

"Just that it indicates that you knew about Kelly all along," I said.

"I didn't!" he countered. "I've never had a thing to do with that dyke. She hates my guts." There was a slight pause, then: "You've been talking to my aunt Mildred, haven't you? What a doormat! She's let Angelina walk all over her for years, and she never had the guts to stand up to her but she can't wait to run around behind her back and try to cause trouble. I'll just bet the minute Angelina wasn't looking, Mildred came running to you—especially if she knows you're out to frame us."

"I'm not out to frame anybody," I said. "But the fact is that Carlene's death was not an accident. You know the man who killed her, and you're the one with the most to gain by her death."

"That's bullshit!" he said. "You think getting saddled with a kid for 18 years is some sort of prize?" There was a pause as he apparently realized what he just said, and he hastened to add: "But he's my kid and I'll do right by him."

Uh huh, I thought.

"And your mother gave you the money for the custody suit?" I said.

"Like shit she did!" he blustered. "I got my own money! I do pretty damned well on the circuit. I don't need her money. That old lady never gave me a dime in my life!"

It's possible that he could be right, but I strongly doubted it. Almost any lawyer could handle a custody case; why would he need the best lawyer in Kentucky—the best *criminal* lawyer, to boot. Well, considering what I'd heard of his family's past, I'd imagine they'd had some experience with criminal lawyers. Maybe this guy was a family friend. Still....

"So," I said. "You had no idea Kelly even existed until your mother told you."

"That's right!"

"And the minute you found out, you filed for custody."

"Well, not the very minute."

"Of course. But within a few days?"

"Right."

"Not even knowing for sure that Kelly was yours."

"He's mine, all right," he said. "I seen pictures."

Oh?

"How did you manage that?" I asked. "Who took them?"

I could tell I'd flustered him. "I…uh…as soon as I knew about him, I asked Angelina to have somebody get me some pictures of him. She had some private investigator she knew get some."

"Frank Santorini?" I asked.

There was a pause, then: "I don't know who took them."

I couldn't tell whether he was lying or not, and it really didn't matter. The fact that Frank Santorini had been found shot dead in his office three days after Carlene was killed had suddenly become another very real piece in the puzzle. I'd take odds that he had been killed to cover up the link between Carlene and whomever had hired him. And if Santorini was taking pictures of Kelly before Carlene died, that proved Angelina D'Angelo had known about Kelly for some time before Carlene's death. Her having denied it was, in my mind, yet another knot in the noose around her neck.

"The thing is," Roy continued, "the kid looks just like me. That's all I need to know."

It suddenly occurred to me that I had never heard Roy D'Angelo refer to his son by name. Real father material, all right!

"One last question," I said. "When is the last time you were in town?"

"That time I saw you. I got in a pretty bad wreck at the next stop on the circuit, and I've been out of commission." There was a pause, and then: "And just so's you'll know, since you're so fucking curious about everything, I'm giving up the racing. When I get the kid, I'm gonna spend full time here, expanding my garage business, stuff like that, so I'll be able to be able to be a real dad."

Well, I must say, he was indeed getting all his ducks in a

row, anticipating all the obvious objections to his bid for custody. And the scary thing was that he just might get it.

We were both silent a moment, until I said: "Okay, I guess that does it. Thanks again for talking with me."

"Yeah," he said, confidently. "You just go ahead and go to the cops and tell them whatever in hell you want. I got nothin' to hide. And the kid's *mine!*"

And he hung up.

His name's Kelly, you jerk! I thought.

* * *

Sigh.

That "going to the cops" thing didn't work out quite the way I'd hoped. But I *did* hope I hadn't made a fatal mistake in bringing it up. Once again I was uncomfortably aware of how things had changed in my life. I didn't have to just worry about myself anymore: I had Jonathan and Joshua to consider. I couldn't afford that old Hardesty "bring it on" attitude anymore.

And I realized that I really should go to the cops—I knew Marty Gresham and Mark Richman would give me an objective hearing without insisting on stepping in and interfering with my investigation. And even if I didn't have all the pieces of the puzzle in place yet, at least I could give them a good heads up in the event that something might happen to me.

I sat there for a while, mulling over what had been a pretty informative day. Maybe it was the lunch, but I mulled myself into that state just this side of sleep, where the mind starts wandering off on its own. I pictured myself holding four brightly colored balloons on long strings: Roy, Jan, Angelina, and Bonnie Bronson. Bonnie's string slipped out of my hand and I watched it rise silently into the sky, becoming smaller and smaller.

So long, Bonnie, I thought.

Pulling myself back to reality, I realized I'd pretty much decided that of the three remaining prime suspects... Roy, Angelina, and Jan...only Roy had the laws of parental rights on his side. But Angelina could get around that little obstacle with her checkbook. So Jan was off the hook, then? Well, let's just say I'd moved her to the number two spot, with Angelina and Roy in a dead heat for first.

The fact that Roy was probably in Louisville when whoever it was tried to kill me might have held a little more weight were it not for the fact that Eddie Styles was very likely the one doing the actual dirty work and, elusive as he was, he could be working for either Roy or Angelina.

Yes, or for Jan, my mind observed. *Eddie Styles* was *her godfather, after all.*

One step forward, one step back.

* * *

I picked up the phone and dialed the City Annex, and asked for Lt. Mark Richman's extension. The phone rang three times before I heard it being picked up. "Lieutenant Richman," the familiar voice said.

"Lieutenant: it's Dick Hardesty. I hope I'm not interrupting something," I said.

"No," he replied, "I was just finishing up a call on my other line. So what can I do for you? It's been a long time."

"I know," I said. "I figured I'd let you work on someone else's problems for a change."

"And don't think I don't appreciate it," he said. "But since we're talking now, I can assume the break is over?"

"Well," I said, "I'm not sure. But there is something going on I wanted to let you know about, just in case."

There was only a slight pause, then: "Ah, yes…the hit and run you're working on. Officer Gresham told me about it. I wish we had something positive we could tell you about this…Eddie Styles, was it?…character, but we still haven't been able to track him down. He's a pretty elusive guy."

"I know you're doing your best," I said, "but I was wondering if we might get together for lunch so I could fill you in on everything, just in case…"

Richman interrupted, "Officer Gresham told me about your brake line accident. You should have made an official police report, you know. That's what we're here for."

"I know," I said, "but I'd be willing to bet Eddie Styles was responsible…Marty's said you'd had a report that he was in town at the time…and you're already looking for him, so…it's a long story, and it's a pretty complicated one."

"Okay," Richman said, "you've got me. How about tomorrow at the usual time and place?"

By that I knew he meant Sandler's, where Marty and I had had lunch. And I knew the time would be 12:15. We'd met there often enough in the past, but I was rather pleased that he thought of it as being "usual." "That'd be great," I said, and meant it.

"And I might see if Officer Gresham can come along. We might as well both hear the story at the same time."

"I really appreciate it, Lieutenant," I said. "I'll see you tomorrow."

We exchanged "good-byes" and hung up.

* * *

I left the office in time to pick up Jonathan at work and make it to Happy Day at the regular pick-up time. Jonathan went in to get Joshua while I waited in the car. Since it was Jonathan's school night, we had established something of a ritual of eating out to save time and, as was becoming "usual," we went to one of the 600 or so Cap'n Rooney's Fish Shack franchises in town so Joshua could watch the fish in the gigantic tanks while eating with his fingers—two of his favorite pastimes. Jonathan was having a test that night, and had brought his textbook to work so he could study during his lunch hour. He brought it into the restaurant with us to do a little more last-minute cramming. Joshua was too fascinated with watching the fish to ask Jonathan to read it to him, so with both of them visually occupied, I spent my waiting time checking out the manager behind the counter. Jonathan glanced up from his book and caught me staring. He kicked my leg under the table, grinned, and went back to his book. He knew me well enough by now to know that for me, looking at hot guys was just part of who I am, and not a threat. Still, he wanted to give me a gentle reminder to keep it that way.

Joshua managed, during dinner, to drop a full, open cup of tartar sauce into his lap, but fortunately his napkin, which I'd just retrieved from the floor for the third or fourth time, was on his lap at the moment and caught most of it.

While Jonathan was in class, Joshua and I returned to the apartment for a rousing game of "horsey" with me in the title role, of course. We also "read" the latest issue of *Time*—which is to say held lengthy question/answer/commentary on the pictures, got out his coloring book and spent some time retrieving crayons from under the sofa so he could get the colors of the cow *just right*—purple and orange, and watched a little television, with Joshua carefully explaining what was going on to Bunny.

I'd just gotten him out of his bath and into his pajamas when Jonathan returned from class. Then it was story time, some quality alone-time for Jonathan and me, a little more TV, and then bed.

Remember hitting the bars and cruising and picking up tricks and not getting home until the next morning? one of my mind voices asked, nostalgically. *God, you've turned into your father!*

Yeah, I admitted reluctantly, then realized that being my father wasn't such a bad thing to be.

* * *

I arrived at Sandlers at a little after noon and got a booth. I ordered coffee and shifted my mind into neutral—I'd been thinking of the case far too much and forced myself to give it a rest, at least until Mark and Marty got there.

I'd just started my second cup of coffee when I saw Mark Richman come in, alone. He saw me and came over, taking a seat, then reaching across the table to shake hands.

"Officer Gresham will be here in a minute," he said.

The waiter came over with a full pot of coffee and filled Richman's cup, and we small talked for a few minutes.

"How's the family?" I asked. We knew each other well enough by this time to know something of each others' personal life. We'd even had a few beers together, and when he was not in uniform or on police business, I called him by his first name, Mark. But on occasions like this, it was always "Lieutenant."

He smiled. "Great," he said. "And Craig finally came out to us."

Craig was Mark's eldest son, probably around sixteen, who Mark had long suspected was gay.

"Good for him!" I said. "How did it go?"

"Not bad," he said. "I know it wasn't easy. His mother's always talking about having grandkids and he was afraid he was disappointing us. He knows better. Our other two can give us the grandkids: we just want Craig to be happy being who he is."

We could use a lot more parents like the Richmans.

"It sounds like he's well on his way," I said.

He grinned and said: "He is. I'm really proud of him. He's already trying to pick up odd jobs to save money for college."

"Great!" I said. "Does he do babysitting?"

Richman cocked his head and raised an eyebrow. "As a matter of fact, he does—so if you ever need one, I'm sure Craig would be happy to do it. And I think it would be good for him to have some adult gay role models."

"I appreciate that," I said, glancing up to see Marty approaching the table. As he pulled out a chair, he nodded to Mark with a crisp: "Lieutenant," then shook my hand. He still looked pretty damned hot despite the added weight.

He must have read my mind because he patted his belly and said "I know: how come us straight guys go to seed once we get married, and you gay guys don't?"

His grammatical incorrectness aside, I just grinned at him, and we all three picked up our menus.

A minute or so later, the waiter came over with coffee for Marty and a top-off for me, and asked if we were ready to order. We were.

After the waiter left, Mark poured more sugar into his coffee, set his spoon on the side of his saucer, then looked up at me. "Okay," he said. "So let's hear it."

* * *

I told them everything I knew including the very strange family dynamics between Roy, Jan, Angelina, and Mildred Collins, and the links that bound them all, one way or the other, to Eddie Styles. I mentioned Frank Santorini's death and that I felt he may have been murdered to be sure no one could fill in the third side of the triangle…who had hired him to trail Carlene. Perhaps, when Carlene was killed, Santorini had made his own connection and might even have tried a little blackmail to keep quiet. If so, it was definitely a wrong move on his part.

The waiter returned with our meals, and I continued talking as we ate.

That Eddie Styles had killed Carlene was a given: that he had killed Santorini was a pretty solid bet. But I still didn't know exactly who hired Eddie Styles, and realized I might never be able to find out—or at least to prove it—until Styles was caught.

The police were doing their best to find him, and probably could step in at this point and start their own investigation. But Angelina and Roy were in Louisville and might be very reluctant to return if they knew the police wanted to question them. And knowing the police were aware of the links between Eddie Styles and the others might well drive him even deeper into hiding.

"So who do you think is the most likely candidate?" Marty asked.

"My money at the moment is split between Angelina

D'Angelo and her son Roy. Roy wants Angelina's money, one way or the other. Whether Mrs. D'Angelo really sees Kelly as a second chance for the kind of son she wants is a little iffy to me, especially at her age. But I can't see Roy having any use for Kelly at all except as a way to get into his mother's bank account and will."

"What about Jan Houston and Mrs. D'Angelo's sister?" Mark …Lieutenant Richman… said.

I shook my head. "A remote possibility," I acknowledged. "Jan could have had Carlene killed out of anger—Styles is her godfather and *might* have done it as a favor. But it's hard to imagine where she might have gotten the money to hire Santorini. And furious at Carlene as she was, she's not stupid. She had to have known she didn't have a chance of getting custody of Kelly with Carlene's sister in the picture. And she truly hates Roy, half-brother or not. I just can't see her doing anything to help *him* get Kelly.

"As for Mildred Collins, I can't see any real motivation. She might have been upset about Carlene's breaking up with Jan, but like Jan, she had to have known that Carlene's sister would be the one to get him."

I sat back and took a long sip of coffee before continuing.

"Roy said he had asked his mother for some photos of Kelly, and that she had hired a private investigator—Santorini, obviously—to get them. So if *she* hired Santorini, it would figure that she's the one who killed him, or had Styles do it. But given the relationship between Roy and his mother, it's a stretch to imagine him asking her for anything or, if he did ask, her being willing to do it. But where Roy could have come up with the money to hire Styles is another question.

"Again, I have no idea what the bonds between all these people really are, and whether Styles might be the kind of guy to kill as a favor. Possible, I suppose, but I tend to doubt it."

When the waiter came to pick up our plates and ask it we wanted dessert, Lt. Richman checked his watch, then ordered a piece of lemon meringue pie. Marty patted his belly again and declined, and opted, as I did, for just some more coffee.

When the waiter had left, the Lieutenant said: "A very sound story. Unfortunately, not one word of it would stand up in court. So while I agree that one of your suspects probably had Ms. DeNuncio—and probably Frank Santorini—killed, the only way we're going to be able to prove which one is to catch Eddie Styles; or get a confession, which doesn't strike me as very likely to happen."

He was right.

"Or try to trick the guilty one into tipping his or her hand," I said, as the waiter returned with the Lieutenant's pie and more coffee all around.

Marty shook his head. "I wouldn't recommend that," he said. "Whoever it is has already tried to kill you once—you keep on prodding a hornet's nest with a stick, you're bound to get stung. And you might not be as lucky next time."

Mark/Lt. Richman/the Lieutenant…whichever was in the process of swallowing a mouthful of his pie, but gestured with his fork until he'd finished. "He's right," he said. "You're asking for trouble if you don't back off."

I shrugged. "Too late for that, I'm afraid," I said. "I already told Roy D'Angelo I was planning to go to the police with what I knew. And even if I were to send everyone a telegram saying 'You can relax now; I'm off the case,' it probably wouldn't do any good. They all know you're after Eddie Styles, and that I know about their ties to him."

"Well," Richman said, "even if the department stepped in right now, I really don't know what we could do with no solid evidence. Plus the fact that we'd be trying to work in two jurisdictions: here and Louisville. At least with Styles the search is already nationwide. We'll just have to step up our efforts to find him. In the meantime, I'd watch my back very carefully, if I were you. Just be sure you keep us posted on everything you do, okay? We'll do whatever we can from our end. But no heroics! In fact, I'd strongly suggest you keep Officer Gresham posted on anything and everything that happens."

I grinned. "I'm not big on heroics," I said. "And I appreciate your being there. But believe me, I'll be careful; I've got more than just myself to worry about now."

I was really pretty pleased that, since I'd worked so closely with the police on a number of cases, now they seemed willing to give me a lot of leeway. They could have officially taken over the case and ordered me to drop it—though Richman, at least, knew that wouldn't work. But they could at least made things pretty difficult for me. But I realized that their leaving it in my hands was partly an indication of appreciation for my past help, and partly an awareness of saving considerable amounts of time and taxpayers' dollars in not having the police do basically the same things I was doing for free.

"I've got a feeling everything's coming to a head pretty soon," I said.

Lt. Richman placed his fork on his now-empty plate and moved it aside.

"Just be careful," he said. "And remember, we're here."

CHAPTER 16

When I didn't think about it, I was okay, but when I did, I had to work to keep it under control: the idea that somebody seriously might want me dead wasn't a pleasant one. I'd already laid myself open to another try when I'd mentioned to Roy that I was going to go to the police. Looking back on it, I thought again what a dumb move that had been. All he'd had to do was make a phone call and, if Eddie Styles was still in town—which was probably unlikely—I might not have lived long enough to make it to the police at all. But the fact that that hadn't happened—thank God!—didn't necessarily let Roy off the hook. Chances were good that Eddie Styles *wasn't* in town...which wasn't to say he couldn't be here in a matter of hours, no matter where he might be. And I hadn't specified to Roy exactly when I might be going to the police.

But regardless who was behind all this, I didn't have much doubt that another attempt might well be made on my life. So I had a choice: I could sit by and wait to see if anything happened in the next day or so, which would indicate that Roy was indeed the one. Then, if nothing happened, I could try baiting Jan. Then Angelina. But that was rather like playing a very long and drawn out game of Russian Roulette. I didn't think I could take the waiting.

Nah, my mind advised, *just get it over with.*

My first call was to Mildred Collins, to get Angelina D'Angelo's Louisville phone number. I asked her, when I got her on the line, if she had any idea as to when Angelina might be coming back.

"No idea at all," she said. "Often I don't know until I get a call from the airport telling me to come pick her up. And if for some reason I'm not home, she just catches a cab and comes over. She has her own key."

I somehow got the feeling it had not been given voluntarily.

She gave me Angelina's number, then said: "Are you close to finding what you are looking for, Mr. Hardesty?"

"I think I am, yes," I said.

There was a slight pause, then: "So you *do* think Angelina or Roy might somehow be involved in all this?" she asked.

"I'm still not positive," I said, mostly lying but, I realized with frustration, with some truth.

"Well, I'm sure you're wrong," she said, but with a rather notable lack of conviction.

"I hope so," I said, totally untruthfully this time. "But that's what I'm trying to find out."

I thanked her for her time and we hung up.

* * *

I didn't even replace the phone on the cradle before dialing the number she had just given me. I didn't want to hesitate on the off-chance that she would also immediately try to call Angelina to tell her of our conversation, and that I considered Angelina and/or Roy a suspect.

The phone rang four times without an answering machine picking up, and I was just moving the phone away from my ear when I heard: "Hello?" I wondered for an instant if I had mistakenly called Mildred Collins back, then remembered the similarity of the sisters' voices.

"Yes, Mrs. D'Angelo…this is Dick Hardesty calling. Your sister, Mrs. Collins, gave me your number."

"Why would she do that? (*hech-hem*)"

"Probably because I asked her," I said, not being able to resist. "I'm sorry to bother you at home, but…"

"Well, you *are* bothering me," she interrupted. "I'm a busy woman, and I (*hech-hem*) don't have the time to waste on a bunch of foolishness."

"I'm sorry," I said. "I didn't think you would consider looking into someone's death as foolishness."

Damn it, Hardesty I thought, *don't antagonize her! She'll hang up on you,*

"(*hech-hem*) You know what I meant," she said, just a shade less belligerently. "Just what is it you want?"

"I'm concerned that Roy might somehow be involved in Carlene DeNuncio's death," I said.

She snorted derisively. "That's utter nonsense!" She said. "He doesn't have the (*hech-hem*) backbone to be a murderer."

"That may be true," I said, "but I really would like to know more about his relationship with Carlene, and why Jan Houston hates him so."

I threw Jan's name in there to see if I'd get any kind of response. There was none. Instead: "I'm coming back there tomorrow," she announced. "If you (*hech-hem*) insist, I suppose I could find a few minutes to talk to you then."

"I'd very much appreciate that, Mrs. D'Angelo," I said.

We hung up and I paused to reflect on just why she might be coming back to town so soon, since she'd just returned to Louisville and her sister apparently had no idea when she'd be back. Based on the fact that from what Mildred Collins had said of her sister, this kind of behavior was apparently not all that unusual, I didn't want to put too much emphasis on a possibly sinister link between my call and her return. But I certainly couldn't rule it out.

* * *

Since I was on a roll in setting myself up as a moving target, I was tempted to call Jan Houston at work, but managed to talk myself out of it. Calling her at home after dinner would be better, and I could force myself to wait.

It was getting close to going-home time, and I had the urge to make a quick swing over to Cramer Motors to see what might be available when my insurance check came through, but then I thought that Jonathan would probably want to be along, so I shelved the idea, putting it on my mental calendar for Saturday.

I was just getting ready to leave when Jonathan called, saying he could get a ride home from Kyle and save me the time of driving the extra distance to pick him up. I told him I'd pick Joshua up and meet him at home.

I arrived at Happy Day about ten minutes early (surprise!), and was sitting in the car in front of the building when I saw Estelle Bronson step out onto the porch and motion for me to come in. A little surprised, I did.

"It's nice to see you, Dick," she said, using my first name for what I think was the first time.

"I just happened to be by the door when I saw you sitting there. The other parents will be here in a few minutes, but I wanted to see if you might have heard anything at all about Carlene's death…even though I know you're not working on the case any longer, and I'm truly sorry about that, but…"

"It's good to see you, too," I said. "And I'm still working on the case…on my own," I hastened to add.

She seemed impressed. "Why, that's very kind of you, but…I mean…can you afford to do that?"

"Well, let's just say it's gotten personal," I said. She looked puzzled but didn't follow up on it.

"So have you found out anything at all?" she asked.

"Yes, I think I have," I replied, "and I think I'm very close to knowing who was behind Carlene's death, and why."

"That's wonderful!" she said. "I…"

At that moment a very nice looking guy, who I recognized from an earlier visit as the father of Happy Day's youngest charge, appeared at the door. Estelle let him in, then excused herself to go see about getting the children ready to go home.

The hunk and I exchanged a few words, though my crotch was too busy scoping him out to pay too much attention to what was being said. None of my other mind voices seemed to object: I guess they all thought I deserved a little guilty pleasure from time to time.

The children began pouring in through the door to the back yard, riding a large wave of kid-sounds and running feet.

Two other parents had arrived at the door, and Estelle came up with the hunk's little girl, handing her to him with one hand while opening the door with the other.

Since I'd only picked Joshua up once or twice before, I still wasn't used to the organized pandemonium of the ritual transfer of power from Happy Day to the parents, and was duly impressed by how everyone just took it in stride.

The hunk kissed his daughter, bounced her up and down a couple of times as she laughed, then gave me a very nice smile and a nod and left.

I felt a tug at my leg and looked down to see Joshua staring up at me as though I were a giant sequoia. "Where's Uncle Jonathan?" he asked.

"We'll meet him at home," I said. "Are you ready to go?"

He nodded his head up and down rapidly, and I took his hand and led him through the door.

"Piggy-back!" Joshua said as we reached the steps, and I instead picked him up and swung him up and around so he was seated on my shoulders, with his legs on either side of my neck.

"You can see better from up there," I said, holding his legs securely so he couldn't fall off. I was very aware that he had put on a few pounds in the short time he'd been with us.

* * *

While I had my Manhattan and watched the news, Jonathan and Joshua fed the fish and watered the plants.

Immediately after dinner, I called Jan Houston.

"Hello?" the now-familiar voice said.

I decided to make it short and to the point.

"Jan, hi, this is Dick Hardesty," I began. I thought I heard a man's voice saying something in the background: probably just the TV. "I just wanted to let you know I'm pretty sure I know who was responsible for Carlene's death, and I'll be going to the police with what I know."

There was a pause, then: "So why tell me?"

Yeah, Hardesty, why tell her? a mind voice asked.

"I just thought you might like to know," I said, "and didn't want for it to come as a shock."

I had no idea what I meant by that last part, but probably meant to imply either her real mother or her half-brother was a murderer.

"So who did it?" she asked.

"Well," I said, "I've got just one more thing to check on before I go to the police, so I can't say right now. But, as I said, I just didn't want you to be surprised when you hear about it."

"Ok," she said. "Whatever. Is that it?"

"That's it," I said, feeling somehow just a little bit foolish.

I heard the click of the phone being hung up.

Sweet girl, I thought. *No wonder I'm gay.*

I'd barely hung up the phone when it rang.

"Hello?" I answered.

"Dick, it's Jake. Jared's coming in to town for the weekend, and we were wondering if we might try to get the gang together for dinner Saturday night. Would that be a problem for you? Do you have somebody who can look after Joshua?"

Well, talk about serendipity! I thought. "Yeah," I said. "We just might. Can I call you back in a little while?"

"Sure," he replied. "I'm in for the night."

"Okay," I said. "We'll get back to you shortly."

I reported the call to Jonathan, and told him about my conversation with Mark Richman at lunch, and that his son Craig might be willing to babysit.

Jonathan was suddenly every inch the concerned parent. "I don't know, Dick," he said. "How old is this Craig? Can he be trusted? I mean…"

I grinned. "He's sixteen, and if he's Mark Richman's kid, I'm sure he's pretty responsible and adult. He just came out to his parents, and that takes a lot of maturity."

"He's gay for sure?" Jonathan asked. I'd mentioned to him before that Mark thought he might be.

"Yeah, and Mark thinks that you and I would be good gay

role models for him."

His resolve visibly softened. "That was really nice of him," he said. "Well, I guess we could try it. And it would be nice to have somebody we can call on every now and then." He glanced around to see where Joshua was (on the floor refereeing an apparent dispute between Cowboy and GI Joe), then lowered his voice. "It would be nice if we could have some time to ourselves once in a while. I miss that."

I hugged him. "Me, too," I said. "Now let me see if I can find Mark's home phone number."

* * *

It was all set. Mark volunteered to bring Craig over at six on Saturday night, and Jonathan or I would bring him home. Jake contacted all the rest of the gang, and everyone could make it but Mario, who as manager Venture, had to fill in for one of his bartenders who'd broken a leg falling off a horse. We arranged to meet at Rasputin's at seven for dinner, then planned to stop by Venture for a couple of drinks after. We—Jonathan and I—wouldn't be able to stay very late, but we agreed it would be really good to get out and enjoy a "pre-Joshua" evening.

* * *

Friday passed without a hitch, though I noticed I was a little more aware of every corner-of-my-eye movement and sudden sound than normal. And I'd made a point of taking the bus to and from work, and even went into the garage to check the car before Jonathan and Joshua left. Probably paranoid of me, but my gut was telling me that this entire case was coming to a very rapid head.

We called out for Momma Rosa's pizza for dinner, and Joshua endeared himself to me even further by refusing to touch the mushrooms on the slice he was given from Jonathan's half of the pizza. Instead, he discovered the anchovies on my half and, whenever I wasn't looking, would try to steal them from my uneaten portion.

"See?" I said to Jonathan. "Even a four year old boy knows what's really good."

"Four year olds are strange," Jonathan said.

"Am *not*," Joshua said vehemently.

"Well of course *you're* not," Jonathan said, hastily backtracking.

After dinner…no dishes to speak of…Jonathan tried to study while Joshua variously wanted to wrestle, play "car", scramble up onto and off the couch to watch TV with me, or went about indulging his active fantasy life, frequently with sound effects and animated dialog.

Bedtime/story time came and went without a hitch, and Jonathan and I were relaxing in the living room and just thinking of going to bed and setting up the goalposts ourselves when the phone rang. Damn!

Hurrying to the phone so as not to wake Joshua, I picked it up and said: "Hello?"

The voice wasted no time. "This is Angelina D'Angelo. I want you to meet me."

"I'd like that," I said, rather surprised to learn she was back…though she said she'd be back Friday and this was Friday. "Whenever it's convenient for you," I said. "Tomorrow at my office?"

"Now!" she said.

"It's a little late, isn't it?" I asked, mildly irked.

"Do you want to know who killed that…that woman, or not?"

"Of course I do," I began, "but…"

"I went to a great deal of difficulty getting you documented proof. I do not want it in my possession one minute longer than I have to. Do you want it or not?"

"Well, of course," I repeated. "Do you want me to come over there?"

"No. Mildred is already asleep. That's why I waited until

now to call. She's not to know anything of this! Meet me in the Pence Avenue parking lot on the north side of Riverside Park in one hour. I don't know why I'm doing this, but I'm not about to have you falsely accuse me or my son."

"I understand," I said. "I'll see you there in one hour."

She hung up without another word.

Jonathan, who had been listening to my side of the conversation and looking totally confused, said: "You're not going to go out at this time of night, are you? Where are you supposed to meet?"

"Riverside Park, the Pence Avenue parking lot."

"But that's in the arboretum," he said. "It's surrounded by trees."

I was still holding the phone as I said: "Yes, and I know a set up when I hear one."

Luckily, I remembered Mark Richman's home phone number, and I dialed it.

* * *

Being in a residential area, the streets around Riverside park were fairly deserted by eleven p.m. The park stretched along half a mile of the river in roughly the shape of an on-its-side V. The narrowest point of the park was a popular spot for teenagers, and there were a few cars parked by the river as I drove by. The widest end of the park was a small forest preserve that had been made into an arboretum. We'd spent a lot of time there for various of Jonathan's school projects. The Pence Avenue parking lot was set within the thickest part of the arboretum and was, as Jonathan had said, surrounded by trees. A great place for an ambush.

Okay, I admit it. I was nervous as all hell. And of course, though I had called Lt. Richman and gave him a three-sentence summary, there was no sign of the police. Well, if they were doing their job the way I hoped they were, there *wouldn't* be any sign of them. But an hour is a hell of a short notice for something like this.

I was counting on the fact that Angelina D'Angelo did not know I had such good police contacts, or that I had already told them as much as I had.

As I expected, there wasn't a single car in the parking lot, which couldn't be seen from the street. There was a dim street light at each corner of the lot, but I doubted you'd be able to read a newspaper even if you were standing right under one.

I deliberately stopped in the very center of the lot. I'd be able to see anyone coming up to the car. But of course, the words "sitting duck" also crossed my mind.

Quiet. Very quiet. Way, way *too* quiet. And warm. And did I mention "quiet"?

A pair of headlights suddenly glinted in my rear-view mirror, and a car pulled up and stopped about twenty feet behind me.

Show time! I thought.

With it's headlights still on, I couldn't see who was in the car, but I saw the door open and a woman step out. It was *not* Angelina D'Angelo, unless she'd had her beehive hairdo removed.

Mildred Collins? What the hell was she doing here? Angelina had said she didn't want Mildred to know anything about this meeting.

I opened my door and automatically removed the keys from the ignition. I put them in my lap—a pretty sure sign I was nervous—while I undid my seatbelt.

"Mr. Hardesty?" I heard her voice call. "Where is Angelina?"

I stepped out of the car and felt my keys slipping off my lap and hitting the pavement.

Cool move, Hardesty, I thought, quickly bending over to pick them up. And the instant I began my bend, I heard the sharp crack of a gunshot and felt a flutter of air past my ear.

It had come from somewhere in *front* of the car, so I yelled for Mildred to get down as I ducked between the open door and the driver's seat just as all hell broke loose!

Two squad cars, their strobes flashing, roared into the lot

and sped past us to the opposite side of the park, where I was pretty sure the shot had come from. And then there were flashlights and cops everywhere and a few seconds later what sounded like a string of Chinese firecrackers going off.

As I ran over to Mildred's car, another car raced into the lot and pulled up beside it, and Mark Richman got out, coming over to join us.

"Thanks, Lieutenant!" I said to Mark, then turned to Mildred, who was standing like a statue by the driver's door.

"Are you all right?" I asked.

"Yes, I'm fine," she said, her voice shaking. "What's going on? Where is Angelina?"

I didn't know how to tell her that somehow her sister had set us both up to be killed. I could understand Angelina wanting *me* dead, but why *her*?

"What are you doing here?" I asked.

"I…I had gone to a movie, and when I got home, I found a note from Angelina telling me you had called and insisted she meet you here, and she was taking a cab, and that I should come out and bring her back home."

"Didn't that strike you as more than a little unusual?" I asked.

She shook her head. "Not for Angelina," she said.

"Why didn't your sister go to the movie with you?" Richman asked.

"Angelina doesn't like movies, and so I go a lot when she's here," she said. "And when she just showed up again without letting me know she was coming, I…well, I just needed to get away for a bit."

Angelina had told me on the phone that Mildred was already asleep. Why didn't she just say Mildred wasn't home?

A couple of officers hurried across the parking lot to the lieutenant.

"Did you find him?" Richman asked.

"Yes, sir," the cuter of the two said.

Cuter of the two? How the hell can you be thinking about cute at a time like this? my mind demanded. I had to admit even I was surprised, but I chalked it up to relief that this whole thing was close to being over.

"Well, I want to talk to him," Richman said.

"Uh, I'm afraid that won't be possible, sir," the other officer said. "He wouldn't surrender his weapon when ordered to, and instead opened fire on the officers. We had no choice but to return fire."

"Damn!" Richman said, then cast an apologetic glance at Mildred.

I couldn't help but notice the expression on her face. Relief?

"Did you get an identity?" Richman asked.

"His wallet says he's an Edgar B. Styles of Louisville, Kentucky."

I looked again at Mildred. There was no expression at all. Don't ask me why, but I was suddenly very uncomfortable. Something was going on in my mind and I didn't know what it was. For some reason, I flashed back to Angelina's set-up call. Something about it. What?

"Well," Richman said as the officers moved away, "I think, from what you've said, Dick, that we should go over to Mrs. Collins' house and have a talk with Mrs. D'Angelo." He turned again to Mildred. "I'm sorry, Mrs. Collins," he said, "but I'm afraid we're going to have to arrest your sister for conspiracy to commit murder—and possibly for the murder of Carlene DeNuncio."

And the light came on! I *knew* there was something wrong with that call from Angelina, and suddenly I realized what it was.

There was no "hech-hem"!

"Excuse me, Lieutenant," I said, "but can I talk to you for a moment privately?"

* * *

I'd had a friend who had been with the same partner for 35 years. The partner was a nice enough guy, but he could not speak more than three sentences without inserting a "…you know?" It drove me and others who knew them completely up the wall. But my friend was totally unaware of it! He'd heard it so often, it just didn't register anymore. Mildred Collins had been around her sister so long that after all those years she simply had become unaware of Angelina's annoying throat-clearing. Since I couldn't tell their voices apart without it, when Mildred called and said she was Angelina, I had no reason to think it wasn't. I wasn't listening for a *"hech-hem"*, so when there wasn't one, it simply did not register.

* * *

Okay. We've reached the wrap-up, and I don't think it's necessary to give a step-by-step account of all the details and legal processes that followed. That was largely up to the lawyers and the police. I'm sure you've pretty much figured out the outcome by now on your own. Suffice it to say that for starters, Mildred Collins was arrested for the attempted murder of one Dick Hardesty and, eventually, directly linked, through Eddie Styles, with Carlene DeNuncio's death. It took, as these things often do, nearly a year, and I learned bits and pieces as they came out and, finally, during Mildred Collins' trial.

Her motive had been simple: she wanted her niece/daughter Jan to have Kelly. She knew the only way for that to happen was if Roy D'Angelo were, as Kelly's father, to get him first. It was Mildred, not Angelina, who put up the money for the lawyer, and who was going to buy Kelly from him. She'd approached Roy immediately after Carlene had left Jan, and it was Roy who put her in touch with Eddie Styles. It was primarily for that reason that when the custody hearing came up, the decision was to leave Kelly with Beth Erickson and her family.

* * *

We had our Saturday evening out as planned. Craig Richman was a really nice kid we subsequently used frequently as a baby sitter, despite the fact that Craig developed a very strong crush on Jonathan. But Jonathan handled it well, as I knew he would.

And our life went on, with Joshua now so firmly a part of it that it is hard to imagine him not having always been there. Samuel and Sheryl, of course, were always with Jonathan and Joshua, but the pain became less and less disruptive until it was just a dull ache seldom noticed unless called up.

Jonathan and I were discussing all this one night in bed.

"We lead a pretty interesting life, you know that?" Jonathan said, reaching over to turn off the light.

"That we do," I said. "And there's a lot more to come."

I could see his grin in the semi-darkness. "I can't wait," he said, cuddling up beside me.

"Me, neither," I said.

I kissed him, and we went to sleep.

THE END